PRAISE FOR *UNSPEAKABLE THINGS*

2021 Edgar Award Finalist—Best Paperback Original

"The suspense never wavers in this page-turner."

—*Publishers Weekly*

"The atmospheric suspense novel is haunting because it's narrated from the point of view of a thirteen-year-old, an age that should be more innocent but often isn't. Even more chilling, it's based on real-life incidents. Lourey may be known for comic capers (*March of Crimes*), but this tense novel combines the best of a coming-of-age story with suspense and an unforgettable young narrator."

—*Library Journal* (starred review)

"Part suspense, part coming-of-age, Jess Lourey's *Unspeakable Things* is a story of creeping dread, about childhood when you know the monster under your bed is real. A novel that clings to you long after the last page."

—Lori Rader-Day, Edgar Award–nominated author of *Under a Dark Sky*

"A noose of a novel that tightens by inches. The squirming tension comes from every direction—including the ones that are supposed to be safe. I felt complicit as I read, as if at any moment I stopped I would be abandoning Cassie, alone, in the dark, straining to listen and fearing to hear."

—Marcus Sakey, bestselling author of *Brilliance*

"*Unspeakable Things* is an absolutely riveting novel about the poisonous secrets buried deep in towns and families. Jess Lourey has created a story that will chill you to the bone and a main character who will break your heart wide open."
— Lou Berney, Edgar Award–winning author of *November Road*

"Inspired by a true story, *Unspeakable Things* crackles with authenticity, humanity, and humor. The novel reminded me of *To Kill a Mockingbird* and *The Marsh King's Daughter*. Highly recommended."
— Mark Sullivan, bestselling author of *Beneath a Scarlet Sky*

"Jess Lourey does a masterful job building tension and dread, but her greatest asset in *Unspeakable Things* is Cassie—an arresting narrator you identify with, root for, and desperately want to protect. This is a book that will stick with you long after you've torn through it."
— Rob Hart, author of *The Warehouse*

"With *Unspeakable Things*, Jess Lourey has managed the near-impossible, crafting a mystery as harrowing as it is tender, as gut-wrenching as it is lyrical. There is real darkness here, a creeping, inescapable dread that more than once had me looking over my own shoulder. But at its heart beats the irrepressible—and irresistible—spirit of its . . . heroine, a young woman so bright and vital and brave she kept even the fiercest monsters at bay. This is a book that will stay with me for a long time."
— Elizabeth Little, *Los Angeles Times* bestselling author of *Dear Daughter* and *Pretty as a Picture*

Praise for *The Catalain Book of Secrets*

"Life-affirming, thought-provoking, heartwarming, it's one of those books which—if you happen to read it exactly when you need to—will heal your wounds as you turn the pages."
—Catriona McPherson, Agatha, Anthony, Macavity, and Bruce Alexander Award–winning author

"Prolific mystery writer Lourey tells of a matriarchal clan of witches joining forces against age-old evil . . . The novel is tightly plotted, and Lourey shines when depicting relationships—romantic ones as well as tangled links between Catalains . . . Lourey emphasizes the ties that bind in spite of secrets and resentment."
—*Kirkus Reviews*

"Lourey expertly concocts a Gothic fusion of long-held secrets, melancholy, and resolve . . . Exquisitely written in naturally flowing, expressive language, the book delves into the special relationships between sisters, and mothers and daughters."
—*Publishers Weekly*

Praise for *Salem's Cipher*

"A fast-paced, sometimes brutal thriller reminiscent of Dan Brown's *The Da Vinci Code*."
—*Booklist* (starred review)

"A hair-raising thrill ride."
—*Library Journal* (starred review)

"The fascinating historical information combined with a story line ripped from the headlines will hook conspiracy theorists and action addicts alike."

—Kirkus Reviews

"Fans of *The Da Vinci Code* are going to love this book . . . One of my favorite reads of 2016."

—Crimespree Magazine

"This suspenseful tale has something for absolutely everyone to enjoy."

—Suspense Magazine

PRAISE FOR *MERCY'S CHASE*

"An immersive voice, an intriguing story, a wonderful character—highly recommended!"

—Lee Child, #1 *New York Times* bestselling author

"Both a sweeping adventure and race-against-time thriller, *Mercy's Chase* is fascinating, fierce, and brimming with heart—just like its heroine, Salem Wiley."

—Meg Gardiner, author of *Into the Black Nowhere*

"Action-packed, great writing taut with suspense, an appealing main character to root for—who could ask for anything more?"

—Buried Under Books

Praise for *May Day*

"Jess Lourey writes about a small-town assistant librarian, but this is no genteel traditional mystery. Mira James likes guys in a big way, likes booze, and isn't afraid of motorcycles. She flees a dead-end job and a dead-end boyfriend in Minneapolis and ends up in Battle Lake, a little town with plenty of dirty secrets. The first-person narrative in *May Day* is fresh, the characters quirky. Minnesota has many fine crime writers, and Jess Lourey has just entered their ranks!"

—Ellen Hart, award-winning author of the
Jane Lawless and Sophie Greenway series

"This trade paperback packed a punch . . . I loved it from the get-go!"

—*Tulsa World*

"What a romp this is! I found myself laughing out loud."

—*Crimespree Magazine*

"Mira digs up a closetful of dirty secrets, including sex parties, cross-dressing, and blackmail, on her way to exposing the killer. Lourey's debut has a likable heroine and surfeit of sass."

—*Kirkus Reviews*

Praise for *Rewrite Your Life: Discover Your Truth Through the Healing Power of Fiction*

"Interweaving practical advice with stories and insights garnered in her own writing journey, Jessica Lourey offers a step-by-step guide for writers struggling to create fiction from their life experiences. But this book isn't just about writing. It's also about the power of stories to transform those who write them. I know of no other guide that delivers on its promise with such honesty, simplicity, and beauty."

—William Kent Krueger, *New York Times* bestselling author of the Cork O'Connor series and *Ordinary Grace*

LITANI

LITANI

JESS LOUREY

THOMAS & MERCER

Text copyright © 2021 by Jess Lourey
All rights reserved.

Published by Thomas & Mercer, Seattle

www.apub.com

Amazon, the Amazon logo, and Thomas & Mercer are trademarks of Amazon.com, Inc., or its affiliates.

ISBN-13: 9781542027014
ISBN-10: 1542027012

Cover design by Shasti O'Leary Soudant

Illustrations by Tony VanDenEinde of Little Elephant Interactive

Printed in the United States of America

To all the survivors, old and young.

AUTHOR'S NOTE

Growing up in rural Minnesota in the 1980s, I heard whispers of a satanic cult operating in the nearby river town of Saint Cloud. The gruesome details remain etched in my memory—dogs and cats and then women and children disappearing, chilling shrieks piercing the night, pentagrams and human blood discovered on the Mississippi's brambled banks. Preteen me swallowed that stuff whole. As an adult, however, I've never been able to verify the tales. They were likely a regional rumor, an example of the "satanic panic" sweeping the nation in the '80s.

Think the Salem witch trials in the age of Reagan.

Horrific stories tumbled out one after another that decade, dark tales centered around Satan worship and the ritual abuse of children. National headlines on the topic veered from the vague (The Best Kept Secret, *20/20*, ABC, June 14, 1984) to the informative (Sheriff Says He Found Evidence of Satanic Cult, *New York Times*, July 16, 1985) to the salacious (Girl Told Officers of Porno Films, Being Forced to Eat Pets, *Minneapolis Star and Tribune*, October 19, 1984).

The most disturbing of the national headlines were reserved for Jordan, Minnesota, a village two short hours southeast of where I grew up. In the first half of the century, Jordan was known for breweries, baseball, and churches. That wholesome image exploded in September 1983, when a mother accused local trash collector James Rud of molesting her nine-year-old daughter. Rud's questioning led to the discovery of an alleged child sex ring that began in a local trailer park but extended to all corners of the town. By June of 1984, twenty-five Jordan residents, most of them couples, had been charged with the abuse of dozens of children ranging in age from two months to late teens.

Even amid the lurid stories of the time, the Jordan case was extreme. It made international headlines, with *People*, the *Washington Post*, and the *New York Times* just a handful of the media outlets covering it. At one point, the revelations blasted out of Jordan—population 2,700—at such a shocking rate that reporters moved to the town so as not to miss any new developments. The case reached a crescendo in July 1984, when two of the alleged victims testified that not only had children been indoctrinated into a sex ring but also some had been murdered, their bodies tossed into the nearby Minnesota River.

Scott County prosecutor Kathleen Morris, the attorney in charge of the case, took these claims seriously. Considered an ambitious and skilled attorney, she was fresh off successfully convicting six members of the Cermak family, residents of a nearby Scott County village, of sexually abusing their own and other children.

However, in an explosive and unexpected twist in October of 1984, with a year's worth of damning testimony gathered, Morris dropped all the untried Jordan sexual abuse charges except those against Rud, who had since confessed to his crimes. The world was left openmouthed. Morris said she pulled the charges to shield the children from the trauma of further testifying and to protect the new murder investigation.

No murder charges were ever filed, and all the accused except Rud walked free.

The public outcry over this stunning reversal led then state attorney general Hubert Humphrey III to order a monthslong investigation into what had gone wrong with the case. His report concluded that while some of Jordan's twenty-five alleged perpetrators had been unjustly accused, many children had, in fact, been molested, their abusers escaping prosecution. Tragically, since the initial case had been so botched—young children asked leading questions, some of them interrogated more than forty times with several of the interviews lasting hours, haphazard searches, the loss of probable photographic evidence that Rud's parents (two of the accused) were allowed to remove from his trailer, inconsistent record keeping, purported mismanagement by Morris—there was no legal recourse for anyone, neither the falsely accused nor the children whose tormentors walked free.

Despite Humphrey's findings, most retrospective articles and books misclassify the Jordan ordeal as simply one more example of the social hysteria erupting in the '80s. These so-called moral panics ranged in severity from the relatively harmless satanic cult rumors I heard in rural Minnesota to the McMartin day-care sexual abuse scandal in California. At the time, the McMartin trial was the most expensive court case in American history and was later depicted in a Golden Globe–winning movie. In the modern retelling of these headline-grabbing dramas, the focus has consistently been on the adults whose lives were destroyed by allegedly false accusations.

Social scientists and media critics have attributed these 1980s "witch hunts" to a perfect storm of civic expediency and sociological factors, including women entering the workforce and the subsequent rise of day-care facilities, which led to fears about children being raised by strangers; an outcry from both feminists and conservatives over pornography's move from theaters to homes, thanks to the growing popularity of VCRs; Freud's theory of repressed memories experiencing a renaissance; and a judicial "tough on crime" approach, a backlash to the supposed lawlessness of the '60s and '70s. This storm was stoked by improperly trained and sometimes unscrupulous psychologists, police officers, and attorneys. The result all across the nation was families no longer trusting one another, neighbors turning on neighbors, and communities destroyed.

As a sociologist, I find this dark chapter in American history both fascinating and heartbreaking. But as a writer, and as a woman who grew up in a home and a community where the unspeakable regularly happened, I'm struck by the voices notably missing from the witch-hunt narrative: the children who lived through this terrifying time.

Theirs is the story that matters to me.

PROLOGUE

According to my dad, there were three perfect smells in this world:

1. Fresh-cut grass.
2. A campfire at the edge of a redwood forest.
3. The jubilance of rich black dirt after a thunderstorm.

He didn't stop there.

He also swore by a trinity of sounds that'd make you smile on your worst day. The first was a baby's giggle. I couldn't argue that. Second was hearing honest admiration from someone you respected. It might earn a slow-burn grin, he'd say, but that still counted.

The final sound guaranteed to tickle you pink?

"A dad joke," he'd say. Then he'd throw back his head and laugh his goose-honk laugh like I hadn't heard the whole shtick a million times before.

Remembering it still makes me smile, which I guess proves his point.

Even now, clad in the dubious armor of adulthood, I clutch those memories like an overboard rope. They kept me above water when I first moved to Minnesota to live with my mother the summer of '84.

Barely, but there were other circumstances at play.

The first was that my mother was basically a stranger to me.

When Mom and Dad divorced, he kept me in Pasadena, and she returned to the Minnesota hometown where they'd been high school sweethearts. Unorthodox for a woman to give up her child, even more so in the '70s, but it was a classic Linda Jubilee move. It'd be three years before she'd request I visit her in Minnesota. I'd been four-almost-five at the time of the divorce, so by then, I didn't remember much about her except the smell of her rose-milk lotion and a faint recollection of her and Dad's not-really fights, them going at each other like county theater actors at the end of the season, when everyone was tired of delivering their same lines.

Dad had been all smiles dropping me off at LAX that day for the flight to Minneapolis, making me promise to be on my best behavior. He'd never talked much about her before that, never remarked that it was odd she hadn't visited, rarely called, and then there he was, acting like it was the most normal thing in the world that she suddenly wanted to see me. I remember feeling wowed by the airplane, special because of the way the stewardesses fawned all over me, and equal parts scared and excited for my reunion with Mom.

When she met me at the gate, she'd been all awkward grins and stammers, which warmed me because of my own shyness. She walked me to her car and tucked my borrowed suitcase in the trunk, her mouth smiling and her jewelry clacking. The Minnesota air was celery green and just as crisp, and Mom promised fun plans as she sneaked glances at me. The inside of her car smelled exactly like the rose milk of my memory, and that's a special kind of warmth, to realize you've recalled something so important so perfectly.

That first night, she painted my fingernails the color of raspberry juice.

She took the next day off, which made me feel special because her job was important. She was the Carver County prosecutor, and she didn't skip work for just anyone, she shared with me, nodding, her eyes serious.

Sounded bomb to me.

And what a day it was. We rolled up to Joyce's Salon and got matching perms before heading over to the Paramount for a matinee of *The Rescuers*, where Mom bought me Jaw Busters. After, we stopped by the five-and-dime, and she let me pick out clip-on ladybug earrings. We ended the day by hitting Albert's Pourhouse for root beers and cheese pizza, which I gobbled up.

I loved all that attention and my hair curled as tight as a fiddlehead fern.

Then, on the third day, as Mom was discussing our itinerary (a baseball game and clothes shopping and a bike ride!) over breakfast, she spotted me worrying on my remaining front tooth. All the baby teeth around it had fallen out. I admit it looked jack-o'-lantern-ish hanging there all by its lonesome, but what could I do? The tooth was barely even loose.

"That one sure wants to come out," she said.

"Yeah, it sure does," I agreed. Then I smiled my raggedy smile. I was seven years old. I wanted to make her happy. I wanted her to like me.

What happened next took less than a minute.

Her eyes narrowed at my grin like she'd solved a riddle she'd been puzzling on for some time. She leaped up and ran down the hall, the carpeting the same then as it was when I returned in '84.

I didn't think much of it. How could I when I had a bowl of Cookie Crisp in front of me? Dad didn't allow sugar cereal back home. It was delicious, despite the strong perm odor dulling my senses.

If Barbie dolls peed, I bet it'd smell like perm solution.

I was giggling when Mom returned with pliers and a rag. Before I could say boo, she popped open my jaw the same way you'd release a snapdragon, thrust the pliers into my mouth, and plucked that straggler straight out of my head.

Whoo-eee was there blood.

I screamed because of shock more than anything. I wouldn't calm down until she let me call Dad, and when I told him between hiccuping sobs what'd just happened, that was the end of that. He demanded Mom stick me on the next flight home.

She didn't speak on the drive to the airport. The whole ride I imagined her kicking me out at the curb and speeding away, the sleep-matted side of her matching perm the last part of her I would ever see. I was grateful when she parked and walked me to my gate.

She led me to the counter, handed the woman behind it my ticket, and walked away.

After that cold goodbye, I heard from her only twice a year for the next seven years: a birthday and then a Christmas card, a five-dollar bill stuck in each. That's a trick that'll stick with you, your mother not loving you back. You'll try to stretch the little things—a secret smile that was maybe meant just for you, that first night when she cooked your favorite meal of chicken strips and oven french fries and it tasted like love—but you know down deep that if you can't belong with your mom, then you don't belong anywhere.

So being forced in 1984 to move in with a woman I didn't really know, hadn't seen since she'd wrenched a tooth out of my head seven years earlier, that was the first reason I clung to the overboard-rope memories of my father.

The second was something the children of Litani called The Game.

By the way, learning that I was forced to move from urban Pasadena to a rural Minnesota dot-on-the-map at age fourteen, you might picture me as a city girl forced to shrink myself, a big, glittery fish trapped in a small, boring pond, me with California hair and clothes and ideas, air-dropped into *Little House on the Prairie*.

You'd be wrong.

Not because back then I was a small-for-her-age nerd who liked plants. Not because the kids in Litani were fast, every one of them sex and cigarettes and sharp-toothed smiles. Not even because Pasadena had neighborhoods that were like small towns, safe and friendly and familiar.

No, you'd be wrong because Litani was danger, pure and simple.

In Litani, the devil lived right out in the open, and there was no one to save you. It didn't matter if you were a kid. In fact, they preferred it that way.

That was The Game.

But the third reason I clutched those memories of my dad like my life depended on it? That one was the strongest.

It was also the simplest.

I'd killed him.

That made it my fault, everything that happened to me in Litani after that.

CHAPTER 1

I took a swipe at the sweat beading on my top lip and eyeballed the living room. White wicker furniture beneath blotchy abstract paintings in light pinks, corals, and sea-foam greens. A glass-topped coffee table, also wicker. No photographs. Everything arranged around the enormous floor-model color television that squatted, broad and muscular like a carnival strongman, beneath a sashed window draped with a floral curtain.

The room reminded me of a *Price Is Right* showcase.

Sterile and unused.

"Bring 'em all in. Yes, I mean *all*," Linda Jubilee shouted into the mustard-yellow handset. At least it would've counted as shouting if Dad had done it. I'd known him as a quiet man. Whether he was born that way or learned it from working in the woods, I didn't know. Linda Jubilee, though? I had no sense of her vocal range. This might have been her normal. Her dress was certainly different from what I was used to people wearing at home in the summer. Formal. She wore a taupe blazer swollen with shoulder pads over a brown corduroy skirt. A loop of plastic pearls reached her waist, slithering across her chest as she paced, their color equalizing her white pantyhose and pumps. The powdery scent of Love's Baby Soft washed over me when she passed near enough.

Had she retired the rose-milk lotion?

My anxious attention slid back to the house. The oak-and-linoleum kitchen was to my left, a hall straight ahead, and an open door immediately off the living room revealed the edge of a rolltop desk.

Linda Jubilee's home office.

As I watched her holler down someone on the other end of the line, demanding they "stop being coy, dammit," her expression reminded me of the brown-haired actress from *Cagney & Lacey*. They both had the same strong face. Linda Jubilee's body was elfin, though, like mine. The JCPenney word for our build was "petite." All I knew was that last year, when I'd been forced to join theater to fulfill an eighth-grade extracurricular requirement, I was small enough that they let me play the star at the top of the Christmas tree.

"I don't care if they think it's a game!" she shouted into the phone.

I'd had a science teacher who'd been a yeller. If a student forgot the periodic table symbol for copper or—*heaven forbid*—couldn't recall the difference between mitochondria and cytoplasm, a deep crack would furrow between Mr. Keller's brows, like the earth had fallen away below his skin. Then out of his mouth rolled the thunder.

Linda Jubilee, though? She looked serene as she yelled. Cheerful almost.

"No, *not* with their parents," she squawked. "Why would you even ask that?"

She'd sent a police car to pick me up from the airport this time. The cop was off duty and doing it as a favor, he kept saying, like he thought I was gonna snitch on him. He played KCLD radio out of Saint Cloud the whole drive, all trendy tunes like Prince's "When Doves Cry" and the Icicle Works' "Whisper to a Scream" (which, come to think of it, could be my theme song). The officer—who couldn't have been more than twenty-five years old—seemed to be hearing each song for the first time from the way he cocked his head when a new one would start playing.

Under normal circumstances, I'd have found his dorky effort to cater to what he imagined I liked to be hilarious, but I was light-years from normal. This new, dark world felt pretend. I had no idea how to behave. I kept expecting to wake up, to step out of this bad dream and return to the real world, but the nightmare persisted.

The Icicle Works finished up singing about how we were just children, and I clutched my twisting belly and tried not to think about me and June humming along to the song back in Pasadena, using fresh cherry halves like lip gloss and giggling as we acted out our own MTV videos, my life regular and perfect, and my biggest concern whether Dad would let me get a retainer to straighten my gnarly teeth.

"Please," Linda Jubilee breathed into the phone, like she'd just heard the stupidest thing legally allowed. "I'm well aware we can't send children undercover. I was joking."

Was this phone call why she'd sent the nervous cop to pick me up rather than come for me herself? Or was it because after that last time, the tooth-pulling time, she never wanted to be at an airport with me again? In either case, after a drive full of more new (to him) hits than you'd think you could cram into sixty minutes, we'd passed Litani's graveyard hill. The town over the rise was shabbier than I remembered, the 76 gas station with the rotating orange ball out front less magical than it had appeared to seven-year-old me, the vast and abandoned Engle Brewery perched on the edge of town more ominous. It was a prisonlike complex, one building attached to the next like a twisting centipede growing larger at each segment, the final and most immense section sprouting a towering smokestack, ENGLE BEER cemented right into it. I shivered looking at it.

Litani had taken up so much mental real estate since I'd last visited that returning was like stepping into a television show I'd been watching for years. It was alien yet familiar, weirdly still beneath the oppressive heat and humidity.

Linda Jubilee's house—my home now, unless I made her mad again—sat on the farthest side of Litani. To get there, we drove past blocky little yards behind ribbons of sidewalk, a haze like golden dust choking everything. No sound except the hum of the police car, no smell except for dirt, no sensation except dull dread, right up until we rolled in front of an ugly blue box of a house with a matching attached garage.

Big box, little box.

Linda Jubilee's.

Both the policeman—who was wearing his uniform, off duty or not—and I stared at the house for a few seconds, like we weren't sure who was supposed to go inside.

"Need help with your bags?" he finally asked.

I didn't want his help with anything. I couldn't articulate why. He'd been polite enough.

"I got 'em," I said, grabbing the hard-sided suitcases from the seat next to me. Linda Jubilee had insisted I bring only two. At first that'd seemed impossible. Then I realized it didn't matter, not really, and I'd tossed in some clothes and my extra pair of Converse sneakers (pink, and the closest thing to dress shoes I owned), a toothbrush, and The Book.

Suitcases in hand, I had no choice but to step out of the police car. I banged the door shut with my hip. My belly still ached. The world outside the car felt hot and close. It was a miserable, record-setting scorcher of a July across the nation, and Litani was small—I knew that from the population sign on the way in. Only 2,700 people, and that's if everyone told the truth when they answered the census.

I leaned down so I could peek inside the passenger-side window. "Thanks for the ride."

He swallowed. His face was serious and vague, a LEGO officer come to life. "Tell your mom hi."

I watched him drive away, grateful for that last bit.

It revealed why I hadn't liked him.

He was a brownnoser.

That and he'd kept shooting his eyes at me in the rearview mirror.

CHAPTER 2

The screen door rattled when I first knocked at Linda Jubilee's blue house, one suitcase on each side of me, the sun cooking my scalp right through my hair. She opened the door immediately, her hand spread like a starfish across the webbing. She must have seen the police car pull up, but she remained committed to her angry phone conversation, the handset cradled between her ear and shoulder pad. She didn't pause to say hello, hadn't even glanced my way, not that I'd noticed. She just kept hollering into the phone.

"What sorts of altars?" she demanded.

My stomach knots twisted tighter.

I squeezed the suitcases so hard my fingers circled back into the soft pads of my hands. My eyes kept finding her, then darting to my feet. The carpeting weave reached higher than the tops of my sneakers, its earth-colored fibers stretching like grass toward the sun. Or maybe the strands were seaweed, waving. That would make me a mermaid. I allowed the suitcases to drop just low enough to brush the top of the shag.

My mom made a sound of frustration. "No, over there!"

I assumed she was still speaking to the person on the other end of the line.

"Francesca!"

I jumped. She'd been talking to me. "Yes, ma'am?"

"Your suitcases belong in your room." She jabbed her thumb down the hall and then showed me her back, the coil of phone cord snaking around her waist.

"Say that again," she breathed into the handset. "I was distracted."

I drew a raggedy breath and padded through the deep carpeting, past the margarine-yellow walls, staring straight ahead, trying to glance inside open doorways without moving my head. I didn't want to cheese her off by revealing that I didn't remember which room she considered mine. To this day, I regretted making such a fuss about her pulling my tooth. My rejection of her efforts had angered her, made her withdraw from my life.

It left a hole.

Dad did his best to fill it.

I squashed that thought almost before it formed. I didn't have room for it, not right then, not in my mom's house when she hadn't even looked at me yet.

"Last one on the right," she hollered in my direction.

I flinched. I'd almost gotten away with figuring it out on my own. The other doorways had revealed a peek of her bedroom, an avocado-tiled bathroom, and a linen closet.

I stepped into the final room, and sure enough, I recognized the furniture. I'd slept there only two nights, but it was hard to forget a lumpy twin bed covered with an elephant quilt, a nightstand holding an elephant lamp, and walls plastered in elephant-gray wallpaper. The suitcases slid out of my hands. They didn't make a sound. The carpet was too thick, shag grabbing like tentacles at my feet.

This was my home now. My life.

Tears stung my cheeks. I wished for them to melt me like water tossed on a witch so I could disappear. Dad would hate me wallowing, had always said you could "find something good everywhere and in everyone," but he wasn't here, was he?

I'd made sure of that.

A clap scared me out of my skin.

My mom stood in the hallway, her lips pulled tight.

"Cozy!" she declared, staring over me into the elephant room. Still not looking at me. "Is it like you remember?"

"Yes, ma'am."

She smiled, but it didn't quite reach her eyes, which finally, unsettlingly, landed on me. "I have a meeting downtown. When I get back, I'll tell you about an exciting project I have for you." Her eyes, so dark brown they were almost black, flicked to the window. "In the meanwhile, why don't you visit the playground down the street, the one you must have passed when Officer Wendt dropped you off."

Her tone was pleasant, but what now? *Go to the playground?*

I was a teenager, not a baby, but that wasn't even it. I didn't have a center, not inside me and certainly not in Litani. If forced back outside, I would float away, a peach-colored balloon gliding up, up, and away.

"I can't leave without The Book," I blurted. It was a gomer thing to say, but it was the first thing that sprang to mind.

She tilted her head, disappeared from view for a moment, and returned with an army knapsack (not a pair of pliers, thank god), more tube than pack. She held it out to me. "Stuff whatever you like in here. It's yours for as long as you need it."

I didn't know what was stylish in Litani, Minnesota, but I was pretty sure the bag she was offering wasn't it. Its olive-green surface appeared both rough and slick, like sealskin, and it reeked of motor oil. Seeing no other option, I grabbed it from her and placed it next to my largest suitcase, which had belonged to my dad. What use does a fourteen-year-old have for luggage? I'd planned to travel after college, maybe visit Japan or Brazil, where there were still plants to discover. But until then, a backpack had met all my needs just fine.

Under Mom's gaze, I laid the luggage on its side, clicked open the closures, and removed The Book. I shielded the precious cargo as best I could as I slid it into the knapsack. It was going to be lonely inside the big goofy tube-bag, but that didn't worry me as much as the immediate threat my mom posed.

Please don't ask me about The Book. Please, please, please.

I needn't have worried.

"There you go," she said after I stuffed it into the knapsack, as if the matter—every matter—were resolved for now and eternity. "Now run along. Be home before sunset."

I stood, looping the straps over my shoulder. I'd never felt lonelier in my whole life, not even at Dad's funeral when all those people from the college and our neighborhood came up to tell me how he was the best man they'd ever known. I forced my voice steady. No way was I going to cry in front of her, not again. "What should I do at the playground?"

"Play!" she demanded. "Make friends!"

I nodded and shuffled toward the front door, hovering just outside myself, hollowed out with only the pain in my stomach to anchor me, a mooring that was sure to give way as soon as I stepped outdoors.

Daddy. Help me.

But of course he wouldn't, not ever again.

Mom had paused too long when my great-aunt called to tell her Dad was dead and that I'd need to come live with her in Minnesota. I knew because I'd been clutching the other phone in the house, straining to hear magic words, hoping against reality that Mom could somehow make things better. Not bring Dad back to life, I knew that, but maybe she could forgive me for what I'd done.

But she hadn't asked any follow-up questions about his death, didn't attend the funeral, hadn't flown to California to help pack up the house, never provided any healing words. All she had to offer was a too-long pause followed by, "Fine."

"Don't go any further than the playground," she said as I passed through the screen door, her voice tight and sharp, aimed like an arrow at my back. "And only play with kids. No grown-ups."

CHAPTER 3

If Linda Jubilee had meant her caution as a joke, it would *not* have cleared the top 100 in Dad's list of things to make a person smile. But maybe that's how mom jokes were.

Or maybe just my mom's because she's evil.

Dad would have scolded me in a New York minute for the unkind thought, but I held firm to it as my high-tops flopped on the strange sidewalks.

It kept me from crying.

The knapsack straps itched, so I adjusted them. I was sure I resembled a kindergartner with her big ol' nearly empty backpack, but I didn't know anyone in this town, so what did I care? Sweat trickled down my neck, the July sun searing it like a cast-iron pan. I spotted people here and there, some of them mowing their lawns, others carrying blankets to what sounded like a Saturday baseball game up the block. They all stared at me, not even hiding their gapes. Was it because I was unfamiliar? Or was it the tube pack I was carrying?

Doesn't matter.

On top of the graveyard hill on the way into Litani, I'd been able to see for a mile in every direction, had taken note of the forest and river marking the west edge of town, but I hadn't been paying attention to how far away the woods were from Linda Jubilee's house. Could I reach them on foot?

I might as well find out, because no way was I going to hang out in a playground in a strange town for hours.

Plus, the woods were where Dad was.

Of course he wasn't *really* there. I knew that. Not even in a "he's everywhere looking down on me" way. No, Dad *was* the acrophyll and chlorophyll, pollen and petals. He'd been a botany professor at UCLA, so it was his job, but it'd been more than that. He said his blood flowed green. Simply put, his whole life had been plants and me. I'd joined him in the Angeles National Forest every summer since I was five, plus some weekends during the school year. He'd probably started taking me because, after he and Mom divorced, he didn't know what else to do with me, but I soon became his assistant.

"Do you see that?" he'd asked during one of our first forest outings. He'd been pointing toward a plant that looked like every other green thing we'd passed on the walk from the car. "How many leaves does it have?"

I counted with my chubby fingers. "One, two, three, four, five, six, seven." I remember feeling proud. That'd been some good counting.

He beamed. "Yep." Then he knelt next to the plant and tugged at it. Slowly, a ghost carrot appeared. He was careful to break it off an inch from the base before reburying the plant's weeping root in the soft earth. Then he snapped off the greenery, rubbed the worst of the dirt off the white vegetable, and handed it to me.

"It's an Indian cucumber!" he said.

I accepted it. The tuber was the size of a finger and hairy. My face must have conveyed my doubts, because Dad laughed and grabbed it back, chomping it in half in a single bite.

"Delicious!" he declared.

The second time he offered it to me, I didn't hesitate. I popped it into my mouth.

I wouldn't have called it delicious, but it was juicy and mild and had appeared out of the ground like a magician's trick. I was sold. After that, I devoured every bit of plant information he offered. The forest became my school and my playground, a place that I associated with the best times of my life.

Could it provide me solace in Litani?

I cruised past the playground full of little kids swinging and sliding and seesawing, the benches surrounding it dotted with moms talking and laughing while keeping one eye on their children the whole time like only a mom (except for my mom) could do.

How had she imagined I would want to play there? *Excuse me, small child, could you give me an underdog?* Please. I kept my eyes trained on the faraway treetops towering over the houses, watching for where they were the thickest, and directed my steps toward them.

The neighborhood ramblers and cottages were soon replaced by the largest trailer park I'd ever seen, a sign reading BLUE WATERS ESTATES spanning its wide front gate. The name suggested I was near the river I'd spotted on my way into town, but I'd have known regardless because the air had grown swollen and froggy.

The woods loomed directly on the other side of the trailer park.

I should have kept my cool and walked toward the trees, but I couldn't stop from racing into their open arms, relieved beyond words to finally feel a measure of familiar comfort. This wasn't California, but the trees turned the light into the same liquid green. Moss and dirt and the sweet musk of composting plants perfumed the air, wetter than the woods I'd grown up in, but the same living fragrance. I inhaled deeply, something in me loosening, my stomach at long last unknotting itself.

Turned out Mom kicking me out of that dry box of a house was the kindest thing she could have done for me, even though she'd done it by accident.

I let the emerald air scour my lungs as I studied the forest floor. There were obvious paths running through it, some narrow and likely animal, others wider and marred with cigarette butts and Hamm's beer cans. The path that led into the darkest heart of the woods was splashed with what looked like dried paint or mud; it was hard to tell with the peekaboo light of the sun playing through the leaves. White-petaled anemones (the root and leaves made an excellent styptic when boiled) and wood nettle (it produced delicious shoots with late-summer seeds like flax) clustered at the edges of the paths.

Squinting at the sun-dappled ground to get my bearings, I decided to walk north, toward what appeared to be an opening in the forest. I used the moss on the sides of trees to guide me. Moss needed water to reproduce. Shade retained water better than sun, and the north side of anything was usually shadier than the south. Ergo, if there was no other nearby water source, moss usually grew on the north side of things. Dorkville, right?

Five short minutes of following the tree moss along the most-used path brought me out of the cozy forest gloom to the river. The flowing water glittered like a promise, not blue but a pretty gray with silver edges. I stood at a narrow point, the river twenty feet or so across. A tire swing hung off a nearby tree. I was suddenly desperate to leap onto it. I imagined myself swinging a wide arc over the delicious water, hooting like a banshee, and then letting go, dropping into the cool river. I scratched a bug bite at my ear, realizing I couldn't do it. Dad taught me you never swim alone, and besides, I couldn't leave The Book unguarded.

Allowing myself a sigh of regret, I settled for hiking farther up the river to a spot where a log had dropped in. I walked across it, arms out for balance, and then plunked myself down into the crook, cradled like a bird in a nest. The log was carved with etchings—initials, hearts, stars inside circles—but none of them interested me. I was here for the cool water. I removed one shoe and sock and then the other, wrinkling my nose at the mucky smell of my hot feet. But when I sank them into the clear river—*ahhhh* . . . bliss. I shivered from toe to tip.

The Angeles National Forest had not been a place where Dad and I relaxed except when he got winded or his chest started hurting. Other than that, we were there to work. That place was a true wilderness, so different from the timid hills and trampled trails surrounding me now. The Angeles Forest had breathtaking mountain vistas, deep canyons, waterfalls, and alpine lakes. There were towering cedars, their roots sipping at the icy mountain streams, and steep trails, all of it spread beneath startling blue skies.

The forest also contained an incredible variety of plant and tree species, and Dad and I were there to study them, not soak our dogs. That seemed like a shame, because this sure did feel good, the silky water momentarily washing away my troubles. I twirled my feet in the river, marveling at how my whole body was cooling from the bottom up, relishing water clear enough to reveal the potato-shaped rocks below.

I was smiling—my first real smile since Dad's funeral—when I spotted it.

There on the riverbank.

A flash of purple.

Wild bergamot!

I grabbed my shoes, hopped up, and danced down the log. Bergamot was a go-to plant whether you wanted a sachet to make your clothes smell fresher, had a bee sting, or needed to treat a headache, cold, sleep problems, or tummy ache. The boiled leaves could even be made into a poultice that would clear the skin. But best of all, wild bergamot had been my dad's plant personality: strong yet soft and everything to everybody.

I reached the purple flowers, the scorchy day slicking my skin now that my feet were no longer cooling in the river. I slid the knapsack off my shoulders and dropped to the ground. Maybe the bergamot would be the first page in The Book I'd make all on my own. To honor Dad (as if I had any right).

I don't remember which of us came up with the idea for The Book, Dad or me. He'd wanted to call it *People's Plant Personalities*, I wanted *Choose Your Plant Personality* because I devoured Choose Your Own

Adventure books like potato chips, but we both agreed that the concept was genius. Basically, we'd let people choose their plant based on their personality. Were they a burdock, sharp and desperate but the first to provide stability where the earth had been disturbed? Or possibly they were more of an American elder, with people always grabbing their berries and missing that their true worth lived in their flowers.

Dad and I drafted the personality profiles together, and then he'd add some medicinal or nutrition information and I'd sketch the plant, giving it human features. It was solid-gold nerdy, the whole idea of it, but since I no longer had Dad, The Book had become my heart, a forever record of our time in the woods together. So maybe it wasn't so gomer that I'd told my mom I couldn't leave it behind, alone in the house with her.

It had originally been a journal, one of those fancy leather-bound ones holding thick, creamy paper inside. Dad had picked it up at some botany conference. When we were looking for something to use for our project, we'd agreed it was perfect.

I was reaching into the knapsack for it when the worn patch caught my eye. I'd overlooked it, hidden as it was beneath the base of a strap. The ink was faded with age but still legible.

Jubilee.

The name squeezed my heart. Had the pack belonged to Dad?

He'd never mentioned being in the military, but I'd never asked. What child imagined their parents' lives before they entered them? I knew he'd lost a brother real young, that his parents—my grandparents—had passed before I'd been born, but the handful of times I'd asked, he'd shut down the conversation as sure as closing a door.

It's better to live in the present, pumpkin. That's where the good stuff is.

I supposed I could ask my mom, or Dad's aunt Edna back in Palo Alto, if Dad had been in the army. I ran my finger over the patch. No, it felt better to simply trust it had belonged to him. It wouldn't hurt a fly to believe that. I was about to reach inside for The Book when I remembered I hadn't packed a pen or a pencil. I smacked my forehead.

Crack.

I yelped. The noise was much louder than it should have been. It took a couple blinks before I realized I hadn't made it.

Someone was in the woods with me.

I shrank, cradling my knees to my chest, my skin suddenly icy. Had my smart and resourceful dad made me feel safe in the woods rather than the forest itself? I did my best to steady my breath. Tugging on my socks and shoes might make too much noise, so I left them next to me, choosing to instead silently thread my arms through the knapsack straps. There was some assurance in feeling The Book close to my body.

Movement caught my eye. Whoever was there was forty feet or so to my right, striding away from the river, more shadow than shape in the thick woods. They stepped on another branch, the crack echoing through the woods.

"Ready or not!"

It was a man's voice.

My skin tightened.

And then he strode into an open patch, the sun spotlighting him. He was now twenty feet away with his back to me, shortish brown hair curled around his neck. He wasn't big—smaller than Dad, who'd been average—except this guy had ropy forearms, Popeye-esque compared to the rest of his body. His right arm featured a blotch so big and intentional looking that it must have been a tattoo, though of what, I couldn't tell from here. I felt a desperate ache to see his face.

Pushing myself slowly off the ground, I leaned against the nearest tree, willing myself to become bark and bone, never peeling my eyes off the stranger.

Until I heard the high-pitched squeal to my left.

A girl maybe five or six, her hair sunshine yellow and twisted up in pigtails, took off toward the trailer park.

The man bellowed at the sight of her.

My belly churned, knotting itself right back up.

Only play with kids, my mother had warned before kicking me out of her house. Here were a man and girl playing together. Surely they were father and daughter?

Didn't matter, because my skin felt like it was crawling with a thousand ticks, and suddenly, violently, I needed to be as far away from these woods as possible. The weird disconnect between the safety I'd expected and the panic I was feeling was dizzying. My backpack over my shoulders, I leaned down to grasp my shoes. I kept my eyes pinned to the man lumbering toward the girl, trying to figure out the best way to escape without running into them.

I was considering a less-used path when a hand clamped onto my wrist.

"Wanna join The Game, Fresh Meat?"

CHAPTER 4

I could hear that the girl's words wanted to be capitalized in how much weight she gave them—*wanna join The Game,* Important Capital Letters, just like for The Book. Except not, because The Book was good and The Game wasn't; that was also as clear as glass. I snatched my wrist away, feeling the snakebite burn of her grip even after my arm was free. I dropped my sneakers in the process.

She was dirty blonde, her eyes hard in a way that plucked my nerves. Two more girls stood behind her, all three of them nine or ten based on their clothes and size. They'd sneaked up while I'd been watching the man play hide-and-go-seek. The ginger-haired girl shared the leader's stony expression, but the third one, a brunette wearing braids, had a softer face, her chocolate-brown eyes magnified by thick glasses.

My heart banged in my ears as we stared each other down. Something told me they weren't here to make friends. It was probably just as well. I was terrible at it. Dad had sent me to camp a few years back. I'd been so intimidated by all the unfamiliar kids that when it came time to introduce myself, I pretended to have a British accent. Too embarrassed to come clean, I was forced to maintain it all week long.

I'd left only one good friend behind in Pasadena. June. Man, did I wish she were here now. She and I had been as close as two fingers on a hand, Dad always said. We'd even started our own business back in fourth grade, a detective agency called Paul's Angels (Dad had loved that—he was a natural choice as our boss; June even called him D2, short for "second Dad"), slapping up flyers all over the neighborhood offering to find missing pets and "get to the bottom of suspicious activities."

We'd actually solved a couple of crimes, June and me. A woman a few blocks away hired us to figure out whose dog was doing its business in her yard. It took three days of stakeouts perched in the thick branches of a Pasadena oak in the park across the street, grinding on Big League Chew and taking notes on everyone who passed by, before we caught the perpetrator in the act.

We'd snapped a Polaroid.

We were thorough.

We'd also caught some kids stealing mail and a neighbor hooking her hose up to another neighbor's spout and running up her water bill, and we'd located a missing cat, though I didn't think this trio would be any more interested in hearing about me and June's solve rate than they were in hearing about the price of tea in China.

The blonde broke the charged silence. "I like your shoes," she said, tipping her head toward where my sneakers lay on the forest floor.

She was wearing a Garfield T-shirt made for a grown man. It was as long as a dress on her. On closer inspection, it wasn't the real Garfield, just a knockoff fat orange cat meant to look like him, cockily leaning against the word "Garfiend." Still eyeballing me, she lifted the oversize shirt, yanked a pack of cigarettes out of her shorts, flipped open the top, and pulled out an Eve Slim and a peach-colored lighter.

I about pooped my pants. She was a *kid*.

I glanced behind me, searching for the man and the girl who'd been playing or Allen Funt to gleefully reveal that I was on *Candid Camera*. I only saw trees, heard the river, smelled the sweet rot of forest.

"I like my shoes, too," I said, turning back to the blonde, my top lip catching on dry teeth. "You shouldn't smoke."

She lit her cigarette, glaring at me. She didn't really inhale, though she probably thought she was. "Who are you?"

"Francesca."

I was surprised to hear that come out of my mouth. Only some teachers and my mom called me that. I suppose I meant to sound like the boss of the situation. It was only nominally better than a fake accent.

"You here on vacation?" asked the ginger-haired child.

"No, I sure am not."

The scrawny Garfiend girl scowled through her cigarette smoke. "Where're you from?"

I'd had enough. I was older than all of them. A teenager. A *Californian*. "What are your names?"

"Crystal," the ginger said, but sullenly.

The girl who'd so far been silent said, "Michelle." She even smiled shyly, highlighting two fresh buckteeth with gaping holes on each side. That tooth situation, coupled with her brown braids, dropped her age from ten to eight. The way her fingers played nervously with the frayed hem of her green track shorts, I wondered what she'd done to fall in with the two clearly rougher girls.

"I asked you where you're from," the leader repeated. "Cuz if you were from around here, you'd know these are our woods. No one comes or goes without paying a price. You've heard of Satan, haven't you?"

She'd meant it as a threat, not a question. She dropped the nearly whole cigarette onto the forest floor and ground it out threateningly with her jelly-shoed foot, like a little gangster. I'd have laughed if I weren't so scared.

I reached for my Cons. "I have to leave."

The slap was so unexpected that I didn't have time to block it. I reeled back, hand to my stinging cheek, as the blonde dived for my shoes. She tossed them to Crystal and then put up her dukes. "Those sneakers are mine now. That's the price you pay for trespassing. You have a problem with it?"

My hands flew to the knapsack straps, instinctually protecting The Book, the only thing of value I owned in this world.

It was a mistake.

Crystal's eyes lit up. "Ask her what's in there, Dawn."

Dawn. That was Garfiend's name.

Rather than yell at Crystal for giving her away, Dawn stepped closer, trying to peer around me to the army knapsack.

My neck skin prickled, my baby hairs rising in response.

"How about your ugly backpack is mine now, too, *Francesca*."

I jerked back, a sharp stick stabbing my bare foot. "It doesn't even belong to me," I said.

"Then you won't mind handing it over," Dawn said.

"No," I protested, blinking stupidly.

She put her hands on her hips, her eyes gleaming. "How about we make a deal? You can either give me the backpack or you can play The Game."

I didn't care to do either. My muscles acted before my brain, springing me sideways in the direction of the trailer park. I began to run, no longer feeling my feet, pumping my legs like pistons.

I made it all of ten yards before the girl gang took me down.

CHAPTER 5

I'd witnessed fistfights many a time on *Knight Rider*, catfights on *Dynasty* when June's mom let us watch, and all sorts of smacking around in *The Outsiders*. In all cases, the violence had a dancing quality, not choreographed exactly but like there were basic rules that everyone followed: *do this and then this and then this*. Those bouts had also been fair, where people gave as good as they got until they didn't.

Real-life fighting wasn't like that at all, I was discovering. It was ferocious grunts, squeals, hair pulling, machine-gun kicking *pow pow pow*, and flesh twisting. I fended off blows as best I could while desperately clinging to the knapsack, but I was seriously losing.

"Get her bag!" one of the girls yelled.

When I felt it being tugged off my shoulders, I went full wild thing. Everything I loved was gone: Dad, my house, Pasadena, June. I couldn't lose The Book, too. The oily cloth bit my shoulders, but I refused to release it, madly punching at air and ground and girl.

"Stop it!" I screamed.

A tiny rock fist landed in my stomach. I wheezed and kicked in the direction it had come from. I felt an instant of satisfaction as my foot connected with something soft, followed by an *oof*. The grim pleasure was short-lived, though, because suddenly the knapsack was gone.

I lifted my face to the treetops and howled, unable to any longer contain the raw-heart loneliness that'd been gulping me down since my dad's death.

Since I'd killed him.

It ached like a field of raw nerves to remember how smart he'd been, how much he'd loved me. I'd loved him, too, and taken such good care of him.

I knew the moment our perfect life had started to unravel.

It was the day his meeting with the dean was supposed to be.

He'd overslept, like he did most mornings.

"You're going to be late for work!" I'd called to him, like it was a plain ol' day, not the beginning of the end.

"Almost ready," he hollered from the bathroom.

I had his breakfast prepared—peanut butter and banana toast, messy but delicious. I'd also packed his lunch, though sometimes he got so busy teaching that he forgot to take it out of his car, and his vehicle would smell like rotten apples the next time I hopped in.

"Don't you have that meeting with your boss today?" I asked, wrinkling my nose at his Grateful Dead T-shirt. He'd never attended one of their concerts, but his grad assistant last summer had thought it'd be a kick to buy him the shirt. Dad liked the tie-dye colors and treated me to a whole excited lecture on how avocado pits could have been used to make the pink swirls, turmeric the yellow, and beets the red. I didn't have the heart to tell him it was probably made in some factory overseas.

"Oh!" he'd said, running back to his bedroom. He emerged four minutes later wearing a button-down and his favorite clip-on bow tie in place of the Grateful Dead shirt. That curl of black hair that always got loose lay across his forehead. "How's this?"

"Much better."

He smiled and took the food I was offering him. "I can rustle up supper tonight."

"Sure, Dad," I said.

We both knew he wouldn't. We'd starve if I didn't cook. My repertoire was limited, but what I prepared, I prepared well: frozen pizzas, grilled cheese and tomato soup (his favorite), macaroni and cheese, and lots of fresh fruits and vegetables. I'd learned how to make all that after he and Mom got divorced. He needed all the room in his head for plants, and I loved that about him. Plus, it felt good to take care of him.

He was almost out the door before I remembered. "Did you take your heart medicine?"

He had one hand on the doorknob and the other holding his briefcase and lunch bag, the peanut butter and banana toast perched in his mouth, just on the edge of dripping down the front of his shirt. I leaped forward with a rag and caught the glop before it hit.

"Dad! You need to be more careful."

"I know," he said around the mouthful. He was difficult to stay mad at. He was so innocent looking, all elbows and wide brown eyes, an actual nutty professor. "And no, I didn't take my medicine. Pumpkin, I couldn't survive without you."

That made me feel good. Important. I was still smiling as I finished cleaning the house and walked to school.

It'd be three weeks until I murdered him, killed him in his own bed.

I couldn't have fathomed such a possibility back then, any more than I'd have believed it if someone had told me I'd transform into a dragon or wake up on Jupiter. But that's how it was with the big life moments, I now knew. You get plucked out of your regular life and dropped right into them. You struggle to escape, to convince someone it's a mistake, that you've been dumped into a scene in a movie you were never meant to be in, but too bad so sad the only way out is through.

That's when you find out what you're really made of.

No backsies.

That was a terrible truth to learn before the age of fifteen, that some mistakes are forever.

And so I wailed in front of these three strange girls. I screamed at the sky in this dirty nightmare of a forest, my knapsack gone, face bloodied, flesh stinging, feeling as empty as a fresh-dug grave.

My unearthly baying froze all three, Dawn about to open the pack, Crystal with her arm cocked to punch me, even Michelle in a feral daze, her fingers arched like claws near my face.

"What the hell kind of noise was that?" Dawn asked when I drew a breath.

"Give me my bag back now," I growled. The cry had at least erased some of the numbness. In its place, I felt ashamed and elated, neither of which made sense.

"Hold her," Dawn said, shoving her hand inside the knapsack.

Michelle and Crystal pushed me against a tree, pinning me in place. I began shaking all over.

Dawn held The Book up triumphantly, sneering at me. "Lookit the baby cry," she said.

I hadn't even noticed the tears streaming down my cheeks. I was too busy being squashed beneath a giant's foot of emptiness. They would steal The Book, these *Lord of the Flies* girls. They'd destroy it. Burn it, probably, cackling the whole time. Turned out there was always somewhere lower to go, a worse feeling below even the most suffocating of depressions.

"Please," I begged. "Don't wreck it. It was my dad's."

Dawn sing-sang my words back to me. "*Don't wreck it. It was my dad's.*" Then she spit at my feet. "Come on, guys. Let's go read the baby's book somewhere nicer."

The emptiness turned black. When Crystal and Michelle released me, I collapsed.

"We'll catch you on the flip side, baby Fresh Meat," Dawn said. "Thanks for your dumb book."

She dangled it in front of my face right before a big mitt appeared, snatching it out of her hand.

CHAPTER 6

My first thought was, *These are mighty busy woods.*

Second was, *Please don't be the creepy tattooed guy who was playing with the kid.*

But then Dawn leaped back, and the stranger was clearly visible even though one of my eyes was already swelling shut.

It wasn't the same man from before.

"Give it back, numbnuts!" Dawn yelled, but she didn't advance on him.

I could see why. He was tall, maybe six feet, though it was hard to be sure from my angle on the forest floor. He was broad shouldered, too, with shaggy hair that fell across his eyes. I guessed he was eighteen or nineteen. The way he held The Book against his stomach reminded me of a TV-show preacher cradling the Bible.

Someone was breathing like a bull. I realized it was me. I tried calming down, but it was possible his presence meant I'd gone from the frying pan into the fire.

Screw it.

"That's mine," I wheezed, reaching toward The Book.

The guy didn't take his focus off Dawn. "You should go home."

"At least I have a home, *Crane*," she said, pronouncing his name like it was something nasty. Then, acting her age for the first time since I'd met her, she stuck out her tongue and spun on her heel, traipsing off toward the trailer park. Crystal glared at me before grabbing my shoes and following Dawn. I didn't have the strength to argue. Michelle left last, pushing her glasses up her nose and sneaking glances at Crane as she turned away.

Crane watched them until they were out of sight and then faced me. "You okay?"

You know how sometimes, when you've been really scared and then are finally safe, you take it out on the person who helped you rather than the ones who hurt you? Yeah. "No, I'm *not* okay. Give me my damn book."

The swear word stung like pepper on my tongue.

Crane tossed his head, giving me a full glimpse of his eyes before his bangs curtained them again. Blue. Too bright. Deep set. Just like the eyes of Marc Singer, star of *V* (and *The Beastmaster*; Dad hadn't let me watch it, but I'd seen the poster).

He offered The Book.

Despite my aggressive demand, I hesitated to grab it. Everything in this sinkhole town had so far been a trap. What the heck was wrong with Litani's kids? And had Dawn really mentioned *Satan*? But I couldn't leave The Book behind. Wincing, I struggled to my full height, all four foot ten inches. Crane loomed at least a foot taller than me, so I'd been right at my guess of six feet. I bent over and grabbed the knapsack, snatched The Book out of his hand, and tucked it inside. I was reluctant to slide the pack on my strap-bitten shoulders, but it seemed smart to keep my hands free in case I needed to fight again.

"My name's Crane."

"I know," I said, all my focus on guiding the first strap around a bloodied elbow. "I heard Dawn call you that." I was being a brat. I didn't care.

He coughed. "You're bleeding."

"Eat my shorts."

"Pass the ketchup," he replied, his voice neutral.

I'd never heard that response before. I felt a smile stretch across my face but stopped when it hurt. "Thanks for helping me."

"They're demons, those three." He shrugged. "It's not their fault."

I bit my tongue. I'd been about to say, *Then whose fault is it?*

He glanced in the direction they'd walked off. "I live over there, if you want to clean yourself up before you head home."

His morsels of kindness felt huge. Still, I hesitated.

"I have a hose," he said, cocking his head so he could study me through his hair. "You don't have to come inside."

There's a denture cleaner commercial that shows an older lady dropping her teeth in this jar with cleaning disks. They fizz and loosen the grodiest buildup, and that's what his offer felt like: bubbles loosening tar.

Maybe I'd found a friend in Litani, just like my mom had asked me to.

Maybe.

I nodded and followed him toward the trailer park.

CHAPTER 7

"Is Crane a nickname or your real name?"

He continued to lead the way out of the woods, silently.

"I'm Frankie."

No response. I watched his back, the way he held himself. Boys don't know how to be uncomfortable in their bodies, I realized, even the ones who don't look great. It's not that they can't be shy, or sad, or scared, just like girls. It's that they haven't been taught their bodies are bad their whole lives, like we are. Dad tried to shield me from the worst of it, but we still owned a TV.

I tried again. "I'm new to town."

Still nothing.

"Just moved here today." We were nearing the edge of the tree line, leaving the fairy-tale forest that had melted into a horror show. The real world beckoned from beyond: the hum of cars, the crack of a baseball connecting with a bat, the whir of lawn mowers. I was almost in it when my bare foot landed square on a cocklebur. I grunted and leaped back, my toes curled, and leaned my hand against a tree to tug it out.

Crane turned to me. "You shouldn't go barefoot in the woods. You shouldn't go into the woods at all."

I tossed the bur off to the side and stood as straight as my skinned knees would allow. He was ten feet away from me, backlit by the sun so I couldn't read his face.

"They stole my shoes."

He nodded, then abruptly turned to continue.

I followed him into the glaring sunshine, blinking away the momentary blindness. Shielding my eyes, I was able to take stock of my injuries as we walked. Both knees bloody from falling and then being dragged, one of them with the tight pink sheen of second-string skin. My denim shorts were okay, but my T-shirt was stretched at the neck, hanging off my shoulder in a way that was nearly fashionable. If I swiveled my head back and to the side, I could see a red burn-bruise emerging on my collarbone where the knapsack strap had bitten my skin. My right arm was scratched up, and one eye was halfway closed, the lid swollen like a fleshy awning above it. When I sent my tongue around my mouth, I didn't discover any loose teeth, though I tasted the blood tang of my split lip.

I coughed. My throat felt scraped raw, like I'd swallowed smoke.

I was prodding my tender belly when we passed under the BLUE WATERS ESTATES sign.

I'd walked by it less than an hour and forever ago.

The part of Pasadena I grew up in didn't have trailer parks, so I'd never ventured inside one. The closeness of the narrow houses made me anxious, and it was immediately apparent that there was a big difference in the types of people living here. Some homes featured immaculate lawns, though they were as tiny as postage stamps compared to what I was used to. The occasional blooming fuchsia hung from hooks, and a few places had flower beds and welcome mats. Other trailers were ringed with scrub and dirt and gloom.

"Holy hell, girl, what happened to you?"

I swung my head to the right, my one and a half eyes homing in on a shirtless man sitting in a frayed lawn chair. His trailer cast an inky shadow over him. A powder-blue pickup was parked in the driveway, rust blooming like cold sores across its body.

My training kicked in: an adult asks you a question, you answer. "Got in a fight."

When he stood and stepped into the sun, I stumbled back. Crane stiffened and moved closer to me.

"You sure did."

The soupy smell of BO radiated off the stranger. He was lean, wiry, his height closer to Crane's than mine. He sported a mullet and a Tom Selleck mustache, a gold cross necklace dangling in his waxy-looking chest hair. The sun glinted off a huge belt buckle that had something carved in it, some sort of rippling animal.

It all felt so private, the parts of him he was showing. I blushed and glanced at my feet.

"Name's Sly," he said, his hand appearing in my sight line. He gripped a Pabst Blue Ribbon with the other. "I'd introduce you to my visiting parents, Victor and Eula, but they're . . . otherwise engaged at the moment."

Crane made a noise I couldn't identify. I squinted up at him. He brushed back his hair so he could glare. I took Sly's proffered hand, shook it because that's what I'd been taught to do. "Frankie."

A grin quirked up beneath his bushy mustache. It was a nice smile, I was surprised to notice. "That's a fan-fucking-tastic name, Frankie," he said.

"You coming or not?" Crane asked. "Because I don't got all day to stand in the hot sun."

I reclaimed my hand from Sly, who was holding it longer than seemed right. I'd never had an adult swear at me. "Nice to meet you," I said, backing away.

A vision of a mushroom as Sly's plant personality bloomed behind my eyelids. Mushrooms were technically fungi, not plants, but Dad had said we could bend the rules. It was our book, after all. I puzzled over which specific mushroom Sly would be as I followed Crane, glancing back toward his trailer as we trudged along. He must have gone inside to check on his parents.

We passed a solid building, the only permanent structure I'd seen in the park. BLUE WATERS MAIN OFFICE was burned on a wood sign out front, a map nailed up next to the sign. My eyesight was too cloudy to pick anything solid off the map, just a general impression that the trailer park was shaped like two big loops over a sharp vee. It reminded me of an owl face, a simple one like Mr. Owl from the Tootsie Pop commercial.

How many licks . . .

Crane stopped five rows down and seven trailers back from the office. I'd been counting, the necessity of keeping track of my bearings burned into my neurons from all that time in the woods with Dad.

Crane's home was middle of the road in terms of quality. No flowers decorating it, no welcome mat, but the small patch of grass was mowed, and there was no crummy lawn furniture or rusting equipment lying around.

"How many people live in the park?" I asked, tugging the stretched collar of my shirt toward my neck.

He pointed at the hose, which was connected to a tap at the side of his trailer and curled into a neat circle. "I don't know."

Something about his attitude annoyed me. "Do you know how many trailers there are?"

He shrugged, but then, the words dropping like quarters from a miser, said, "About a hundred singles, the same number of double-wides, and the office."

"Thank you." My voice sounded bossy even to me, but I couldn't seem to help it. Why was I being mean to the one person in this town who'd been nice to me so far? Well, other than Sly, if you counted a handshake as nice, and the bar was low enough that I did.

"Your parents home?" I asked.

It was my sneaky way of trying to find out his age. He was right at the cusp where he could be a high schooler or a grown-up. If he was still in school, it confirmed that Litani kids were grade-A messed up. If he was an adult, I shouldn't have been alone with him; I'd have known that without my mom telling me. Crane didn't fall for my trick, though, instead bending down to wrench on the faucet with a rusty screech. The water pulsed before running clear.

Suddenly, the thought of anything touching my battered skin, even water, made me feel like ralphing. I sucked in a breath past my cut lip and clenched my hands.

Crane brushed his hair from his eyes, studying me. "It's gonna hurt whenever you do it," he said, not unkindly. He crimped the hose and held it out to me.

My shoulders slumped. He was right. And I'd draw less attention walking through town if I lost the biggest clumps of dirt and blood. But I was in no hurry to feel the razor pain of water on my raw meat.

"Crane, what's The Game?"

My question made him release the rucked hose, spraying water everywhere. I squealed and jumped back, the quick motion awakening every agony in my body.

"Who told you about that?" he growled, leaning over to twist off the faucet.

I swiped dripping water from my eyes. "Dawn."

And then I remembered something my mom had yelled into the phone. *I don't care if they think it's a game.* That was a common saying, referring to nothing and everything. But then Mom'd followed it with, *I'm well aware we can't send children undercover.*

"Dawn said something about Satan, too."

He re-coiled the hose. "I meant what I said before about staying out of the woods. Don't trust anyone in Litani, especially anyone who asks you to play The Game."

It was the longest string of words I'd heard him say, and his grim attitude chilled my guts. "But what is it?"

"Don't ask." He was scowling at me, his T-shirt and blue jeans surely as hot as a personal sauna in this oppressive heat.

I fisted my hands on my hips. "You realize you can't say 'don't ask' and not expect any questions, right?"

"You wouldn't believe me if I told you."

"Try me." I was mad, but I still liked how grown-up those two words sounded.

Crane angled his head, studying me. He was Marc Singer all the way when he was being intense like that. "There's Satan worshippers in town," he finally said. "They hurt kids. Some people say they even murder 'em, using their virgin blood in rituals."

That had not been at all what I'd expected, and a snort escaped before I could help it. "Come on."

He tensed up, and his hair curtain fell back across his eyes. "I said you wouldn't believe me. It's your funeral. I'd watch out for strangers if I was you, though."

"*You're* a stranger."

His lower face, the only part I could see, appeared on the brink of smiling before he locked it up real quick. "You should go home," he said gruffly.

"You're not going to tell me anything else?"

Rather than answer, he walked inside his trailer.

Jeebers. What the heck was wrong with this place?

CHAPTER 8

The sun crisped the part in my hair as I limped back to Linda Jubilee's house. If I was stared at, I didn't lift my head high enough to notice. No one spoke to me, either. Half of me was grateful no one offered to help, the other half surprised. People thought big cities were standoffish, but Pasadena had neighborhoods where everyone looked out for one another. The one time I'd fallen off my bike cruising to the playground to meet June, a neighbor—the same one who hired us to locate the mystery pooper—dashed out with antiseptic and another was on the phone to Dad almost before I hit the ground. I might be exaggerating, but the point is that small-town stereotypes were turning out to be even less accurate than big-city ones.

In any case, I made it home without anyone talking to me or me talking to anyone.

A police car was parked out front when I hobbled up. My heart bounced into my throat—had they discovered what I'd done to Dad?—until I remembered my mom's connection to law enforcement. It might even have been the same car that'd dropped me off. I sure didn't want to explain to a police officer why I looked like I'd taken a shortcut through a meat grinder. It wasn't that I wanted to protect the weirdos who'd attacked me. It was more . . . shame. Yeah, that was it. It'd be humiliating to admit I'd been beaten up and had my shoes stolen by three little girls.

If Mom and the officer were in the wicker living room, it would be impossible to sneak past without them noticing my condition. If they were hanging out in the kitchen or her office, though, their attention on something else, I stood a chance.

Near the open front door, I cocked my ear, listening for their location.

". . . ten years old, Linda," I heard a man's voice—likely the policeman's—say. "There might be more children."

Mom responded, but she sounded like the *Peanuts* teacher. *Whah whah.*

"The trailer park," he answered, like it was a given.

That iced my liver, because whatever they were talking about wasn't good. I could tell it from the stiffness in his voice. Maybe there was more than one trailer park around here.

Or maybe not. Maybe they were talking about the one I'd just left.

Mom said something back, but I still couldn't pick out her words. That meant she was standing in her office, him closer to the living room. Shoot! Unless I was lucky (lately, I wasn't ever lucky) and his back was to the front door, no way could I sneak by.

I drew a deep breath. Might as well get it done and over with. I tugged open the door. A quick glance to the right revealed the back of a uniformed officer standing in the doorway to Mom's office. A sliver of good fortune? I tried to close the screen door quiet as a mouse, but he still turned. I spotted the worried flash of his eyes as I fled down the hall.

I slipped just inside my bedroom and strained to listen, leaving the door cracked.

"She's home," he said.

Mom made a neutral noise.

"She looks like she fell out of a moving vehicle."

Mom must have entered the living room because I could suddenly hear her loud as a bell. "She's dramatic, that one," she said. "Remind me to tell you about the time I helped her pull a loose tooth."

I cringed. She *was* still mad at me about that. I didn't stand a chance.

Muffled footsteps padded down the hall toward me. I jerked back and closed the door right before the surprisingly gentle knock.

"Francesca, are you all right?"

"Yes, ma'am." I struggled for something to tell her that wouldn't be a lie. "Skinned my knees. No biggie."

"Do you need help?"

I leaned against the door, my day—week, month—tied like a cement block around my neck. What would happen if I opened it and let her help me? All my pain could tumble out and my mom—who better than a mom?—could kiss every scrape and make my heartbreak somehow bearable.

I dragged in a deep sigh. "No, I'm fine. But thanks."

A pause.

"Let me see."

No way could I defy a direct order. I dragged the door open, my pulse fluttering like a trapped bug in my throat. Mom's jaw tightened as she took in the scope of my injuries. I wished I'd used Crane's hose without him, wished I could hide from Mom's gaze, wished the carpet would swallow me whole (if any carpet could, it'd be this one). Mom was still wearing the work clothes from earlier, but before she'd taken in my war wounds, before she'd had a chance to button up her face, I'd seen something wilted about her, something beyond her heat-squashed hair. What had her and the officer been talking about?

"What happened?" she asked.

A sound from the end of the hallway. The police officer was listening.

"I fell off the top of the slide at the playground." The lie burned like acid.

Mom crossed her arms, disturbing the string of fake beads. Her dark eyes drilled into me. "Did someone do this to you?"

"I swear, I did it to myself." That was the truth, though not the one she was after.

"Anything else you want to tell me?"

I itched to lean forward and glance down the hallway. I imagined the officer taking notes. "Um, I met some girls."

She tapped her foot. "What were their names?"

I rubbed my palms together anxiously. "I don't remember. I got so shocked when they talked about Satan worshippers in town . . ."

Mom grimaced. "Did you tell them your last name?"

I shook my head.

"Good. Hold on." She swiveled to the linen closet and pulled out a towel and stacked on top of it a washcloth, a pot of ointment, a bottle of hydrogen peroxide and another of Betadine, and a roll of gauze. She looked down the hall, her lips pursed, then back at me, handing me the pile. "I'm glad you're here, Francesca, but there's something going on in town that's taking my attention. It's got old roots, all the way back to your dad."

A part of me, something important, fell away. "What?"

"That Satan talk. It started with your dad, back when he was still in high school. You look like him, you know."

The officer cleared his throat, and Mom glanced at her watch, then back at me. "We'll have time together soon to catch up, and I have that surprise to tell you about. But right now, I have to go out again. Work. There's some hotdish in the fridge you can warm up for supper."

She just kept talking like she hadn't just said the most outlandish thing. My dad the agnostic and Satan didn't fit in the same sentence. We didn't even believe in Satan, so how had I ended up in this upside-down world? I only nodded.

She smiled faintly. "I can tell you're a tough cookie, just like me. You'll want to take care of this all on your own, won't you? Get cleaned up, then."

I stayed in place, frozen, as she walked away.

She must have been almost at the door when she called out, "Don't stay up too late."

I turned toward my bed. A movement at my window caught my good eye. I blinked, watching for it to repeat itself. It didn't. Must have been a trick of the sun.

"I won't," I said, but the slam of the screen door told me she was already too far away to hear.

❖

The hot shower was a perfect blend of agony and ecstasy.

The water stung every bit of wrecked flesh it licked, but it washed out the grit, black and red pooling at my feet and swirling down the drain in a marbled eddy. The powerful stream also kneaded my aching muscles. I used a washrag to scour myself, even though the scrubbing almost hurt worse than getting beat up in the first place.

Better to feel the pain now, my dad had told me that day I'd fallen off my bike, *than suffer the infection later*.

I let those thoughts wash down the drain with the dirt and my blood. Once the water ran clear, I shampooed my hair with Mom's Prell, kneading the clean-smelling lather into my scalp before rinsing it out. Then I used a squirt of the green liquid to rinse out the washrag until it was no longer muddy with gore. When everything was as clean as it was going to get, I twisted off the water, wrung out the washcloth, and draped it over the side of the tub before stepping onto the bath mat.

I used the towel Mom had given me to aggressively dry my hair before dabbing gently at my body. Once I was as dry as I could bear to make myself, I laid the towel across the toilet, planted my butt on top of it, and went to work with the first aid supplies. Holding my right arm over the sink, I poured hydrogen peroxide on my scratches, delighting when it fizzed white like Zotz. I considered pouring some over my raw knees, but the Law of Peroxide mandated that it frothed pleasantly in deep cuts and killed like the devil on surface scrapes. I settled for dripping some Betadine on my knees, catching the coppery overflow with a wad of toilet paper. Then I slathered antibiotic over the arm wounds and looped gauze around them.

Once my injuries were tended to, I brushed my middle-of-back-length hair, starting at the ends and working my way toward the scalp so as not to create a massive Prell snaggle. Next, I gently pulled on a rainbow tank top, white cotton underpants, and dark-green shorts before I worked up the courage to look in the mirror. I wiped the condensed steam off it with my uninjured arm and leaned forward.

And let out a deep breath.

It wasn't as bad as I'd feared.

Sure, my one eye was fat and droopy, the cheek below it sporting a purpling bruise, and my lip was split, but it wasn't too swollen, and with some ice, the shiner would cool right down. Satisfied I'd done my best, I tossed my dirty shorts into the laundry hamper and my ripped shirt into the garbage, where I hid it under used tissues so I didn't have to be reminded of the fight.

I made my way to the kitchen, where I rustled around the fridge, located the CorningWare holding the casserole Mom had mentioned, and scooped out two heaping piles. I microwaved the dish for two minutes, salted it, and walked into the living room.

It was a little after 7:00 p.m. in Minnesota, so five-ish in California. What was on television here at this time? As I flicked on the TV, I realized I was ravenous. I hadn't eaten since the dry turkey sandwich they'd given me on the flight. I dog-ate a bite of hamburger macaroni gloop, figuring I'd need my free hand to run through the channels. But when the TV brightened, I was happy to discover no channel changing would be necessary.

Greatest American Hero reruns!

I plopped onto the couch—as much as a person can plop with wicker furniture—and dug into the salty, soothing casserole, using a fork rather than my mouth this time. It had been a crap day, but something about being clean, having my worst cuts and scrapes bandaged, and filling my belly made me feel more human than I had in a couple weeks.

Dad had lots of ways to support me when I had a bad day—listening, mostly, letting me figure things out by talking my way through them, but sometimes, if I was really wound up, he'd brush my hair. He started doing it when I was little, and I guess he never found a reason to stop. Did that sound like someone who had anything to do with Satan? The further I got from that conversation with Mom, the crazier it sounded. I must have misunderstood her. We'd clear it up the next time we spoke.

Back to my hair. Dad'd joke about giving it a hundred strokes, but I bet it was more than that. I would try keeping track, but even as a teenager, something about the motion put me right to sleep. The highest I ever counted was sixty before, *zonk*, I'd be out on the floor and between Dad's knees while he sat on the couch. At some point he'd carry me to bed and tuck me in, and I'd half wake up in that snuggly bubble of safety and comfort. He kept it up right until the end.

I was smiling at the bittersweet memory when a loud thump came from my bedroom.

CHAPTER 9

I leaped off the couch, cracking the drying wounds on both knees. I swallowed a cry. Was someone lurking in my room?

The front door—escape—was ten feet away. But what if the noise had merely been the house settling? I'd look like an idiot for bolting outdoors, and where even would I run to? I had no idea where Mom's meeting was being held, and the only people I'd met so far were not exactly the hospitable types.

I should go to my room, check it out with my own eyes.

Trust your instincts, Frankie.

Dad had first said that to me when I couldn't decide if the towering plant I was eyeballing was an extremely poisonous giant hogweed or a delicious Indian celery.

Trust your instincts and use your brain, he'd said.

Start with your gut, he meant, but consult your head, too.

I'd been almost positive it was a giant hogweed. It was a feeling, a knowing in my body. But then I remembered: giant hogweed had purple splotches. Being careful not to touch the potentially toxic leaves, I discovered that the plant in front of me did, too.

Gut and brain.

So yep, check my room, but from the outside so I could escape if I needed to.

Remembering the flash I'd spotted on the other side of my bedroom window when Mom had been talking to me, I quietly rested the plate of half-eaten casserole on the coffee table. I tiptoed to the front door, turning the knob slowly so the tumblers barely made a bump when they released. I glanced quickly down the hallway behind me.

It was empty.

But that didn't mean someone wasn't creeping in my bedroom. My nose was on high alert, sniffing for trouble. It didn't take much to imagine those three holy terrors, Dawn, Crystal, and Michelle, had sneaked into my home to finish what they'd started.

I slipped outside, silently closing the door behind me. The sun wouldn't set for two more hours, and it was still as humid as a jungle outside. I spotted a glimmering television through the bay window of the house across the street. The distant screech of swings echoed from the playground two blocks down. Drawing a deep breath, I glided around the side of Mom's place, appreciating the softness of the cut grass beneath my wounded soles.

Wild rosebushes (the leaves made a poultice for bee stings) beneath the windows—Mom's office window, the bathroom, and then my bedroom—held sweet pink blossoms. The grass alongside the rosebushes didn't appear trampled, though there was a well-trod path between Mom's house and the neighbor's. I made my way down it and stopped at my bedroom. Nervous about what I'd discover, I pressed my face against the glass and cupped my hands around it for shade. Both my suitcases were open on the floor, clothes spread out, exactly as I'd left them. A dresser drawer and the closet were ajar. I'd planned to unpack after dinner.

Unless someone was hiding under my bed, there was no trespasser in my bedroom. Relieved, I turned my back to the house and leaned against it. That's when I noticed the cigarette butt beneath the nearest rosebush. My heart clutched as I reached down. The smoked end was still hot. I sniffed the air.

Dawn.

My head whipped right and left.

Nothing.

I glanced back at the cigarette. Pall Mall. So probably not Dawn, but somebody had recently been walking through here. It could have been a neighbor, or a person using the path as a shortcut, *or someone who'd tried to crawl inside my window, someone who'd fled when their efforts made too loud a noise.* My skin crawled with the sensation of being watched.

I dropped the butt and hurried to the backyard, searching for more evidence of intruders.

"You must be Linda's girl."

The voice startled me. I whirled around to face a woman in her fifties wearing a housecoat, her hair in curlers, standing in the next yard over. She was smoking.

"Yes, ma'am," I said tentatively, stepping closer. Was she smoking a Pall Mall? "I just moved here today."

"I'm Joyce," she said. She jerked her thumb toward her house, a duplicate of Mom's except for its green shingles where Mom's were black. "My husband's Gerald."

"Frankie," I said.

She tipped her head to study me through the blue haze of cigarette smoke. "You look an awful lot like your father."

Even though she was echoing my mom's words from earlier, they sounded loads different dropping from her mouth, like maybe it wasn't a bad thing. My whole mood shifted toward the pink. "You knew my dad?"

She coughed. "Hard not to know him around these parts."

The smile stayed on my face while my stomach dropped away. *Did you tell them your last name?* was the first thing Mom'd said when I'd mentioned Satan worshippers. "What do you mean?"

She shrugged.

Too much had slid off the edge of the world today. At least one thing had to make sense. "Did you mean it's hard not to know him because of his last name? Jubilee?" I asked, my voice shrill.

It's an uncommon name, a memorable one, please say that's it.

"Sure," she said, holding the cigarette in the vee of her fingers, near her face, but not taking a drag. "Because of his last name."

I licked my lips, my mouth suddenly so parched it was sticky. "Say, did you see someone just come between the houses?" I pointed toward my bedroom window.

Her eyes glinted as she watched me for a second too long, and then she ground out her cigarette into an ashtray perched on the edge of her patio table. She yanked a pack out of her housecoat and lit a new one.

Eve Slims, same as Dawn.

"Why do you ask?" she said.

"I thought I heard something."

She arched an eyebrow. She wasn't wearing any makeup. She must have spent the whole day in her housecoat and curlers.

"You should tell your mother," she said. "She certainly has the police chief over often enough." One corner of her mouth bunched up into a smirk. "He might as well do some honest work while he's around."

Then she chuckle-coughed, said, "Nice meeting you," and disappeared into her house.

I wanted to scream.

I couldn't imagine how she could have been less helpful.

Numb, I walked back inside, clicked off the television, and peeked behind every door, inside every cupboard and closet, and beneath every piece of furniture. I figured it was better than imagining the worst. When I felt sure that I was truly alone, I cleaned up my dinner, unpacked both my suitcases, stored the empty luggage in the basement next to moldy-looking boxes marked XMAS and WINTER COATS, and started a load of clothes.

Once everything was in order, I was still too unsettled to watch television or read. I considered creating my first solo page in The Book. It felt sacrilegious, the thought of adding to it without Dad.

I blew hair out of my eyes. I might as well admit it. I wasn't going to be able to relax in the house until Mom got home even though I was (pretty) sure nobody had crept in. A walk was my best bet. I could stick close to the house, pacing to the park until Mom returned. I tucked The Book inside my dad's knapsack, pulled on my pink Cons (Dawn had stolen my everyday pair), and made my way to the playground, a million miles past worrying about looking like a big baby.

The park was empty except for two black-haired, slouchy head-bangers, teenagers by the size and shape of them, riding the merry-go-round. They seemed far too old to be at a playground, but who was I to judge? I dropped into one of the swings, dragging my feet through the sand, thinking about my mom, and June, and Crane, and The Game and Satan and Dawn, and what Joyce the neighbor had said about everyone around here knowing my dad, her voice gloaty and mean. Dad had done something back when he lived here, when he was a kid. Mom had hinted at it, and Joyce had driven that nail deeper. I would find out what, and I would set things right. I owed him that much.

I owed him everything.

The sun finally began to tap the horizon, painting the sky tangerine and rose. The headbangers skulked off toward the trailer park.

I was about to turn toward home myself when a noise at the far edge of the playground, over by a brush pile, caught my attention. I pushed myself off the swing, glancing around. No one in sight. Swallowing my nervousness, I walked toward the sound, aware of the ominous direction I was headed. The trailer park crouched just beyond the rise, and behind it, the shadowy woods and river. But I wouldn't venture that far, not even close. I just needed to peek inside the brush pile.

The smell hit me first, too-sweet and rotting, its *wrongness* soldiering up the baby hairs at the back of my neck for the second time that day. Then I noticed the lazy black flies swarming over the pile, and I went full-on body ice.

Something had died in there.

Had I imagined the sound?

But there it was again, a scratching most definitely coming from the stack of skeletal branches at my feet.

A squirrel or a chipmunk must be trapped inside.

At least that's what I was thinking right up until it screamed.

CHAPTER 10

I was so jittered from my first day in Litani that I heard the shriek as a human sound, was all screwed up to run, but then the sun dropped to a perfect angle and I spotted little eyes glowing back at me from inside the pile of sticks, followed by the tiniest of mews.

A kitten.

"Hey, you," I breathed, sliding onto my sore knees and holding out my hand. The kitten spat at it and then began licking my fingers. Had I washed them after eating the casserole? No matter. I gently grasped the creature and tugged it out, sitting cross-legged so I could rest it in my lap. The tabby was trembling, so young that its eyes were still blue.

"It's okay," I said. "I won't hurt you. Are you lost?"

I stroked it until it stopped quivering. Its ribs were poking out.

"What am I going to do with you?"

The kitten squeaked in response. It was a high noise, more of a chirp than a meow. I smiled despite myself. "Take you home, I guess."

I would need kitten food and litter. Plus Mom's permission. That last one was my biggest hurdle. She didn't seem like the kind of lady who allowed pets. My brain was scrambling to come up with a plan when I spotted a couple walking toward me from the direction of the trailer park. I recognized Sly but not the woman beside him. I kept petting the scrawny kitty as they approached.

"My girl Frankie!" Sly called out. He was still wearing the jeans with the giant belt buckle, but he'd pulled on a yellowed Iron Maiden T-shirt, its image disturbing me, a grinning skeleton shoving a sharp-poled British flag right into the center of the United States. Sly's bushy mustache twitched as he caught me staring at the image. "How's it hanging?"

I didn't stop stroking the tabby. I also didn't respond, thinking about my mom's and then Crane's warnings. I was outside, on a play-ground, in plain view of houses, so I felt safe enough but not partic-ularly friendly, even though it was crazy uncomfortable to ignore an adult.

"This is Darlene," he said, jabbing his thumb at the woman. "Darlene, Frankie here got in a fight earlier today, which is why she looks so tough."

Darlene stared at me, her eyes vacant. She appeared at least a decade older than Sly, in her mid- to late thirties, but it might have been the bags under her eyes and her ashy skin that aged her. She was scratching at her scalp.

"We're together," she said, though I hadn't asked. "A couple."

I squirmed in place. "Nice to meet you."

She nodded at my lap. "Where'd you find the cat?"

"Brush pile."

"You gonna keep it?" Sly asked.

A rusty purr, maybe its first, rumbled out of the furball. "I'd like to. Don't know how I'd pay for food and litter, though."

Sly rubbed his chin. It made a bristling sound. "You could join the babysitting club."

My heartbeat picked up. Was I about to get my first taste of good luck in ages? "What's that?"

Darlene coughed wetly. There was something hard about her face, like her skull was extra close to the surface. "It's a group of girls. Based out of the trailer park. We need a sitter, we call the number, and they pass it down the line until we find someone who's free."

"Pays okay," Sly said. "For a kid's job."

"What's your last name?" Darlene asked, as if the question had just occurred to her. She scratched her scalp again.

I thought again of Mom's question and Joyce's smug face. Well, their reactions didn't change my name. "Jubilee."

Darlene's eyes widened, then relaxed, so quick I might have missed it if I hadn't been watching for it. "You Paul Jubilee's girl?"

"Yep," I said defiantly, pointing my chin at her.

Something slid-bumped behind her eyes, no missing it this time. It worked its way to the center of her face, which tightened as sure as if a drawstring were closing it from the inside.

"I heard about you," she said. "You must be visiting your mom, yeah?"

"Not visiting," I said. "My dad's passed."

The strangest thing: her face relaxed when I said that.

"Did you know him?" I asked, heartbeat thrumming.

"Small town," she said vaguely.

Frustration burned my throat. It was another version of what Joyce had said. I had no idea what a follow-up question to that would sound like.

Sly pulled a toothpick out from behind his ear and stuck it into his mouth, breaking the spell between me and Darlene. "Jubilee. Your momma put them Zloduks into prison, didn't she?" he asked.

"Maybe," I said, stroking the kitten. I wanted to keep talking about my dad, about how wonderful he'd been, how caring, how whatever bad thing they'd heard he'd done when he was younger wasn't true. "I dunno."

"Nasty business, what that Zloduk family did to their own," Sly said, his voice gone dark, his eyes bouncing off my bare shoulders.

He cocked his head, like he expected a response from me. When I stayed silent, he kept on. "Some people need power that bad, they'll darn near form a religion." His chuckle rolled toward me like bone dice. "Most of us, we just need relief from the grind, you know?"

"Yes, sir," I said, not in agreement but as a shield. I didn't know what the Zloduk case was and was sure I didn't want him to tell me.

He nodded, his posture loosening. "We should go, Darlene. Leave the girl with her kitten."

But it wasn't my kitten. It was a stray. I knew I didn't deserve something so nice as this, not after what I'd done. I hadn't told anyone about it, not even June.

What could she have said?

That's fine that you killed your dad, Frankie. Kids do that all the time. Wanna come over Saturday? We can watch Gimme a Break!

The kitten shivered in my hands, and Darlene made a sympathetic noise.

"Here you go, doll," she said, tugging her purse off her shoulder, her voice suddenly lavender and honey. She fished out a ten and handed it to me. "Consider it a loan. You can pay me back after you start babysitting."

I took the money. I knew I shouldn't, but I was desperate to care for the kitten. "Thank you. I promise I'll repay you."

"She trusts you," Sly said.

I didn't know if he meant Darlene or the animal, and in either case it was weird of him, but I didn't have time to puzzle that out because I had real solid money.

"I'd like to go to the store right now," I said. "Do you know the nearest one?"

"What'll you give me to tell you?" Sly teased in that mean-slippery way some men did, hooking his thumb behind his huge belt buckle. From my position on the ground, I could see that a wolf was stamped into the center of it, its muscles poised, its head cast toward the viewer so it appeared to be leaping straight out.

I glanced at Darlene, hoping she'd simply tell me where the store was, but her face had grown brittle.

"I'll find it on my own," I said, beginning to stand, feeling every bruise and scrape.

"Let me give you a hand," Sly said, offering his. "I was pulling your leg about the store, you know. It's Von Hanson's. Two shops down from the old brewery. You know where that is, don't you?"

I nodded, doing my best to keep my eyes off his belt buckle as he helped me stand.

His hand was hot, and he held mine for too long again, as if we were shaking on something.

A deal with the devil popped into my head, and my blood shivered despite the sultry air.

CHAPTER 11

As I trudged toward downtown Litani, the kitten tucked in the hammock of my shirt, I tried to imagine Dad ever living in this strange, bleak town. Pasadena was so vibrant and Dad so comfortable there, at least up until those last couple weeks when everything began unraveling. That day I'd talked him into swapping out the Grateful Dead T-shirt for a button-up and tie, when he'd returned home, he'd told me changing into formal wear hadn't been necessary.

The important meeting had been rescheduled.

I didn't think much of it.

I should have.

If I'd been paying attention to how pinched his eyes were, how his hands fluttered at his neck before removing his tie, I *would* have.

But he dived straight into talking about how excited he was to hit the Red Box Picnic Area of the Angeles Forest the next morning. He wanted to gather samples of pineapple weed and creeping Charlie. He called it a real "battle of the ground covers" in that section of the forest, and he wanted to collect enough of each to make tea. He said they were both grossly underestimated plants. (To be fair, he thought this about most plants.) Pineapple weed lived in rocky areas where nothing else could and resembled a knockoff chamomile, its leaves lacier and bitterer. Only the blossom—a tight little bud that was floral tasting, green, with a hint of pineapple—should be eaten. It was a natural sedative and soothed the stomach.

Creeping Charlie was the real rock star, though, according to Dad. It thrived in the shade on the edge of forests and sometimes on rocky soil, and the world saw it as a greedy invader. They didn't know, Dad said, that creeping Charlie was a jack-of-all-trades. It kept soil from sliding, sure, but also its dry leaves could be made into a tea that was great for colds and coughs. Eaten fresh or boiled, the leaves were a delicious source of vitamin C. But that was just the start. Creeping Charlie, and most ground ivy, was *magic*. It had strong antibacterial properties, rid the body of excess mucus, was an astringent and a diuretic, could be turned into a balm that sped up healing, and treated everything from tuberculosis to tumors to tinnitus.

"And people think it's an invasive weed," Dad had said, shaking his head like he'd just heard about someone walking past a pile of gold.

So saying he'd been excited to go to the Red Box Picnic Area was an understatement. But the next morning, he didn't wake me up. When I shot out of bed, it was past nine. Dad wasn't in the kitchen or the bathroom, and his bedroom door was closed.

He didn't answer it when I knocked.

"Dad?" I said, cracking it open, my pulse beating hollowly in my throat. His outline was below the quilt, but that didn't make sense. As scatterbrained as he was, he'd *always* been an early riser. "Are you okay?"

He didn't respond for a doomed minute.

"Frankie?" he finally said, his voice hoarse, small. "Can you get my medicine?"

His heart.

I rushed to the bathroom, my hands shaking so hard that I dropped a bunch of pills. I didn't have time to pick up more than the one I needed. With a frustrated groan, I dumped our toothbrushes into the sink, filled their holder cup with water, and dashed back to Dad.

"Here you go."

He tried to lift his head, drops of perspiration dotting his gray skin. "Can you help me?"

I could. I had before.

After years of worrying about his poor health, last year he'd finally revealed that he had bicuspid aortic valve disease. I suspect his concern that I might have it, too (it was genetic; I looked it up after he confessed), won out over his not wanting to worry me. Before that, when he'd suddenly grow weak on hikes or clutch his chest, he'd tell me it was "just a spell" and that it'd quickly pass.

It usually did.

But sometimes, when he forgot to take his medicine for a couple days or was under a lot of stress, he'd get like this, and I'd have to help him. It never got any easier.

"Sure, Dad," I said. I placed the pill on his dry, cold tongue and then lifted his head, so much heavier than a head should be, and brought the water to his lips. He tried swallowing, but more water ran down his neck than into his mouth until eventually gravity won and the pill went down.

"We should go to the hospital, Dad," I said, knowing he wouldn't. One of the rare times he'd cooked supper, about six years earlier, he'd been dicing carrots and accidentally sliced his finger to the quick. Gruesome flashes of bone were visible as he ran water over it, shocking white quickly covered by a gush of red. He'd refused to get stitches. He never did regain full motion of that finger. When it rained, it hurt him something awful.

"I'll be fine, pumpkin," he said, his voice still sounding far off. "Just forgot my medicine. I think we'll have to skip the woods today."

"That's okay," I said. But it wasn't. I was terrified, just like I was every time this happened, my pulse thudding in my throat. What if I hadn't gotten up when I had, hadn't peeked in on him? "You need rest. I'll keep an eye on you."

His lip twitch was the only response.

I pulled up a chair and watched him, chin in hands, elbow on knees, for hours. I promised myself I'd call an ambulance if his breathing slowed down, no matter how mad he'd be. But his breath never lagged, not the whole time I was there, and by early afternoon it grew steady. He was almost back to himself by nighttime.

When people found out I'd killed him, would they go easier on me if I shared that story? If I told them that I'd loved my father so much I'd spent an entire day watching over him, not leaving to eat or use the bathroom even though my body had screamed at me to do both?

Probably not.

And it wouldn't matter, because I'd never forgive myself even if someone else did.

The kitten mewled in the crook of my shirt, bringing me back to the present. I was on the edge of Litani's downtown, two square blocks of shops and offices anchored by the Engle Brewery, which loomed in front of me. I craned my neck to eyeball the top of the chimney. The brewery's abandoned, centipeding warehouses could be the illustration for the word "haunted" for people interested in learning English, all bloodred brick and gaping windows clinging to knives of broken glass. It was huge and heavy, this empty factory, its decay extra unnerving so close to the heart of town.

Yet as I glanced around, I realized the brewery wasn't that out of place. It couldn't have been later than eight, and there wasn't a soul in sight. The whole town was ghost-quiet, the only sound the creaking of the 76 station's orange ball revolving. The lights were on over the gas pumps, but no one moved inside the station. Same story with Albert's Pourhouse—the light over the door was on, faint against the still-bright sunlight, but no one walked in or out.

It was eerie, rows of windows staring at me like vacant eyes.

I shuddered.

I'd have raced back to Mom's house if not for the kitten.

Instead, I forced myself toward Von Hanson's, its simple black-on-white hand-painted sign stretching across the whole front of the building. Instinctually, I kept one eye on the haunted brewery complex as I passed it, half expecting a grinning doll to appear in one of the busted-out windows or one of the buildings to sigh before lumbering over to swallow me whole. So intent was I on getting to the grocery store without letting the brewery sneak up that I almost missed the library tucked between the two.

The library was recessed, thirty feet or so from the sidewalk, CARNEGIE PUBLIC LIBRARY across its face. It wasn't a large building, especially compared to the brewery, but it was sweet, reminding me of a tiny mansion. I walked to its front door, one eye still on the brewery. The sign said it was closed but would open up again tomorrow morning at ten.

Still, I was elated. Not only could I stock up on books to read, but I could dig into the local archives to find out what I could about Dad in high school. I was confident he had not been a Satan worshipper. That was partially because neither he nor I believed in Satan, but also because, *come on*. I was sure it was a misunderstanding that had grown into something larger over the course of time and without Dad around to defend himself.

I would clear it up.

Feeling lighter than I had all day, I made my way into Von Hanson's. It was the smallest store I'd ever entered, just one big room, the middle lined with everyday necessities—canned soup, breakfast cereal, toilet paper. The far wall contained the freezer section, the near wall the refrigerated. The clerk glanced up briefly from his magazine as I entered, did a double take at my bruises, lifted a shoulder, and went back to reading.

The kitten stayed calm while I shopped, even when I had to balance it against a bag of litter and a box of 9Lives. When I made my way to the counter, the clerk—who looked only a couple years older than me, his forehead shiny and dotted with acne, his wide-collared shirt about a decade out of style—didn't ask about the animal I'd brought in, and

I didn't offer. I also didn't say anything to Crane on my way out of the store when I spotted him in the shadows, lurking in the slice of shade between the library and the brewery, face down, hands shoved in his jeans pockets. Everyone in this town was a weirdo, that was a solid-gold fact, and it didn't matter because I wasn't alone anymore.

I had the kitten.

Mom's house was empty when I returned. I settled the creature into my bedroom, then returned to the kitchen for a cookie pan, which I lined with newspaper before covering it in litter and tucking it in my closet. Then I filled a dish with water and another with kibble, which I doused in tuna water to soften. I needn't have bothered. The sweet beastie was so hungry it'd have eaten a whole fish if I'd set it down in front of it. I apologized as I peeked under its tail while it ate.

She was a girl.

"I'm going to call you Motherwort," I whispered, petting the baby fur as she scarfed down the food. "Wort for short, because motherwort is so good at healing girls, and this one right here"—I jabbed my thumb at myself—"has had a day."

Watching her eat, I felt touched by something like mercy, a loosening of a knot that I had no right to release, but there it was. Making small movements so as not to distract the kitten, I dug through the stack of books I'd brought from California and pulled out Dad's favorite botany text. I knew the basics of motherwort but needed more.

I slid my finger down the *M*s in the index, found what I was looking for, and turned to the indicated page. According to the book, motherwort was named for its ability to nurture and its particular connection to the female reproductive system. An infusion of the leaves, soft upper stems, and flowers could be used to strengthen the uterus, soothe anxiety and grief, lower blood pressure, and regulate heart palpitations. Sounded perfect to me. I read a little bit more and then drew The Book out of the knapsack, turned to a clean page, and began sketching.

CHOOSE YOUR OWN PLANT PERSONALITY
YOU'RE CAPTAIN OF YOUR OWN DESTINY!
WHICH PLANT PERSONALITY DO YOU CHOOSE?

MOTHERWORT

You are a secret friend to girls in a bind. Your tenderness heals hearts
and calms minds. But you're not for the impolite,
because when treated poorly, your prickly flowers bite.

Tummy full, Wort started batting at my shoelace. I smiled. I was
scared to hope, but there it was, a tender green shoot poking up through
the crust: something had finally gone my way.

CHAPTER 12

"You slept in," Mom said when I appeared in the kitchen the next morning.

I glanced over my shoulder, toward my bedroom. Mom had peeked in on me when she'd returned home near midnight, according to the elephant clock next to my bed. Wort had been curled up in the crook of my neck. Mom hadn't noticed. My plan was to wait until the time was right to tell her about the new arrival. Together, she and I could figure out what to do with the kitten. That sounded like something moms and daughters would do. I knew I was living in a fantasy, but it was better than the alternative.

"I guess," I said, not pointing out that it was Sunday and not yet 8:00 a.m.

She put down the knife she'd been using to butter her white toast. Dad had allowed only wheat in the house. "You look like hell on wheels."

I blinked a couple times before remembering. I'd been so focused on concealing Wort that I'd forgotten to hide my injuries. The swelling had gone down far enough that I could see normally out of both eyes, but I still had a bandage over my scratched arm, and my knees were an angry red. Probably my face was bruised.

"I feel okay," I said. It was true. I was stiff, and my new scabs felt tender, but it wasn't so bad. I wished June were there. I bet I looked like a real tough guy. It'd give me serious bragging rights.

Mom watched me for a few seconds from her seat at the kitchen table, her head at an angle. She was showered and dressed, her powder scent strong, her hair neatly feathered above carefully applied makeup. Other than our small size, we definitely did not look related.

"Remember that surprise I had for you today?"

I was caught off guard by the surge of gratitude I felt for her changing the subject from my injuries to something safer. "Yes, ma'am, I sure do remember," I lied. Sort of. It was a white lie, anyhow, though I wondered if lying was my new thing. Dad would *not* have approved.

She returned to buttering her toast. "You're going to love it. I volunteered you for the Litani time capsule project. You'll be assistant to Theresa Buckle, whose idea it was originally. I wasn't a fan at first—now isn't the best time to memorialize the town—but then I thought it would be a great way for people to get to know you. You'll go door-to-door, asking them to vote on what to contribute. What do you think?"

I cleared my throat. "I appreciate it, but . . ."

She waited, her mouth relaxed. She wasn't going to fill in any blanks. I felt like a fool saying it, but it needed to come out, and so it did, as one long sentence.

"Well, those kids yesterday mentioned Satan worshipping and I know it's foolish but then you said it started with Dad, and then your neighbor"—I flicked my eyes at the house next door—"got all weird when I told her whose kid I am, and so did another lady I . . . I met at the playground yesterday."

Amazingly, she appeared neither angry nor surprised. "And you want those rumors cleared up before you meet more Litani folks?"

I nodded. That wasn't exactly right, but close enough.

She nodded—smugly, I thought—and poured whitener into her Sanka, the clicking of her spoon against the rim of the cup hypnotic.

"That's all they are now and all they were then: rumors. Fantastical stories people tell themselves when they witness something they can't explain, stories that take root when people are afraid. Your father told you about his brother, Benny?"

"A little bit." I knew Dad had had a brother. I knew that brother had died.

It's better to live in the present, pumpkin. That's where the good stuff is.

She took a sip of her coffee, scowled, set the mug back down. "So you know he drowned. On your dad's watch. It was an accident, but it upset your father terribly. He wasn't himself for some time after."

I didn't know any of that. I reached for the wall as the floor slid away from me. Mom didn't seem to notice.

"During the same period, there'd been a few pentagrams spray-painted around town, some suspicious activity at the brewery, talk of an altar, though I never saw it myself. Somehow, the devil talk got conflated with the drowning, all of it pinned on Paul. He couldn't move away from Litani fast enough, and who could blame him?" She tapped her chin, thoughtfully. "Something similar is going on now, though Chief Mike and Officer Wendt are investigating it, so you have nothing to fear, particularly when people learn you're *my* daughter."

I opened my mouth and then closed it. She'd hollowed me out with only a few sentences. "How old was Dad when Benny drowned?"

She squinched her eyes, staring back through time. "We were in high school. Juniors, maybe? Benny was considerably younger, eight or nine, if memory serves. That jug-eared boy followed your dad everywhere, hung on his every word. Paul was more into bugs than plants at the time, and him and Benny would traipse through the woods. They could spend a whole day there, so entertained that they'd forget to eat." She shook her head. "Who does that?"

Me. Me and Dad. That's who does that.

If I'd had anything in my stomach, it would've been pushing its way up right then.

67

I didn't know where to fit any of this new information, but Mom had already moved on, circling back to the time capsule. "When I say 'go door to door,' I mean exactly that. Don't step inside anyone's house. You stay in the sunlight, where it's safe and you're in plain view of the world. Also, when you meet folks this next week, don't believe everything you hear about me or your dad. If you have any questions, you come straight to me. Understood?"

"Yes, ma'am," I said instinctually, the words sticky in my mouth.

"Good. Because small towns are like elephants," she said. "They have long memories and a tendency to cherry-pick."

I nodded, thinking about the elephants she'd decorated my room with. Maybe they'd been a message. Then my stomach growled loud enough for her to hear. It was a sick rather than a hungry sound. The rude noise made me feel shy.

Mom didn't acknowledge it, and her spoon clinking the side of her cup covered the next stomach rumble.

"You start on the time capsule today," she said. "Theresa lives in the trailer park. I'll give you directions. And I packed your lunch."

❖

Back in Pasadena, there were fast kids, sure, but June and I kept to ourselves, the Dorky Duo. We had our walks to and from school, our Paul's Angels business, occasional sleepovers, Sunday night homework-a-thons that we broke only to watch *V* and then *V: TFB*. (Boy, did we go through the popcorn those nights! Dad even watched both miniseries with us. He declared that they were unnecessarily violent, but he said it from the edge of his seat.) We weren't into sports, me or June, had never kissed a boy, we both earned good grades, and we were equally scandalized by the Angelyne billboard when it went up.

You'd think this lifestyle would have been good preparation for moving to a small town, but trudging toward Blue Waters Estates after a breakfast of Shredded Wheat (it was that or Grape-Nuts) and whole milk with a tablespoon of sugar to give it flavor, I might as well have been marching toward the worst neighborhood in LA for how nervous I was.

To distract myself, I contemplated the only thing worse than returning to what was likely Dawn, Crystal, and Michelle's stomping grounds, the thing that I'd been desperately shoving down since Dad's funeral: the thought of Mom finally questioning me about what had happened to him. On the flight to Minnesota, I'd sworn to myself that as soon as she asked me how he'd died, I'd confess the whole thing. She was a lawyer. She'd know what to do.

I hadn't realized how much I'd been counting on her asking.

But I'd been in Litani twenty-four hours, and other than her handing me some first aid supplies and packing me the lunch I was carrying in my dad's knapsack, there hadn't been any affection, no hug or even a handshake, no "I'm sorry for your loss," and certainly no "his death sure was suspicious, anything you want to tell me?" Given her lack of curiosity, her stoicism, I couldn't imagine how the two of them had ever been attracted to each other, unless maybe my mom was a *V*alien who'd fooled Dad. I suspected she'd kept his last name after they divorced just to seem cheerful, at least until a person got to know her.

The good news was that her leaving the house immediately after telling me about the time capsule meant I'd gotten to tend to Wort in peace. I'd fed her and changed her water and scooped the tiniest Tootsie Roll of a poop out of the litter tray. I'd even coaxed a purr out of her before I left, petting her until she was fuzzy, whispering in her ear to be quiet and stick to my room until I returned.

The back of my neck tingled as I passed the playground, pulling me out of my reverie.

I stopped, looked around.

The few people I'd walked past this morning had appeared normal, if a little stiff (maybe they were all *V* aliens here), dressed in church clothes or watering their lawns with a hose in one hand and a cigarette in the other, somehow avoiding looking straight at me while still managing to make me feel stared at.

So if it wasn't the people, what had set me off?

The brush pile I'd rescued Wort from was nearby, more flies than ever buzzing around it. I didn't want to step near enough to smell it, didn't want to imagine that Wort's momma, or brother or sister, was decomposing in there. That was how the system worked, Dad had informed me when on one of our hikes we'd come across a dead possum with her babies still lingering nearby waiting for her to wake up.

Life follows death follows life, he said. You just had to get used to it.

But I didn't need to linger by it. I sped up to reach the trailer park, squaring my shoulders when I passed the dark woods. Today was gonna be another hot one, the glaring sun already sizzling my skin, its piercing heat feeling particularly focused on my scabbed lip. The lack of breeze made it all that much more intense. That, and the silence in the trailer park once I passed under the Blue Waters sign, like I'd stepped out of the real world and into a bubble. I stopped, toes curling. It was as empty as downtown had been last night. That silence amplified the feeling that I was being watched. Somewhere toward the back of the trailer park, a baby wailed, breaking the mood. The world was normal. The sun was shining.

I glanced over at Sly's trailer. He wasn't sitting out front, and the rusty blue pickup that'd been parked in his driveway yesterday was no longer there. Sooner or later, I would need to talk to him to find out where Darlene lived so I could pay her back.

Might as well be now before I lose my nerve.

I strode up his walkway. "Act like you belong" was one of the first rules of detective work, and probably life. I knocked. When no one answered, my curiosity got the best of me, and I glued my face to the glass strip above his doorknob. Inside was a small kitchen, the counters and sink piled with dirty dishes, the garbage can overflowing. The only other visible space was a combination dining/living room. Clothes strewn around. A chair overturned. A stack of videocassettes, but no television in sight, though it was probably against the wall on my side of the trailer, invisible from this angle.

It was gross. Made me not want to stop by later. Maybe Theresa Buckle knew Darlene.

I hopped off Sly's front stoop and walked by the map shaped like an owl's face. A lonely little bike leaned against a nearby telephone pole. The baby I'd heard earlier had stopped crying. The torched silence was heavy, ominous, like there was something in the air waiting to break. The residents must still have been in bed or somewhere else—working the tail end of a night shift, on their way to work, at church.

Though I knew I should now head directly to Theresa Buckle's, I found my feet leading me to Crane's trailer instead. Turned out I *did* want to know what he'd been doing outside the grocery store last night.

His place appeared exactly like it had yesterday—neat, orderly, and empty.

I considered knocking, but it felt like a violation here where it hadn't at Sly's.

"The boy's not home."

I whirled. Sly stood ten feet behind me, his thumb hooked through a belt loop. He was wearing a baseball cap and what looked like the same T-shirt and jeans as yesterday, that massive wolf belt buckle leering at me.

I bit back the *yes, sir* that was bubbling up on its own, my stomach twisting. Had he been inside his trailer when I'd been snooping? Had he followed me here?

"I don't like being snuck up on," I said, pushing back against all my training. June would've cheered, me standing up for myself like that, but it made me feel seasick.

"Whoo-eee, I like a girl with spirit!" Sly pushed his hat back on his head, letting the sun shine directly on his enormous mustache. He was grinning, but his smile felt sharper than it had yesterday. Like he was showing more teeth. "How's the new pet?"

"The kitten's fine," I said reluctantly. I didn't like him, I realized, just like I hadn't liked Officer Wendt. I felt an insect crawling up my leg and went to swat it away, but when I leaned down, there were no bugs. "I wanted to talk to you, actually. To get Darlene's address so I can pay her back."

He scanned the trailer park like he had all the time in the world. Then his stare returned to me, eyes as bright blue as a husky's. I hid a shudder.

"You have the money?" he asked.

"Not yet." My voice sounded higher than usual.

He nodded and stepped closer, his voice soft. "I can help with that."

I backed up. I wanted to swallow, but my mouth was too dry. "How?"

He shrugged and adjusted his hat again, shading his eyes. "That babysitting club I told you about. Why don't you come by my pad right now? I can get your number. Get you on the list."

I pictured the filth of his house, could almost smell the rotting food, but that wasn't why I was so scared my heart felt like it'd stopped beating. "No, thank you. I, um, I'm supposed to meet someone. They're expecting me."

It sounded lame, like a lie. I felt all stretched out and vulnerable and didn't know why.

Sly nodded. "Crane's a good kid," he said, his glance wandering to the trailer behind me.

The abrupt topic change startled me. "What?"

"Crane." He tilted his hat back again. His eyes were normal. Cool almost. Why had I expected them to suddenly be slitted, like a lizard's?

"Do you know him pretty well?"

"Sure," Sly said.

I wanted to end the conversation.

"Yep, a good kid," Sly repeated. His face lit up with that welcoming smile of his, the one he'd shown me yesterday. It was disconcerting how different it was from the way he made me feel. "They're all good here. Every kid in Litani. You too, I bet. Hey, did you ask your lawyer mom about the Zloduk case?"

The one he'd mentioned last night. I'd forgotten about it, but now that he'd reminded me, I didn't think he'd said anything about asking her about it. "No, sir."

That smile again, wide and white beneath his bushy mustache. "Well, it's a doozy. If she keeps a filing cabinet at her house, you'll want to avoid looking for that one."

The first breeze of the day blew through the trailer park, fluttering the leaves, bringing with it the charged smell of storm, though the sky was clear. Far off, a car roared to life, and with it, a radio. I strained to hear the song so I could label it, attach to the reality of it, feel something solid and familiar.

Phil Collins. The drum break was unmistakable. My shoulders relaxed the tiniest bit.

Sly was watching me. His smile grew impossibly larger, welcoming, *we're all in this together*. "You hear it, too. It's a great tune, man. You know the story?"

I shook my head.

"This friend of Phil Collins watched another dude drown. Totally let him die on his watch." He closed his eyes, began singing. "If you were drowning in front of me, I'd pretend I couldn't see. I know where you play, so wipe that grin away . . ."

I'd never really listened to the lyrics before, not closely enough to pull out a story, but what Sly was saying made me think of my dad's little brother, Benny, drowning. "Really?"

Sly's eyes snapped open, two blue lights. "Yep. It's a true tale. If you liked that one, come back when you're older, and I'll tell you the real story behind Rod Stewart's trip to the hospital."

Then he cackled.

It made no sense that I'd need to be older to hear a story about a singer being hospitalized, but the laugh made me feel that imaginary insect creeping up my leg again.

"I have to go," I said, finally locating the words that he'd somehow held over my head, just out of my reach. "Like I said, I'm meeting someone."

The laugh moved from Sly's mouth to his eyes. "Don't let me stand in your way, busy girl like you." He stepped aside and made a great show of bowing.

I hurried past him. I did not glance back.

CHAPTER 13

"Frankie!" The strange woman who answered the door smothered me in a hug, and I found myself in a cloud of fresh-baked cookie smells and trembly flesh. "It's so nice to finally meet you."

"Nice to meet you, too," I mumbled into her pillowy boobs. I sure hoped she was Theresa Buckle. I should have double-checked the numbers on the trailer before knocking. Her double-wide stood at the rear of the park, a thin ribbon of river visible through the trees. I'd had to walk up a strip of plastic grass to reach the front stoop. The doorway was centered between window boxes filled with artificial flowers that hurt to look at, a wax museum to nature right in the middle of the outdoors.

The woman, built like Nell Carter with a great bouf of bottle-red hair that reminded me of Charlotte Rae's, finally released me and stepped back, her gentle smile tipped toward soft crow lines. "You poor child. Look at that busted lip and those skinned knees. It's tough being the new kid in town, isn't it?"

In that moment, for the first time since Dad and I had begun The Book, a complete plant personality page fell into place in my head, image and all, with a solid thunk. Usually, these things took some thought and even more research, but I could tell on the spot that Theresa was a daisy daisy daisy, one of the most underestimated plants in the world.

CHOOSE YOUR OWN PLANT PERSONALITY
YOU'RE CAPTAIN OF YOUR OWN DESTINY!
WHICH PLANT PERSONALITY DO YOU CHOOSE?

DAISY

Bright and humble, willing to let any bee bumble,
You soothe every pain, inside and out, again and again.

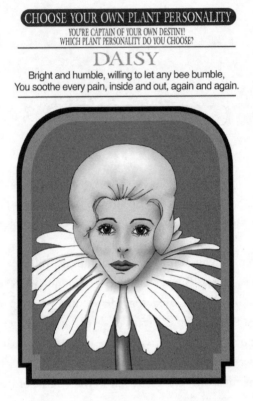

Salve made from daisy heads soaked in almond or sunflower oil worked like magic when used on bumps and bruises. And because daisies contained nearly as much vitamin C as a lemon pound for pound, daisy tinctures were great for treating the common cold. Daisy tea made of the leaves and flowers soothed a twisting tummy, and nothing beat daisy petals for decorating a birthday cake in a special way.

"These are my babies," Theresa said, smiling warmly, her denim skirt swishing as she turned so I could get a better look at the two kids hiding behind her. "Kyle is eight, and Sarah's six. Say hello, kids."

Kyle, with dark hair and eyes to match, smiled shyly and moved his mouth in the shape of "hi." Sarah popped her thumb from her

Kool-Aid-stained lips—six seemed old for thumb-sucking—and tossed white-blonde hair that was more snarl than curls over a shoulder. "Want to play with my Barbie dolls?"

"Hello there, children," I said unnaturally. I didn't really know how to interact with kids. If I was honest, they made me even more uncomfortable than grown-ups did, and that was before getting thrashed by those lame-os yesterday.

"You're going to be the best of friends, all three of you, I just know it!" Theresa said, gripping my hands and tugging me into her trailer. The smell inside was heavenly, though the heat was stifling despite the air conditioner rattling away in the kitchen window. The television was on, Super Grover (my favorite *Sesame Street* character, though I'd eat my own hair before I'd admit that) explaining the importance of patience in his sweet, burpy voice. The kids plopped down in front of it, probably returning to their pre-me positions.

"I'm over the moon that you're gonna help with the time capsule, hon," Theresa said, still holding my hands. She released them when a great breath of wind shuddered the trees and slammed her front door closed. "Mylanta! I don't care how clear the sky is. There's a storm blowing our way. Count on it."

"Yes, ma'am."

She laughed, her body quivering like a tray of Jell-O. She was officially my favorite person in Litani.

"'Ma'am,' already. You are so sweet!" she said. "Now come here in the kitchen and let me show you the project. What's your mother told you?"

My cheeks burned. "Not much."

She studied me, a crease worrying her forehead, before pulling me into another hug. This one was short. She let me go and led the way to the open kitchen. The space was crowded but clean. A pitcher of red Kool-Aid and a plate of chocolate chip cookies—fresh out of the oven, guessing by the smell—rested on the yellow Formica table in the center of the room.

"Help yourself to the cookies and juice," she said before dropping into a padded kitchen chair and reaching for a blue notebook, "and I'll tell you all about the project."

She launched right into it as if we'd been best friends for years while I nibbled on one of the still-melty cookies. She loved Litani, she explained. Her family went back three generations born and raised, and she didn't care one whit for the patch of bad luck the town had been mucking through.

"What kind of bad luck?" I asked when she took a breath.

Her expression grew overcast, her long lashes throwing shadows on her plump cheeks. "Things that could happen anywhere. It just hits harder when they find your hometown." Her face light turned back on. "That's why I proposed the time capsule. It allows us to remember all of Litani's history, not just this difficult stretch, and when we open it up in thirty years, we'll see how far we've come. Another cookie?"

It would have been rude to turn her down, even ruder to request the milk I so desperately desired. The last cookie had sucked every bit of moisture with it. I supposed I could pour a glass of sugary strawberry Kool-Aid—the empty packet lay at the top of the garbage—but drinking that on the heels of eating a chocolate chip cookie felt all wrong. Juice, she'd called it.

"Thank you," I said, selecting the smallest cookie.

"I wish everyone had your manners." She smiled. "They'll serve you well on this project!"

She'd already canvassed businesses to raise money for the actual capsule and had even gotten the city council to set aside a corner of the Carver County Park to bury it in, she explained.

"The businesses who donated get to select one item each to place in the capsule," she continued. "All that's left to do is find out what the regular townspeople want in there. That's where you come in. You're going to go door-to-door, surveying local citizens to ask what they'd like to see included."

"*All* of the citizens?" I asked. Twenty-seven hundred was a lot of doors to knock.

"Wouldn't that be nice?" She patted her cloud of hair. "We don't have the resources for that, I'm afraid. I have a list of around two hundred addresses divided into twenty a day. They're all within walking distance of your house." She laughed again. "Walking distance for someone young and healthy like you, in any case. When someone's home, I have questions for you to ask them. If they're out, there's a leaflet for you to leave behind. They have a couple weeks to mail it back if they want some input into what goes into the time capsule. Sound good?"

It sounded like punishment, which seemed about right.

"Wanna play with my Barbie dolls?"

I glanced to my right. Sarah must have had a glass of Kool-Aid in the living room, because the red circle around her lips had expanded. A person would really have to work hard to get that much beverage around their mouth. Were all kids so bad at drinking?

"No, thank you," I said. "I have work to do."

"*Volunteer* work," Theresa said apologetically. Then she tilted her head, as if something had just occurred to her. "But I tell you what. I have to run some errands in town. Why don't you sit with Kyle and Sarah for a couple hours before you start the project. Make a few extra bucks. It'll be fun!"

I could tell by the way she offered it that she thought she was doing me a favor, and I guess that meant she was. In my experience, though, the idea that babysitting was "fun" was the lie of the century, right up there with erasable pens. I'd done it a handful of times back in Pasadena, all for Dad's colleagues, and I hadn't enjoyed a lick of it. But if I couldn't screw up the nerve to ask for milk, I certainly couldn't tell her I didn't want to watch her children. Besides, I had a debt to pay, and a few bucks would be a good start.

"I appreciate it," I said, just then remembering the babysitting club Sly had mentioned. Was I jumping rank before I'd even joined?

"Then that's that," she said, reaching for her gray-green purse. It was cracked at the edges but seemed to get the job done, which described pretty much everything in the house.

A few dollars was probably really something to her. A clump of regret slid down my throat. I should have been more grateful. "I'm really looking forward to getting to know your kids. I bet you were right that we'll be friends."

She beamed, resembling a daisy more than ever. "They're good kids. My whole world, really. Them and Tom, of course, my husband. He might stop home for lunch. There's tuna hotdish to microwave and a fresh apple pie. You eat as much as you like. I should be back before one."

She smiled with finality, then her body tensed at a funny angle. I thought she was deciding whether to hug me a third time, but then she leaned in and put a hand on my shoulder. "We have only three rules in the house. Always say 'please' and 'thank you'—you won't have a problem with that one—never let the kids out of your sight, and no games with grown-ups."

I paused with the small cookie halfway to my mouth. The linoleum tilted below me. "Are you talking about The Game?" I whispered.

Her eyes grew hooded. "Which game?"

I licked my split lip. "*The* Game."

Her face twisted, and I thought she was going to yell at me. Instead, a belly laugh erupted. "There's a lot of games, hon. They're all fine, just not with grown-ups. Some of the adults around here are a little friendly for my taste, that's all."

"All right," I said, nodding, but it wasn't all right, not even one little bit.

❖

June's father was a salesman, her mother taught fourth grade. Dad had been a professor. I'd never considered their house or mine as particularly nice. I'd never thought about money at all, really. There had been kids at school who dressed fancier than me—*a lot* fancier—and kids like me who didn't much care what they wore, and kids who cared a whole lot and were trying out something new like goth or Valley Girl or preppy, but none of it seemed tied to money.

It was Sarah's "Barbie dolls" that made me realize what a luxury my ignorance had been.

"*I* didn't cut their hair," she said, yanking them out of a cardboard box with windows and a door crayoned on the outside. We were playing in her small bedroom, decorated in pinks and oranges. "The girl we bought them from did."

"You bought your dolls from another kid?"

She nodded, the hideous stack of leggy, off-brand, hacked-hair dolls growing, some of them with garish forever-lipstick scrawled outside their mouth that reminded me of Sarah's Kool-Aid smile.

"One of them came with boots. You can put them on another doll if you want."

It was clearly a precious offer, the way she said it.

For my seventh birthday, Dad had bought me a Malibu Barbie with her cute aqua swimsuit and yellow towel, twelve separate outfits and pairs of shoes for her to wear, and a Barbie Townhouse for her to live in. I'd loved it for all of a week before turning my attention to the Magna Doodle June had gotten me. Imagine staying this excited for a single set of boots.

I glanced over my shoulder at Kyle, who was still watching TV, a grim prospect for a kid on a Sunday morning once *Sesame Street* was over. He'd at least been able to find an Abbott and Costello movie, though it was in black and white.

"Think your brother would like to play with us?"

She rolled her eyes so hard I was worried she'd fall backward. "Boys don't play with dolls."

I didn't know any little boys, so I had to take her at her word. We sprawled on her floor and played teacher and student, ballerina, and actress in a soap opera. After a bit, I forgot how gruesome the dolls were and fell into the imagination of it, wondering what I'd missed out on not having a sister, a thought I'd never really considered before. Why had Mom and Dad only had one kid? That got me to wondering when they'd left Litani in the first place. Had they hit the road together, or had they met up after Dad moved away? And why had Mom returned?

"I'm hungry," Kyle said from the doorway.

I blinked, glancing down at the doll I was holding in a pirouette. Sarah had lost interest I didn't know how long ago and was lying on the floor next to me coloring a puppy outside the lines with a nubby grape-colored crayon.

"I'll heat up lunch," I said, hopping to my feet.

Kyle nodded and returned to his spot in front of the television. Two men were talking to each other on the screen.

"What're you watching?" I asked.

He shrugged and held up a comic book.

"Nice," I said. I was glad to see him reading, though I didn't know why. I couldn't understand why I felt responsible for these kids at all. I mean, I knew I was babysitting, but I hadn't expected to take it so seriously. I guess I liked them. Sarah was sassy and Kyle shy. Grown-ups mistake shy for smart, but sometimes quiet is just quiet. With Kyle, though, I suspected he had a big brain.

I called them into the kitchen when the casserole was heated up. They both picked at it, and I couldn't blame them. Theresa had put corn in the tuna noodle dish, and corn ruins everything. It's the texture. You're chewing away on a nice mushy hotdish, as my mom and Theresa called casserole, and all of a sudden there was a corn kernel, popping like a pimple in your mouth.

"You guys want to go straight to the pie?"

I was gratified at how happy that suggestion made them. They even helped me to clean up the casserole before I served up the pie, which Kyle went full Augustus Gloop on.

"You must be a growing boy," I said, unsure where I'd heard that phrase before.

"He is," Sarah agreed. It made me smile. We were a little family, the three of us, for this safe moment. I was reaching for a slice of pie when the wind knocked at the window. It'd been picking up all day, working toward the storm that Theresa had promised.

"The man is here," Kyle said around a mouthful of cinnamon apple filling.

Sarah nodded sagely, her heart-shaped face sorrowful. "Don't let him in."

CHAPTER 14

I gasped and ran to the window. I'd had my back to it when I'd heard the noise. If anyone had been lurking, they were gone by the time I reached it. I hounded Sarah and Kyle for more information about "the man," but they refused to talk about it. It broke our safe little bubble as sure as a hammer on glass. When Theresa returned home a half hour later, I thought about bringing it up but decided not to. What would I say? The wind made a noise against the window and your kids thought it was a man who'd visited before?

Theresa and I agreed that I'd start the time capsule work tomorrow, and then to my great surprise, she handed me ten dollars for my babysitting time. That was good money *and* enough to pay back Darlene.

When I offered Theresa Darlene's name and a description of her, she gave me directions to Darlene's trailer along with the addresses I'd need for tomorrow's canvassing. I was to bring the list back at the end of the day, discuss how it went so Theresa could make any necessary adjustments, and pick up the addresses for the next day. I shoved the papers into Dad's knapsack, tucking them alongside The Book and the lunch Mom had packed. I felt a little bad not eating it. She was a busy woman, and she'd taken the time to make it special. I'd toss it into the trash in the park on the way home so she wouldn't find out it had gone to waste.

The sky was a burnished copper when I stepped outside, slate clouds rolling fat across it at a speed that turned my skin electric. I felt a quiet warning, but it wasn't just the weather. It was Litani, with its weird people and shadows at the windows. I gripped the knapsack straps and kept my head down walking away from Theresa's.

If it weren't for a gust of wind strong enough to lift my chin, I wouldn't have spotted Crane standing in front of the owl-shaped map and staring at the trailer park office door as if it held answers.

"I bet they're closed on Sundays," I called out, wondering how long he'd been standing there.

He turned, slowly, the wind lifting his hair and revealing his clear, close-set eyes. "I'm not waiting for them to open."

It might have been the weather or the desperation to connect with someone, but a thought popped into my head, and I blurted it out. "Is every other grown-up in this town crazy?"

Crane studied me. A twitch I prayed was a smile danced on his lips. "I'm only seventeen."

I stepped closer, grateful he'd answered one of my questions, even if it wasn't the one I'd just asked. "I'm fourteen."

"Good for you," he said, the wind again lifting that sheet of hair like a shower curtain. "And yes, I do believe that every other adult in Litani is crazy."

An ion-scented gust rattled an empty beer can past my feet like tumbleweed. I remained still, afraid to move, scared it would break the spell and he'd stop talking to me. "Why?"

His shoulder jerked but he said nothing, not at first. But the wind dropped for a moment, creating a vacuum, and he stepped into that space.

"It's Litani's curse," he said. "It gets us all, eventually."

I had no clue what he was talking about. "Did it get you?"

He whirled to punch the map owl right between its eyes, his fist making a *smack pop* sound on contact. "Why are we talking about this?"

85

I jumped back. His sudden burst of emotion startled me. I hadn't heard pain like that before, not coming from a kid. It made me want to offer up some hurt of my own, but the only equivalent pain I could think of was sharing what I'd done to my dad, and I couldn't tell him that. "I'm sorry," I said instead.

"Sometimes I wish I could live in the woods and never meet another person," he said, brushing his hair behind his ears, showing his face full-on, all the way to his clear, broad forehead. It was the most vulnerable gesture he could have made. And that's how I found myself following him to his trailer to show him The Book.

❖

"You want a pop?" he asked.

I shook my head, plunking myself down at the kitchen table. "Your parents home?"

He paused before ducking his head into the fridge. The knuckles of the hand he'd punched the owl with were purply and bleeding. "No."

His trailer was a single-wide, half the size of Theresa's and more like what I expected inside a mobile home: tight, thin walls, a kitchen that bled into a living room that narrowed into a hallway that must have led to bedrooms and a bathroom, the whole thing a shotgun blast from one end to the other. Similar to my mom's house, there were no personal touches, no photos on the walls or magazines fanned out on the table that would give you hints about the type of person who lived there.

Unlike my mom's, though, none of the furniture matched, and it all looked comfortable.

"My dad just died," I said when he turned with a Shasta Twist in his hand. "I moved to Litani to live with my mom."

He popped it open, took a swallow. "That bites."

I liked that he didn't ask any questions. "My dad grew up here. So did my mom, for that matter. I don't know anything about what he was like when he was young."

He dropped into a chair across from me. "You should ask your mom."

Didn't I know it. "My mom's not the kind of person you ask personal questions."

He immediately tensed up, his flap of hair dropping over his eyes. He didn't bother to shove it away this time.

"Does she hurt you?" he said from behind his curtain.

I thought about it. "Nah, not really. I don't think she likes having kids around, is all. Even one as spectacular as me." I grinned to show him I was joking, at least about that last part.

He answered me with that mouth twitch again. I wondered if he ever smiled for real.

"Do you like to be around her?" he asked.

I studied my fingers. My nails were dirty and jagged. I'd taken up fingernail chewing since the funeral. "I don't really know her."

That got him to tuck his hair behind his ears. It made me happy that I'd cracked his code, at least a piece of it: no eyes = he didn't like what he was hearing; eyes = he did.

"I didn't really know my mom, either," he said, all fast like the words were burning his mouth. "She moved out a while back. Can't even remember what she looked like."

I swiveled to stare around the living room pointedly. "Some photos might help."

When I turned back, I was delighted to see actual teeth, small and tight for his big frame, his two incisors twisted in that way that had always struck me as British looking.

"I have crooked teeth, too!" I exclaimed, opening up and pointing. "Well, they aren't all crooked. Just a few of my front ones. When

WarGames came out, June swore I looked just like a fun-size Ally Sheedy. After that, I secretly wished everyone would have to watch the movie, like a global homework assignment, so I wouldn't have to cover my mouth when I laugh."

I giggled at how silly it sounded. It was all true, but I'd never said it out loud before. Something about Crane put me at ease.

Rather than join me in laughter, he tucked his own smile away quicker than the lightning that had flashed across the sky, but it was too late. I'd seen it.

I opened up the knapsack and tugged out The Book. "This is what you saved yesterday when you helped me in the woods."

He didn't respond.

"When Dawn, Crystal, and Michelle were attacking me," I offered helpfully.

"I remember."

I opened The Book to Motherwort's page and slid it over to him. "This is what's in it."

When his jaw clenched, I felt compelled to explain more. "Dad was a botanist. We'd go into the woods together for his job, and we made up these plant personalities for people."

"But that's a cat."

I giggled for the second time. Crane brought that out in me. "Yeah, I drew this one last night. I found this kitten in the brush pile over by the city park, the one with a playground on one end? I don't know what to do with it."

"The drawing?"

"The kitten."

"Can't you keep it?"

"I don't think my mom'll let me," I said, skirting the problem of whether I deserved it.

"Your mom doesn't know?"

I shook my head, eyes on my janky fingernails. My pointer finger one was ragged from the chewing, the cuticles ripped down one side.

"You must be good at keeping secrets."

My glance shot up because I was sure he was making fun of me. But he wasn't. "I guess," I said. "You want to see the rest of the drawings?"

He did. I showed the half-full book to him, even found myself sharing my plans for future pages. He agreed a mushroom would be perfect for Sly, who he warned me to avoid at all costs, refusing to offer details.

When I told him about Darlene lending me money for Wort, he suggested she might be an herb, one that people misuse. When I asked how he'd come to know stuff about plants, he said biology had been his favorite at school, plant biology specifically.

"Where are you going to college?" I asked.

His eyes grew cloudy, his mouth tight. "I don't know," he said evasively.

"I can help you! Well, maybe I can. My dad was a college professor, after all. I know some stuff about it."

"Yeah," he said, the same time a crack of thunder rattled the trailer. "You should probably head home before this storm breaks."

I'd made him mad, but I couldn't imagine how, and I was suddenly angry myself, all this tiptoeing around his moods. "Fine. But I have to go to Darlene's first."

"What for?" he asked peevishly.

"Pay her back," I said, grabbing The Book and shoving it into the knapsack, which I hoped was waterproof. The air was so full of moisture that it was beading across my skin. "See you later."

"See you," he said with finality.

I glowered at him. Part of me had figured he'd offer to walk me over there. We'd been having a lot of fun hanging out, right up until he transformed into Crabby Appleton. Well, I didn't need his company. I was fine on my own.

I let his front door slam behind me even though I knew it was rude and stepped into the charged air, stomping over to Darlene's trailer. Her front door was open. The sounds of a game show I didn't recognize zigged and pinged their way through it.

I was deciding between knocking or calling out for Darlene when Demon Dawn appeared on the other side of the screen wearing my favorite sneakers.

"Lookit that, Fresh Meat is at my house," she said, her smile wicked.

CHAPTER 15

"Who is it, Dawn?" someone called from behind her.

"Why don't you come see for yourself," Dawn said dismissively, not taking her vicious eyes off me. In addition to my favorite sneakers, she was sporting the same oversize knockoff Garfield T-shirt she'd been wearing when she beat me up the day before. Her dirty blonde hair looked legitimately dirty, like she hadn't washed or even combed it since yesterday. I was gratified to notice the bruise on her cheek, though. I hoped I'd given it to her.

Darlene appeared behind Dawn. Standing close together like that, it was clear they were mother and daughter. Even through the mesh of the screen door, Darlene's exhaustion was obvious. She'd either worked a night shift or had had a terrible night's sleep.

"Hello, ma'am," I said, ignoring Dawn, who I couldn't believe had spoken that disrespectfully to her own mother. "I'm here to pay you back."

Darlene nudged Dawn to the side and opened the door, squinting at me. "You're the girl who found the kitten."

"Yep," I said, holding out the five and five ones Theresa had paid me with. "Here's the money you lent me to buy cat food and litter. I sure appreciate that."

She took the money, staring at it for a moment as if she couldn't remember what it was. "You gave Dawn those shoes, didn't you?"

My gut twisted. Those gray sneakers had been a prized possession, broken in just right so they fit like a pillow but still new enough to look sharp.

"She sure did," Dawn said, elbowing her way back in front of her mom. "Said I could borrow them for as long as I liked."

Darlene hauled a pack of Eve Slims out of the front of her robe. "Don't outwear that invitation, Dawnie. You see how this girl settles her debts? You should be more like that."

I hoped I managed to keep the gloating off my face. The little I knew of Dawn, she wouldn't take kindly to being negatively compared to me, and she seemed like one of those small-town elephants with a long memory.

"Why don't you come in," Darlene suggested. "Take a load off."

It'd be raining inside of ten minutes. "I better get home before it pours."

Darlene blinked as if she'd just noticed the weather. "Well, now that you're here, we have extra 9Lives you might as well take. Dawn had a cat, but it ran off months ago. Didn't it, Dawn?"

Dawn scowled at me.

If it had been up to me, I'd have gone straight home, but I wasn't in a position to turn down free food for Wort, so I stepped inside, staying clear of Dawn.

The inside of the single-wide was a war zone, clothes tossed on every surface, empty Swanson TV dinner boxes and chip bags lying around, flies buzzing in a far corner. The liver-colored carpet appeared decidedly sticky, the sour smell suggesting the oppressive heat was cooking whatever had been spilled.

"What're you staring at, Fresh Meat?" Dawn said angrily.

I glanced over at the television, surprised to spot a new JVC VCR on top of it. "That," I said, pointing. My school in Pasadena had had one, and you could rent them from the West Coast Video a few miles from June's house, but I'd never seen one in a person's home before. "Where'd you get it?"

The question shrank her for a moment, but then she puffed right back up. "I'm never giving your shoes back," she hissed.

I nodded, my gaze still traveling. A gallon-size glass jar of buttons rested on the center of the nearby kitchen table. They were all different colors and sizes, reds and yellows and greens with glints of metal. The container glowed like a jar of jewels beneath the bare kitchen light bulb. "How long have you been collecting buttons?"

Dawn followed my gaze and then made a scoffing noise. "We don't *collect* buttons. Those are if a button falls off."

She sounded so young when she said it. "You're ten years old," I said, guessing.

"So what?"

My eyes flicked to her feet. "So I want my shoes back."

She leaned close, only an inch shorter than me, and shoved her finger in my face. She had a sprinkling of pale freckles across her nose. Her brown eyes were squinting, her mouth twisted. "You want your shoes?"

"I just said that."

"Then you have to play The Game." Her expression was fierce and disorganized. For a scary second, I thought she was going to cry.

"What *is* The Game?" I asked. I was never going to play it, not in a million years, but I needed to know.

She crossed her arms defiantly. "You gotta play to find out."

That memory again, of my dad telling me to use my gut but also my brain. Yet here in this junky trailer with a storm brewing and this quivering nerve of a girl standing in front of me, I recalled something else about that talk. It hadn't been something Dad had told me directly, not like I'd remembered. Rather, it had been a scene he'd relayed, something he'd witnessed on a television show, something a make-believe father had told his make-believe daughter and that I'd applied later. Had it been from *The Brady Bunch*?

Lightning flashed, adding to my unsettled feeling. How could I have remembered it so wrong? Well, it didn't really matter, did it? It was still good advice.

"I'll play The Game if it's just you and me," I said. "No one else."

She scratched at her scalp, the gesture reminding me of her mom. "Fine."

"You want to play right now?"

Darlene appeared from a back room, a box in one hand and a bag in the other. "Found some old litter, too. I imagine you can use both."

"Not now," Dawn said to me, as if her mom hadn't interrupted us. "We'll play this week. I'll let you know when."

If she was going to say anything more, it was lost in the sudden pounding at the screen door. We all three jumped back. Before Darlene could answer it, the door was ripped open and a brown-haired woman charged in, eyes as wide as plates beneath square-framed glasses, tears streaking her cheeks, her mouth drooped at a corner. She was wearing a waitress uniform, the flecks of food across the front of her shirt and matching skirt suggesting she'd recently gotten off a shift.

"They've taken Michelle!" the woman shrieked.

Next to me Dawn made a small noise, like air leaving a tire.

"They promised they wouldn't," the woman said, collapsing into sobs. "They're gonna kill my baby, I know it!"

CHAPTER 16

I heard enough to gather that the hysterical woman's name was Karen, she worked at the Pourhouse and lived in the trailer park, and she was the mom of Michelle, the girl with thick glasses and brunette braids who'd joined the beat-me-up crew my first day in Litani. Though to be fair, Michelle had done less pounding than the other two, and I thought I'd detected a note of apology behind her Coke-bottle glasses as she was swinging.

But maybe I was remembering it that way because Michelle had been abducted.

Darlene had charged straight to the phone after Karen yelled that Michelle was kidnapped, and the police chief peeled into the trailer park not fifteen minutes later. I recognized him as the officer who had been at our house when I'd returned from my beating (and, if neighbor Joyce was to be believed, who visited quite often). Officer Wendt pulled up a few minutes after. The two men sat Karen at Darlene's kitchen table and began hammering her with questions, but not before they ordered Dawn and me to wait outside.

They'd closed the front door—the wooden one, not just the screen door—behind them, but it was an aching hot day, and Darlene's windows were open to catch a breeze. Every fifth word or so was loud enough for me to hear. Game. Molested. Kidnapped. In that order.

The words made my stomach cramp. Every girl in my grade knew about molesters, had since *Fallen Angel* aired. The movie starred a thirteen-year-old girl whose dad had just died. Her mom was dating, ignoring her, when this older guy started giving her all this awesome attention. He coached her softball team, but really he was a photographer who wanted to take nasty pictures of her.

We'd all whispered like mad about that movie after it aired on CBS's Tuesday night lineup, weirdly proud that someone close to our age was starring in such an important role, while at the same time ashamed at ourselves for craving the sort of attention she was receiving. What girl in America didn't want to be photographed, discovered, adored? The trick was getting noticed by the right person, we decided, though how to tell the bad from the good was never really explained to us. It made sense there would be real-life cases like what happened in *Fallen Angel*, terrifying ones, where a girl accidentally posed for a creep rather than someone who could make her into a star. I just didn't want to confront that reality so *concretely*.

I glanced over at Dawn. She was holding a lit cigarette despite police officers being right on the other side of the wall. Her hand was trembling.

I squared my shoulders. "What do you think happened to Michelle?"

A gust of wind picked up her limp hair and laid it back down. The air felt impossibly swollen, like an engorged wood tick ready to burst, but the sense of electricity was gone, and the clot of gray clouds that had threatened the sun were rolling east.

"I think she's dead, that's what." Dawn didn't even bother pretending to smoke the cigarette. She just held it. "And I'm next. Me and then Crystal and the rest of the babysitting club."

"I bet she's alive." Because a kid couldn't be kidnapped and killed. That didn't happen, not in real life. "Maybe she got lost."

Dawn grunted. "Maybe *you* should get lost."

I didn't have a response to that, and it didn't matter. Officer Wendt appeared outside the door, his wide, shiny face looking like crumpled paper. I found myself thinking he could use some facial hair to anchor all that white skin. "Dawn? Chief Mike would like to speak with you."

She dropped the cigarette so it landed at my feet and stomped inside.

Wendt held the door for her, then addressed me. "Chief Mike says I'm supposed to give you a ride home."

"I can walk," I said, wondering how The Game and the babysitting club and Michelle's disappearance were all connected.

"Not today you can't."

CHAPTER 17

The storm never broke, just released a brief, unsatisfying burst of rain as Officer Wendt drove me back to Mom's. Rather than pierce the heat, the short-lived squall magnified it, drawing it close. The radio in Wendt's brown sedan had been set to a country station, but he flipped it to KCLD as he pulled away from Darlene's. I bet he thought he was doing me a favor by playing pop music.

He tried making small talk—Mom had told him what I was doing with the time capsule, he said, and I should drop by his place because he had some stuff to show me, and I shouldn't worry too much about Michelle because "those sorts of kids" always made trouble, and it wasn't their fault, not really, they just liked the attention—but after what I'd overheard, my insides felt like they'd been scrubbed with steel wool, and I wasn't in the mood for surface conversation. I hopped out of his car almost before it came to a complete stop, tossed him a quick goodbye, and hurried into the house.

Mom wasn't home. I paced in my room, played with Wort while listening for the front door, paced some more. When the phone rang, I about jumped out of my skin. It was Mom calling to tell me not to wait up for her because of the missing girl, which she knew I knew about because Wendt had told her. That left nothing but listless TV for me. I even watched the corny shows me and June used to make fun of her mom for loving.

June.

Of course! Just because I felt like I was on a different planet didn't mean I couldn't reach out to my best friend. I dialed her number from memory. This was going to be an expensive phone call, and I didn't care. I pressed the handset to my ear, twisting the cord in my other hand.

Whir chirp. Whir chirp. Whir chirp.

No answer.

I hung up. I'd try later. A flash of tabby caught my eye. Wort had gotten out of my bedroom and was running loose from one end of the house to the other like her tail was on fire. As soon as she saw me, she charged at me sideways, her back arched and her tail twice its size.

"Wort!" I said, laughing despite myself. "You can't leave my room. I told you that. If Mom sees you, who knows what'll happen."

By way of answer, she dashed down the hall and disappeared into Mom's bedroom. Still smiling, I followed. The kitten's silliness was a balm. It wasn't just Michelle disappearing that had me so unsettled. It was the encounter with Sly, the hot and cold communication with Crane, the mention of Satan even though Mom said it was nothing to worry about, the way people talked about my dad, the moody hot weather.

Litani.

It was Litani, 100 percent.

Mom and Dad's hometown, and the creepiest village on earth. Now that I was getting a feel for the town, it was as plain as the nose on my face why Dad'd had to get out of here after Benny's death, especially with his poor heart.

His heart.

He and I didn't return to the woods until a week after that last scare, the one I'd decided to refer to as the Grateful not-Dead Incident, where that meeting had been canceled and then he didn't get up the next morning and I fed him his medicine and watched him sleep.

By the time we finally made it to the Red Box Picnic Area, the creeping Charlie was at the end of its bloom, the fairy-size pineapple weed blossoms exploded and bitter. But Dad was himself, solid and happy and at home in the forest in a way he never was anywhere else. He was in such a good mood that he suggested I invite June for a sleepover that night.

He had to head into the office for a bit when we returned home, he said, for his rescheduled meeting—something about his grant funding, he mumbled—but he'd rent a VCR and some VHS tapes and grab a pizza for us on his way home.

I was surprised by his suggestion. Usually our slumber parties were held at June's house. We could watch whatever we wanted at her place, and her junk food selection was primo. Plus, even when he was himself, Dad was delicate. He loved June, and she loved him—he was a good guy, anyone could tell it, and his kindness was a magnet—but he tired easily. That's just how he was built.

But between his heart and the pressure this meeting was bringing him, I didn't want to appear ungrateful. "A slumber party's a great idea!" I'd responded.

"Thought so," he said, smiling, his cheeks flushed. "And you don't need to worry. I'll clean myself up for the meeting this time without you having to remind me."

I beamed at him.

"You're the best daughter a guy could ask for, Frankie, you know that?" he'd said, rustling my hair. "Now, can you take notes? I need to use both hands for digging."

I couldn't yank out my notebook and pen fast enough.

I was lucky, I knew that. Not many kids got to be best friends with their father. Even fewer girls had a dad who loved them enough to check on them sleeping, which he sometimes did when it was only me but always did on the rare occasions June slept over. I'd catch him when I'd wake up needing to pee. There he'd be, head poked in the doorway, gazing intently at me and her in my bed, a soft expression on his face. I'd always lie still until he left so as not to scare him.

The memory made my eyes hot. I shook my head to return to the present, to Litani and to Wort.

"Here, kitty kitty," I called out, stepping into my mom's bedroom.

I felt a thrill of unease. I'd never been in there before. It was a standard bedroom, the peach of her bedspread complementing the cream of the walls. The only furniture besides the bed was a matching dresser and nightstand of dark-brown wood. There was a closet on the far side of the room. The air carried a distinct cologne smell, different than Mom's perfume, more masculine and earthy, but underneath that, could it be . . . ? Yes, the smell of rose-milk lotion! It was faint but unmistakable. I looked over her furniture, hoping to spot the tub of lotion, to finally learn the brand, but her surfaces were empty of anything except for a lamp and a jewelry box.

I took a step inside and turned back toward the door I'd just walked through. A low whistle escaped my mouth. Bookshelves lined the entire wall. This was where my mom kept her personality! There were even a handful of photos sprinkled among the law books and the romance novels and the encyclopedias. I plucked the nearest one off the shelf.

It featured my dad, my mom, and a woman I didn't recognize but who looked vaguely familiar (she had one of those faces) leaning against a bright-yellow VW Bug. Dad had an arm tossed around each of the women. All three were grinning and so young it almost hurt to look at them. Dad had sideburns, Mom her hair high in a ponytail.

For the first time, I wondered about the age difference between them. He looked at least five years older than her, but it could have been her hair making her appear younger than she was. I brought the photo to my nose and sniffed, hoping that it would smell like him, like Dad, Old Spice and strength and maybe a little sweat.

It smelled like dust.

I slid the frame back onto the shelf, an idea bubbling in my brain pot. I couldn't ask my mom about the Litani curse Crane had mentioned, or the divorce. It felt too weird. But I could ask her about her life growing up here, and then she'd naturally talk about Dad. When she did, she'd have to ask how—and why—he'd died.

She'd *have* to.

And then I could finally, mercifully, unburden myself.

My hangnail caught on a book. *Your Body* read the spine in a cartoony font.

I pulled it out, glancing down as Wort twined herself between my legs, purring.

"You're a regular self-petting machine, Worty," I said, flipping open the book. It was one of those *Free to Be You and Me*–ish books to teach girls and boys about their bodies. Some of the illustrations were pretty funny was what I was thinking right up until I got to the page showing a sketch of a naked girl, old enough to have tiny breast buds but too young for pubic hair. The image wasn't anything they hadn't shown us in fifth-grade health class. It was the notes on the margins that stopped my breath.

DD, age 10, breasts and buttocks, penetration

The words bit me like a snake. I dropped the book. Wort yowled and took off across the hall. *Your Body* lay at my feet, thankfully closed.

Age 10?

I didn't want to handle the book again, but I had to put it back. I plucked it from the floor using only my pointer finger and thumb, touching as little of it as possible, returning it to its spot on the shelf, my stomach gnashing at the thought of the dirty thing resting so close to a photo of my dad.

Images of Michelle, her shy smile as she introduced herself to me, tried to elbow their way in. I had to escape Mom's room. I regretted ever trespassing in her private space. I hurried out, vowing never to enter again.

CHAPTER 18

I spent the rest of the day sketching, pacing, watching more lame TV, trying June again with no luck. I fell asleep fully dressed on top of my covers. When I woke the next morning, out of sorts, Mom had already left for the day. I caught a whiff of her perfume, so I must have just missed her. She'd left a note attached to the fridge.

Hold off on going door to door. I have some good news. Will be home for supper.

She hadn't signed it. I knew it was from her, of course. I just wanted to know if she'd sign "Mom" or "Linda." I chewed my way through another bowl of Shredded Wheat doused in sugar, imagining myself a giant frog swallowing bog water. Then, more television, more sketching, tending to Wort, going to the window to check for Mom, rinse and repeat. When she finally flounced through the door around five, I was out of my mind with boredom and worry.

"Just the girl I wanted to see!" she said, using a light voice I hadn't yet heard. "What do you say to meeting the people who make Litani tick?"

Of all the things I'd expected her to say when she came home, that hadn't been on the list. Cold oil slid down my spine. Had Michelle been killed, like Dawn said, and Mom was trying to distract me? "Um, did the police find that missing girl?"

Mom rested her purse on the table by the front door. She looked as fresh as if she'd just woken up, her hair huge and feathered despite the wall of heat she'd brought in with her, coral lipstick in place, cheeks rosy. She wore a white blouse with a ruffled collar, a shin-length prairie skirt, and taupe boots. She was hesitant in answering me, something like concern flitting across her face. "They haven't. But they will soon. I have it on good authority that she ran away."

I fell into the couch with relief, the unforgiving wicker meeting me with a smack. "I knew it."

I hadn't, obviously. But I'd wanted it to be true so bad. That counted.

"Then you're a very smart girl." She appraised me. "Clean yourself up and slap some foundation over those bruises. You can use mine. In the vanity."

"Where are we going?"

"We've been invited to a dinner party at the mayor's house." She grinned wide, tapping her chin with her pointer finger. "Prepare to learn all of Litani's dirty secrets."

Except she didn't seem to be directing that last part at me.

CHAPTER 19

I gripped the frosty mug of Dr Pepper, sucking the almond-cherry-cinnamon flavor out of a shard of ice. I'd been formally introduced to the five people at the table besides Mom and me. The first was the mayor of Litani and our host, a woman by the name of Clara. If she had a boyfriend or husband, he wasn't here. Second and third were Ronnie and Patricia McSorley, both shorter folks, a feature I appreciated, though Ronnie looked like he lifted weights, and he pumped my hand a lot when he shook it. Ronnie and Patricia were about Mom's age, so old, but they seemed friendly enough, smiling and saying they'd known my dad.

Next was Chief Mike Sickhaus, who I'd yet to officially meet, though I'd seen him at the house and then again at Darlene's trailer. He gave me a curt nod. He wasn't in uniform but carried himself like he was, standing straight as a soldier. His curly hair and sideburns framing a generous nose brought to mind a stern Mr. Kotter. Last and totally least was Chad Wendt, the wide-faced dweeb officer who'd twice been my chauffeur. I wondered who was policing the town tonight with these two at dinner.

I was the only kid present.

Everyone had gussied themselves up, the men in long sleeves and neckties, the women wearing summer dresses. I hadn't packed a dress—the only one I'd owned my great-aunt Edna had bought me for Dad's funeral, and I hadn't bothered bringing it with me to Minnesota, especially since I was only allowed the two suitcases. Mom settled for me wearing a pair of tan cords that might as well have been made of rubber for how they trapped in the heat and a white button-down blouse with a ribbon collar that I normally liked but that scratched my skin like fiberglass insulation.

"Pass the bread, dear," Patricia "call me Patty" McSorley warbled from across the table.

The ice I'd been sucking slid sideways down my throat unexpectedly. I covered the cough just in time, ignoring my mom's glare, and grabbed the bread basket. Clara was serving spaghetti and meatballs, which was a smart oven-free choice when cooking for this many people in this heat. She'd also set out two bowls of chopped iceberg lettuce decorated with tomato slices and croutons, one bowl on each end of the table, three dressing selections (Thousand Island, French, and Italian) between them, and off to the side, a dish of aquarium-rock bacon bits with a fancy silver serving spoon stuck in them. Chad had really struggled with that last one. I could tell he wanted to taste what was in that bowl by how he kept glancing at it, then looking at his boss. Was it possible that Chad knew as little about bacon bits as he did about pop music?

When Chief Mike chose the bottle of orange French dressing, doused his lettuce with it, then reached for the spoon to scoop out a dusty pile of bacon, Chad appeared so relieved. He immediately copied Mike's every move, down to avoiding the tomato slices and choosing the same dressing.

I knew Clara was the mayor because Mom and then Clara had told me, but she acted just like everyone else around the table. In fact, if I had to name the person who was in charge here, I'd say it was Mom. That gave me a strange sense of pride. Dad had been a decent teacher; I'd seen it firsthand when I'd tagged along to the university either because my school was closed for the day or I had a cold that made me too sick to attend my own school but not too sick to go to his.

He knew his stuff and people respected that, but he'd never commanded a room like Mom.

". . . and those fuckers will never make that mistake again," Mom was saying, startling me off my thought train. Had she actually dropped the gonzo swear word? I furtively glanced from face to face, expecting raised eyebrows, but instead, everyone but Chad was laughing like they'd just heard the best joke. Chad appeared as shocked as I felt, which warmed me toward him the tiniest hair.

"How about you, Frankie?" Patty asked, smiling at me across the table. "Are you going to be a lawyer like your mom when you grow up?"

All eyes were suddenly glued on me. I wished I'd been listening to what had led up to the question.

"You're lucky to have such a good role model," Clara said, saving me as I scrabbled for an answer that wouldn't come across as an insult. I'd only ever imagined myself as a botanist. My blood flowed green.

"If I'd chosen my mom's path, I'd be a homemaker," Clara continued.

"Worked out fine for me," Patty said, good-naturedly.

"You know I didn't mean it like that," Clara said, though I could tell she *had* meant it like that, a little. "Nothing wrong with choosing that route. It's when you don't know there's options that it becomes a problem."

My eyes traveled to the men at the table. I'd never attended a dinner party before, but even if I had, I was positive women dominating it like this wasn't the usual. Chad was going at his spaghetti like it'd done him wrong, Chief Mike was observing my mom, and Ronnie's arm was looped around Patricia as if he hadn't a care in the world.

"It's not like on TV shows," Mom said, bringing the conversation back to law and to her. "It's not all arguing in a courtroom, demanding justice. There's a lot of paperwork. And investigating."

Chief Mike coughed.

Mom's eyes flew to him. "Yes, I said it. We can call it research if you want, but God's honest truth is that I have to investigate the claims I hear. It's the only way I can win."

"Now that you brought it up," Clara said, twirling her noodles round and round, worms dragged through tomato gore, "what 'claims' have you heard lately?"

Mom's smile sharpened itself across her teeth—I could hear it *swick swick* like a knife against a whetstone. "And here I thought you invited me because you wanted to meet my daughter."

Like I wasn't there, like I was a new pet.

Frankie, I said in my head. *Because you wanted to meet* Frankie.

Clara set her fork on her plate and wove her fingers above it, resting her chin on them. "Don't be difficult, Linda. Of course I wanted to meet your daughter. We all did."

No one seconded that motion. My face blazed.

"And I also wanted to get the truth about the buzz I'm hearing," Clara went on. "The town's on fire with it."

Ronnie and Patty nodded at this. Chief Mike was motionless, but his knuckles popped white as he gripped his water glass.

Mom swirled a forkful of spaghetti, slowly, spearing a meatball at the very end, somehow fitting it all in her mouth. I watched her chew and then dab at the corners of her lips with the cloth napkins Clara had provided.

I realized I was holding my breath. We all were. What poise. What entitlement. It was magnificent to watch, and it made me so uncomfortable.

But she wasn't finished.

She took a sip of water, set her glass down, ran her pointer finger through the condensation. "Why don't *you* tell *me* what you've heard."

"Cut the crap," Clara said, her voice high. "Everyone's talking about it, saying the satanic cult's back. Pets disappearing, turning up dead if they turn up at all. Pentagrams spray-painted on the sides of buildings. Unholy altars in the woods."

"And they kidnapped that poor child," Patty said.

Ronnie's arm draped over her shoulder had grown a fist.

My fork clanked to my plate, the sound echoing in the shocked silence.

"She ran away," I said, before I lost my nerve.

Mom's eyes slid to me. "That's right. She ran away."

"Yep," Chad said, glancing from Mom to Chief Mike. "She was an aggressive kid, we heard. Been in a lotta fights, found her share of trouble. She'll turn up."

I made a gurgling noise but no one noticed, all their attention focused on Mom, who appeared none too happy that Chad had interrupted her. But he'd lied about Michelle. She'd beaten me up, sure, but she was a follower, not a troublemaker. I'd bank on it.

Took one to know one.

"I can neither confirm nor deny the rumors, but if there is a cult, we'll get to the bottom of it," Mom said, her eyes locked on Chief Mike's like they shared an inside joke, except he didn't look in on it—he looked *mad*. "I can, however, tell you we're interviewing a lot of people."

"Like who?" Ronnie demanded, taking his fist from Patty's shoulder to slam it on the table.

We all jumped, all of us but Mom.

"Like the children swearing that older men have invited them to play 'a game,'" Mom said, her eyes slicing him. "Four kids and counting. A mother came to Mike last week to tell him she believed her daughter had been invited to play, and the girl hasn't been the same since."

"It's happening out of the trailer park, isn't it?" Ronnie asked, his tone making clear he was not a fan of the location. "That's where those kind of men live."

Mom paused for too long. "The children won't or can't identify who's invited them to play, so we don't know where the perpetrators live. All I can tell you for sure is that you'll want to keep your kids away from the old brewery."

Clara shot to her feet. "For god's sakes! Not in my town. We're all family here."

A cloud passed over Mom's face. "Family is where it starts."

I was glad she didn't look at me when she said it. I actually felt like I'd become invisible, and I was A-okay with that.

Patty had gripped Ronnie's clenched hand, trying to weave her fingers between his with zero success. It was awkward. "You don't know *anything* about these men?" she asked.

Chief Mike made a noise of disgust and tossed his napkin on the table. "That's enough," he said. "It's an open case. We can't discuss any more."

Mom leaned back, her expression grim. "People should know that we're taking it seriously. That if someone is hurting children, we're going to take them down."

"Like you did with the Zloduks," Ronnie said, his jaw tight.

My blood grew thick.

"Like I did with the Zloduks," Mom agreed.

CHAPTER 20

"Mom," I said timidly on the ride home, "can I ask you something?"

My words startled her, I could tell. I think she'd forgotten I was there.

She'd been driving with her elbow resting on her open window, ozone-charged air lifting the baby hairs at my neck. It must have dropped twenty degrees since we'd first gone to Clara's house. It was now what Dad had called "feel alive" weather, the temperature—just this side of requiring a sweater—making your skin dance. In California, a sudden drop in temperature like this plus the smell of charged air meant a storm was coming, but after yesterday's fake out, I didn't trust Minnesota.

"Sure," she said. "What is it?"

Back at the dinner party, she'd refused to answer any more questions: about a satanic cult or what exactly was happening at the eerie Engle Brewery or which children had been hurt or what adults she suspected. She clearly delighted in being asked, though. From Chief Mike's body language, he had a whole different take. In fact, if I had to guess, I'd say he was really, really cheesed off at Mom.

Once everyone around the table got the message that Mom wasn't going to spill any more than she already had, they'd changed the subject to more everyday things, including the time capsule, which was an eye-roll-worthy topic for them. (I couldn't tell if they didn't care for Theresa, if they didn't like the idea of a time capsule, or if it was something else altogether.)

But no one had asked any more about the Zloduk case, the one topic I was most interested in. Sly had mentioned it twice, and the way everyone at the dinner table had reacted when Ronnie brought it up was driving my curiosity crazy. Mom was so relaxed on the drive, in her own head but in a drowsy way, that I figured it was now or never.

"What happened in the Zloduk case?"

I'd almost expected a return to the arrogance she'd worn like a mink coat at the dinner party, but her shoulders drooped. She was driving slowly, the wind fluttering her hair. Passing streetlights outlined her sharp profile. I looked more like her from the side than the front, and it was disorienting, being with someone so familiar yet such a stranger.

"I'll make a deal with you, Francesca," she said, her voice soft, "but you have to agree to it."

"Yes, ma'am," I said, a thrill twinging my spine despite the alarm bells.

"Here it is: I'll speak to you like an adult." She glanced over at me, quick. Her eyes were deep, inky pools in her face. "I know that might sound great to a kid, but it's not. Not always. But it's the only way I know how to talk, and I really want us to be best friends. So, do you want me to speak to you like I would a grown-up and tell you the real, hard truth, or do you want baby fluff?"

I felt light-headed, like I'd just blown up a pile of balloons. "Like a grown-up, please."

She seemed to approve of that answer. "The Zloduk family lived just outside of town, the parents in a farmhouse, their adult children in two different trailers on the same property, three grandchildren in each trailer."

The sky was split by electric yellow. Mom and I both froze in the startling brightness of it, but no thunder followed.

Heat lightning.

She dropped the rest like a scorpion in the confined car. "Wagner Zloduk was the head of that clan. He and his wife and their adult children were molesting the kids, all six of them."

My hands shot to my ears, but it was too late. The words had gotten in. "Grandparents? Doing . . . that to their grandkids?" It was an evil too dark to comprehend.

"And parents to their own children."

I shook my head, first to deny such a thing could happen and then to keep the image of it from landing. "Parents don't do that."

Mom slowed the car down for a stop sign but didn't come to a complete stop. Now that its seal was broken, the heat lightning was dancing across the sky, enchanting and spooky. I'd almost decided she either hadn't heard my last comment or didn't think it needed a response when she said, quietly, "There's a lot you don't realize about your dad, you know."

If she'd balled up her fist and driven it into my stomach, she would have hurt me less. I thought of the knapsack with the name "Jubilee" on it. "What?"

Her eyes narrowed. "It's true of every kid, I suppose. So much they don't know about their parents."

That hung in the air for a moment. If she noticed me white knuckling the door handle, she didn't give a sign. "That goes for me, too," she continued, with another quick glance at me.

I wished the car floor would stop churning below my feet. "There were things that surprised you about your parents?" I asked.

She made a bitter, drowning sound. "What I meant is that there's stuff you don't know about me, either."

"Yes, ma'am." *No shit.*

"Just as my own mother was inaccessible to me."

Like Dad's, both Mom's parents had died before I came on the scene. At least that's what I'd been told. I knew enough to stay quiet as Mom continued. She was warming up to something, something big.

"She was an English teacher here in town. Everyone who knew her called her outspoken," she said, her lip curling. "And she was, as long as it didn't require speaking against her husband. Your grandfather."

We'd reached a part of Litani I recognized. Home was four minutes away, five tops.

"She hated scenes, your grandmother. She cooked great meals, kept a neat house, worked a respectable job, but the face she showed the world wasn't hers, not her real one."

My spit turned to vinegar.

"The problem, I think, was that she had spent her whole life covering for my father, making excuses for him, sacrificing friendships and family, until it was just the three of us. And when it came time to choose between him or me, she chose him." The raw anger in her voice scared me. She swiped at her eyes before gripping the steering wheel like a life preserver. "It had been too long since she knew where she ended and he began."

Heat lightning danced its frenzied jig across the sky. What was the moment Mom was remembering, the one where her mother had chosen her father over her? I couldn't ask. Mom wasn't talking to me any longer, not really. She was walking some zoo-creature path in her memory, circling again and again in a too-small cage.

"That's why I fell in love with your father. I believed he was the opposite of my own. A good man. A *safe* man."

She'd finally mentioned him. Dad. I waited for more words to drop like rain on my parched heart—what he'd been like, how much they'd loved me, their private jokes. And in that warm space, I could finally lay down my load. She would understand, I saw that now.

"We're home!" she chirped instead, her voice fake cheery as she pulled into the driveway and away from me, our connection gone so fast I wondered if it had been there at all. "I'm beat."

Her box of a house squatted in front of us, flat and ugly, its blue the color of a bruise at night. Mom stopped the car in front of the garage and jumped out to open the large door. I could have helped her, should have offered, but I'd stayed motionless for so long that I couldn't figure out how to move again.

Mom popped back into the car and pulled into the garage. She flipped off the ignition and started to step out but then stopped herself, turning to peer at me. Her face was shadowed, its sharp angles showing me the shape of her skull in the flashes of heat lightning.

"Are you all right?" she asked.

I couldn't even bring myself to blink.

"Remember those perms?" she asked. Then she reached over and ruffled my hair. It was the first time she'd touched me since she'd yanked that tooth seven years ago.

I was leaning over to melt into her arms just as she slid out of the car.

Her window was still open, so I heard her as she walked into the house. "I don't know what I was thinking back then."

❖

Wort was curled in my lap, sleek and warm. I'd stroked her until she fell asleep. "It's only for a while you can live here," I whispered, "until we find your real home. So don't get too comfortable."

The heat lightning was still tattooing the night sky, but it was all talk. No storm was coming, no wave of water to slice through the miserable heat, to fight that electricity in a dangerous, crashing battle. It made me sad. I wanted a biblical flood to flow through Litani and cleanse its streets, washing away the cult that had been mentioned at the dinner party, the greasy fear I felt at the idea of children being molested, The Game (it couldn't be the same one Dawn had asked me to play because she was a kid, yet my gut told me it *was* the same one), the confusion around who was good and who was bad in this terrifying town.

But no rain came to save us, only this cruel, feverish air punctuated by the wicked grins of heat lightning. My hair pasted to my neck, too hot to sleep, not wanting to wake up Motherwort, I leaned over for The Book and flipped to a clean page. I couldn't bring my dad back to life. I couldn't make my mom act like a mom. I could at least start to organize who was what in this town.

Paul's Angels, back in business, 50 percent fewer detectives and 100 percent more terror than before.

I clutched my favorite four-color pen, clicking the plunger for the green ink and then nibbling on the end as I tried to envision Crane as a plant. He was hard to read, that was for sure. I'd gotten hints of what was inside before he'd snapped closed. Venus flytrap? No, that didn't feel right. Crane was more solid than that, less carnivorous.

Wasn't he?

I thought of Darlene next. She was an herb; I believed that because of Crane's suggestion but also because she'd helped me, giving me money so that I could save Wort. But which herb? And what kind of plant was her daughter, dirty blonde Dawn? Had to be something prickly.

Thinking of mothers and daughters brought my own mom into focus. Was she a rose? Pretty, sharp? Or was I only thinking that because of the rosebushes planted along her office and my bedroom?

"Gah." This was frustrating. Always before, Dad and I had started with the plant, not the person. I didn't know how to do it this way. It was too hard.

Sly is a mushroom.

That had been my first impression after meeting him, and Crane had confirmed. Why not start there?

"Mushroom" was a term used to describe anything with a stem, a cap, and gills. I normally preferred the term "toadstool" because it did a better job capturing how most people were suspicious of mushrooms. I couldn't blame them. Pop the wrong one in your mouth and you could lose your mind in a hallucinogenic brain scrape or die in a foamed-mouth frenzy.

Choose the right one, though, and it would melt on your tongue in a most sublime way.

Plus, *their colors*. Vivid oranges and sunny yellows and bioluminescent greens and my favorite, the inky blue of a *Lactarius indigo*, a huge toadstool that looked as if it had been plucked straight out of *Alice in Wonderland*.

But Sly wasn't vivid, or sublime. He was toxic. My belly told me that, and if June, my Paul's Angels partner, were here, I was sure she'd agree. Of course, the thing about toxic plants was that most of them had a useful side. I wasn't particularly in the mood to extend that forgiveness to people, but I was my father's daughter and so had to be honest in the plant classification. And if I was truthful in reviewing my interaction with Sly, he'd been nice to me.

Hadn't he?

What a mushroom.

I ached for June to be here so we could talk through it. But she wasn't, and I needed to get something on paper. I started sketching, beginning with the stem. That could apply to any mushroom. It was when I reached the cap that I'd need to get more specific. The green ink scratched the paper, filling, fleshing out. What mushroom looked delicious but tricked you? Something you'd find in pockets, hidden. Something that lived in the Midwest.

I grinned and clicked my ink to black.

I had it.

Sly was a false morel.

A true morel was a king's feast. That's what Dad had called it when a student brought him a bag a couple Aprils ago. Dad had carried the package into the kitchen like it contained diamond-encrusted eggs, calling me over for the unveiling. Inside was a pile of delicate-looking mushrooms, each as long as a hot dog with a head like a honeycombed grocery bag. Dad explained there was controversy over how many species of true morel existed, but the world was in agreement: every one of them was delicious.

After he cleaned and then sautéed them in garlic butter and sprinkled them with sea salt, I had to agree. They tasted like heaven, delicate and nutty, melting like caramel on my tongue.

"Food for a king," Dad said, his eyes closed in ecstasy.

It's funny because you never think you look like your opposite-sex parent, but in that moment, I realized I did. There was no missing it. I had his dark hair and wide-set brown eyes, his too-small nose. Our mouths were different, and I was glad for that because it'd be creepy if we looked like brother and sister.

"Can we get more?" I asked him after we'd devoured the last of the morels and one of us (me) had licked their plate.

"I wish, pumpkin," he said. "True morels are hard to come by."

Not so much false morels.

The false ones could pass as real, he told me, which was why so many people fell for them. There were hints, with their cap appearing more brain-like versus the true morel's honeycomb pattern. They were also more of a murky brown color, which was why I was alternating the red and black ink of my pen, scribbling furiously now that I knew what I was drawing, an angry morel with Sly's slicked-back mullet and Tom Selleck mustache and deceptively friendly smile. Despite those hints, you could never be sure which mushroom was poison and which was pleasure until you cut them open.

A true morel was hollow.

A false morel? Its interior was a maze of tunnels that looped back on themselves, confusion and clots, a mind trapped inside itself. Dad said some people didn't have a negative reaction to eating the false morel, which made the fungi even more dangerous because you'd tell others it was fine—and it *had* been fine, to you—and they'd taste it and get sick. Dad said the false ones wouldn't kill you, not usually, but they'd twist your head and your intestines and make you feel so awful that you wished you were dead.

CHOOSE YOUR OWN PLANT PERSONALITY

YOU'RE CAPTAIN OF YOUR OWN DESTINY!
WHICH PLANT PERSONALITY DO YOU CHOOSE?

FALSE MOREL

You trick those searching for a king, but to others,
you don't do a thing. If a person isn't sure what they've got,
they best toss you rather than tossing you in a pot.

I realized I was panting. I licked my lips, tasting the tang of salt. "Wort?"

She was no longer on my lap. I glanced around the room, panicked. She was nowhere to be seen, and my door was cracked! I shot off the bed. If Mom spotted the kitten, it was over. She'd probably drive her to the pound in the middle of the night. I knew that was unfair—probably—but that was my fear.

I yanked open the door, expecting the worst, but there she was, licking herself just outside Mom's closed bedroom.

"Wort!" I whispered. "Naughty kitten. What are you doing out here?"

I was reaching for her, vowing to never again be so careless about making sure my door was shut tight, when she darted into the living room. My eyes shot to Mom's bedroom. It was past midnight. Hopefully she didn't need to use the bathroom.

I dashed down the hall. Wort danced ahead, crab-walking, certain we were playing some sort of fabulous game.

"Come here, you goofball," I whispered.

Instead, she hopped into Mom's office.

I about swallowed my tongue.

I had no choice but to follow her even though I'd never entered Mom's office before, not even that first visit, back when I was little and she still liked me. There was something hushed about the space, a well of deep stillness inside the sleeping house.

A church quiet.

I stepped into it.

Her rolltop desk stood near the door, its rounded front closed tight. Bookshelves lined two walls, though I didn't see any of the novels I'd spotted in her bedroom. These were all thick, serious. The fourth wall contained file cabinets.

Sly's mushroom voice came to me.

Hey, did you ask your lawyer mom about the Zloduk case?

No, sir.

Well, it's a doozy. If she keeps a filing cabinet at her house, you'll want to avoid looking for that one.

Was there more to it, something Mom had kept to herself? I found myself in front of the second filing cabinet, kneeling (Z, at the end), my hand on the warm metal handle.

I witnessed my thumb mold itself into the curve of the closure button, pushing it.

Heard the tumbling *clunk* of release.

Watched the drawer glide open.

I would have pulled the Zloduk file, even knowing what Mom had told me on the drive home, if Wort hadn't hissed and crawled straight up my back, my T-shirt no protection against her piercing claws.

It hurt, but I was relieved to be distracted. I slid the drawer closed and stood, turning my back to the filing cabinet.

"What is it, Worty?" She was crouched on my shoulder, trembling. I stroked her, worried. She was shaking almost as hard as she had been the day I discovered her. "What has you so upset?"

A slash of heat lightning answered me, revealing the monster outside the window.

Horns.

Knives for fingers.

Crouching.

Watching.

Everyone's talking about it, saying the satanic cult's back in town. Pets disappearing, turning up dead if they turn up at all. Pentagrams spray-painted on the sides of buildings. Unholy altars in the woods . . .

My senses fell away, leaving only a two-word drumbeat in my skull.

Run. Hide.

Run. Hide.

But I was paralyzed, a bug trapped in sap. I'd seen only the demon's outline in the flash of lightning. I couldn't have stood it if the next round of brightness had revealed its grinning, horrible face, sharp fingers reaching for the window sash.

But I couldn't move.

Great whale bones of terror had taken shape, my heartbeat revealing them as sure as the ocean tide.

Run. Hide.

Run. Hide.

I struggled to close my eyes, wished desperately, stupidly, for the monster to kill me without me having to see it (small mercies), but the next rip of lightning came too soon.

Which was when I saw what was really there.

Not a demon—only Mom's rosebush, grown tall and wily.

The wind and light and everything I'd heard since arriving in Litani had preyed on my brain. Satan hadn't come for me after all. How could he? He was a creature of the imagination. Not real.

That's what I told myself as I returned to my room on trembling legs, gripping Wort, who was still shaking worse than me.

CHAPTER 21

I woke up needing to talk to June so bad that I was honestly worried I'd die if I didn't. I planned to ask Mom's permission, but once again, she was gone by the time I made it to the kitchen. She had left a note on the sack lunch she'd packed for me.

Gone to work. Good luck with the time capsule project.

Well, I'd find a way to pay her back for the call, just like I'd found a way to pay back Darlene, because I was frantic to talk to June. I needed to connect to something normal.

I dialed. I crossed my fingers, toes, eyes, and knees. The phone rang and rang, and I was about to give up when she answered.

"Hello?" She sounded sleepy. My gosh, it was only 6:00 a.m. in California. I should have apologized, but I was too happy.

"Hey, June."

"Frankie?" she squealed. "Is it really you?"

Just like that, the tears started gushing.

"You knob," June said, laughing, but I could hear the concern in her voice. "Did you miss me that much?"

From anyone else, that might've sounded mean. Not from her. We'd been best friends our whole lives. She was the kind of kid who held funerals for dead butterflies and would chase after you if she saw you drop a dollar. *My* kind of kid.

"Minnesota is messed up, June."

"Tell me all about it."

I could picture the way she usually looked as clear as if she were standing in front of me: her gap-toothed smile firing up her dimples, wearing her favorite strawberry lip gloss and blue mascara even though she had nowhere to go, her streaked blonde hair teased to the sky. I'd bet The Book that she was leaning forward on the other end of the line, giving me every inch of her attention.

I listed the big stuff that had happened since I'd arrived in Litani, and with every word that spilled out of my mouth—a recap of the people I'd met; the mysterious game Dawn had mentioned; the cult rumors; the scary-looking brewery perched like a greedy buzzard on the edge of town; Michelle, who Mom said had run away but I wasn't so sure; the time capsule; nearly everything except what Mom had told me last night about the Zloduks and then her own parents—I felt better. June wasn't easing my load, but it wasn't any longer all on my shoulders, either.

She'd interrupted only once, when I described getting beaten up. "What was their damage?"

"I know!" I started to giggle. It was so ridiculous when said out loud. Three girls, none of them older than ten, roughing me up and stealing my high-tops. By the end of that part of the story, she and I were laughing so hard that she actually snorted. I didn't tell her that the girl who'd disappeared was one of the ones who'd beaten me up. I didn't want to poison the mood.

"Can you believe I hallucinated Satan outside my mom's office window?" I said, bringing us back to an earlier topic.

To my surprise, she stopped laughing. "You're not supposed to say his name."

"Good one," I said, rolling my eyes. "I thought you were serious for a minute."

"I am serious!" she said, her tone suddenly defensive. "There's a satanic cult that meets under the Hollywood Sign. They kill cats, and they're coming after kids next, girls mostly. Everyone's talking about it."

"So wait," I said, dropping onto the wicker couch. "You believe in *Satan*?"

"I believe in Satan *worshippers*," she said, her voice cool for the first time in our conversation. "And you should, too. They're all over the country, living among us. Mom says it's an epidemic."

June's mom liked soap operas and gossip magazines. We'd always joked about it. The warm feeling inside me took on a rusty edge.

"Thanks for the hot tip," I said.

"Don't get snotty," June said. "You're the one who called *me*."

That was true. And she was the only friend I had. "I think you'd like Crane," I said, changing the subject. "He's real serious. I bet he's a good student."

"Is he cute?"

I thought about it. "Not really."

"Hmmph," she said.

We both sat with that between us, feeling strange inside our friendship for the first time. I didn't like it. "I revived Paul's Angels," I said, threading pretend excitement in my voice.

"Without your dad?" June asked.

The way she asked it made me feel ashamed. She didn't know about those last two weeks with him, about the unraveling.

That day he'd suggested June join us for a sleepover, I'd never been able to get hold of her, not that time. I'd learned later she'd been running errands with her mom.

Dad said he and I could still do the pizza and movies, though, even without June, and he cleaned himself up for the rescheduled meeting and left for the university. I was nose deep in algebra homework when he charged through the door a few hours later. His pace was the first thing that set off my alarm bells. Dad rarely moved fast. Plant life didn't call for it. Slow, gentle, methodical was the name of the game, and he was built for it.

"I've got great news!" he announced.

But his mouth was tight, and his hands were shaking so much they rustled the paper sack he was clutching. That was the second warning.

"What is it?" I asked, feeling the unraveling, unsure what it was, powerless to stop it.

"You're always telling me I work too much," he said, setting the sack on the kitchen counter and pulling out some branches that reminded me of a currant bush, with its serrated leaves and red berries. "The college has fixed that problem for us."

The calmness in his voice against the oddness in his body scared me. He'd been so calm and normal at the Red Box Picnic Area earlier, and now he was like a stranger wearing my father's skin. "Dad, what happened?"

"Got laid off," he said, grinning a mannequin smile. "I burned through my grant more quickly than expected. They said I can finish out the semester, and then I'm done."

"Dad!" I jumped up from the kitchen table. "What'll we do?"

I might have been only fourteen, but that was old enough to know Paul Jubilee was not suited for any work other than tromping through the woods and talking to plants, his days punctuated by occasional wandering lectures in a classroom. Unexpectedly, an image of Mom burbled up from somewhere deep inside me. By that point in my life, I thought of her only when my annual cards arrived and sometimes when June's mom would hug her and look at me with something in her eyes that felt oily, an emotion between pity and pride. Otherwise, my mother had faded in my memory enough that she'd become background.

But Mom was a lawyer, I knew that. Could she give us money? I'd been too scared to ask Dad that day, though.

Everything would be different now if I had.

I jerked myself back into the moment. I was gripping the phone so tight that my fingers were cramping. "Yep," I said. "I'm reviving the Angels without Dad."

"I'm so sorry," June said, true remorse in her voice. "I never should have said that. I think starting up Paul's Angels again is a great idea. He'd want that."

"You think so?"

"Sure. You can get to the bottom of what that game is. You can call me up to consult, just like you're doing right now." Her voice dropped to a growl. "I'll tell you to keep your nose out of trouble, young lady."

I smiled. It was a phrase that always made us giggle, imagining our noses off on their own adventures. "Thanks, June. You're a pal."

She said it was no biggie, told me that she was attending summer camp in a couple weeks and that Jason, this boy that we'd both liked, was going to be there, too, and maybe my mom would let me go (I doubted it, but it didn't matter because I couldn't abandon Wort), and that our house hadn't sold yet, but then it had been only two weeks since it'd gone up for sale, and so on.

By the end of the call, we'd found our way back to each other.

"Don't be a stranger, Frankie," she said when we'd both wound down.

"You either, June Bug. Maybe you can come visit me?"

"Maybe," she said, though I knew it wouldn't happen. No way would I put her in that kind of danger.

❖

I scooped Wort's litter box, hiding the turds at the bottom of the kitchen garbage. I rinsed out and refilled her water dish and topped off her food, promising I'd be back to play before she knew it. Then I grabbed the lunch Mom had made for me (bologna sandwich and an apple, and what was with her packing me a lunch every day?) and tucked it into Dad's knapsack along with the paperwork Theresa had given me before it had all hit the fan in the trailer park.

Today's set of addresses brought me downtown, nearer to the brewery than I would have liked. Mom mentioning last night that kids should stay clear of it just added to the disturbing vibe it naturally exuded. Fortunately, a few more people were out and about, though they all seemed to be in a hurry to get somewhere. I'd spot them out of the corner of my eye, someone walking between a couple houses or leaving a shop, and then I'd turn, and they'd be gone. Litani definitely lacked the peaceful, steady hum of Pasadena, where on a hot summer day, people worked in their yards or walked babies or dogs, stopping to chat with neighbors beneath the shade of an orange tree. And kids played outside, calling to each other, biking and racing and running through sprinklers.

I dead-stopped in the middle of the sidewalk, halfway to the door of the first stop on my list, a white house behind a white picket fence. A heavy rock had dropped into my belly.

That was it.

There were no kids around.

It was summer. Where were they all? Besides the odd smattering of children I'd met my first day here—Dawn, Crystal, and Michelle; that little girl playing hide-and-go-seek in the woods; and the headbangers at the edge of the playground—there were no kids outside on their own in Litani.

Just to be sure, I made a full circle, hoping no one was watching me. I saw parked cars, a healthy crop of wild catnip near the brewery, a cloudless blue sky, but not a single child in sight, no far-off laughter, no gang of friends heading to the river to swim on this blistering day.

Although nothing else had changed, that new awareness made me feel exposed. I swallowed past the paranoia and walked up to the door.

I pushed the doorbell, hearing the shrill echo it set off inside, followed by frantic barking, but no one answered.

I was almost relieved.

I steadied my breath, tucked a leaflet behind the screen door, and moved on to the next house, this one more of a cottage where the other one had been a rambler. The door opened before I even had a chance to knock.

An elderly woman, hair white, eyes puddling behind gold-rimmed glasses, stepped out onto her front stoop holding the door partially open behind her. "Yes?"

She smelled like she'd been frying bacon. It was a good smell. "Hi. I'm—"

"I know who you are. You're Linda Jubilee's daughter."

I liked the smell less. "I am. I'm working with Theresa Buckle, and—"

"And you want to know what I think should go into the time capsule. Well, I think the whole idea should be stuffed in a rocket and shot to the moon. What do you think of that?"

I blinked rapidly. I'd had my pen hovering over the paper Theresa had given me to record answers, using a notebook of my own to provide stability. I clicked the ink back into the pen. "Thank you for your time, ma'am."

The next house was mildly better, with the woman who answered offering me ice water. The house after that, a woman talked to me for ten minutes. All of it was about her granddaughter, who lived in the Cities—which was what they called Minneapolis and Saint Paul here, as if it were easier than just naming the one city or the other—and who she was going to babysit while her daughter and her husband traveled to Las Vegas. It was a pleasant-enough conversation. I soon found a rhythm with the interviews, and I even began to enjoy my time. Mostly women at home with little kids answered the door, and they acted as relieved as me to have someone to talk with.

Their time capsule suggestions, when they had them, were good but not particularly inspired: a high school yearbook, a letter jacket, a can of beer from the Engle Brewery (the guy who'd suggested that said I'd need to buy the can from an antique store because no beer had come out of Engle since 1947). I didn't spot anything that explained why there were plenty of children indoors and none out, but going from house to house began to feel like building something good. This new hometown of mine was dull and ugly and lonely, and there was talk of a cult, and as far as I knew Michelle was still missing, but with the sun pouring its warm yellow liquid on my shoulders and a lunch packed by Mom in my knapsack and Wort waiting for me at home, well, I was feeling okay. I even made a little room to imagine starting school in the fall. I'd have a chance to make new friends.

Dare I say I was smiling as I knocked on the door of the fourth Oak Street house, a structure different than the rest on the block. This one was two stories to their one, and it was wide and somehow off-balance, with a bay window on the front jutting out from what looked like an addition. In fact, it appeared as though there'd been several additions, one built on top of another. It reminded me of a miniature Winchester House, the twisty, quirky mansion Dad and I had toured on one of our rare visits to his aunt Edna.

My smile widened when I recognized the man who opened the door.

"Francesca Jubilee!" Ronnie McSorley said. "Did I accidentally wear your jacket home from Clara's spaghetti party the other night?"

It was a nice joke to make me comfortable, especially since all the men at the mayor's dinner had been wearing long-sleeved shirts that were already too warm for the evening, no jacket required, and it was that thought that made me notice his bare arms.

My smile fell off my face with a thud.

Ronnie's long sleeves had covered his arms at Clara's, but up close, him wearing a T-shirt, I could see they were ropy and bulging, one covered with a blotch so big and intentional looking that it must have been a tattoo, and it was, of an anchor. That must have been why I'd thought of Popeye when I'd spotted him my first day in Litani, playing in the woods with a little girl, the sight making my skin crawl with worms.

Ronnie had been the man in the forest.

I stumbled back involuntarily, my eyes shooting to his face.

He still held his smile.

And then the blonde girl he'd been chasing appeared at his legs, her hair in pigtails, and twined her arms around his thigh.

CHAPTER 22

"Who is she, Daddy?" the girl asked, staring at me with eyes as blue as a summer sky.

"This is Francesca Jubilee," he said. "She's new to town."

And then my paralysis broke. Ronnie was her dad. Of course he was, just like I'd first imagined when I'd seen them playing. The panic I'd just felt was nutso, probably arising because of what Mom had told me about the Zloduk family last night. I needed to stop being such a jumpy fraidy-cat.

"Nice to meet you," I said to the girl.

She scowled and disappeared into the house.

He shrugged. "Kids, you know?"

I liked how he said it, implying that he and I were on equal footing. "I'm here about the time capsule. We were talking about it at the spaghetti party," I said, using his term for Clara's get-together.

He scratched his chin. "I don't recall you speaking up on the subject. Theresa Buckle recruit you to help her?"

"Yes, sir. I'm asking townspeople what they'd like to put in it."

"Vintage newspapers."

His quick answer, right there all cued up, caught me off guard. "That's a great idea," I said.

And it was. An old newspaper was its own sort of record, so it'd become a time capsule inside a time capsule, a snapshot of what was going on at any given period in Litani. I scribbled his idea down on the form, right next to his address. I added "Ronnie" to give him the credit I thought he deserved.

"You think Theresa'll think it's a good idea?"

"I bet she will," I said, smiling up at him as I finished writing. He'd stepped back, so I couldn't see his face. "The trick'll be to figure out which date. Was there anything big that happened in Litani?"

He didn't respond at first. He was still in shadow, dust motes scurrying across the sunbeam that sliced his chest. "Not since what happened to your dad that day at the river."

My breath went sideways in my throat, and I started coughing. Ronnie was certainly referring to Benny's drowning, but his tone was way different than Mom's had been when talking about it. Ronnie's version had teeth and a tail. I got control of my cough and wiped my eyes. "You knew my dad?"

"Paul Jubilee? Yeah, he was pretty famous around here, even before he married your mother." A sound like a laugh, or a wheeze. "Not to mention he was my best friend. I think I still have the newspaper from back then, from before he moved out and left us all here to grow old without him. You wanna see it?"

For the first time in my life, I knew what it meant to be of two minds. I suddenly, desperately needed to read the article, and reading it was also the last thing on earth I wanted to do. Both things were true. I thought of Mom's warning not to step inside anyone's house. Surely she hadn't meant her friends' homes.

A car door slammed, startling me. I glanced over my shoulder. Someone had parked in front of the last house I'd been to, the little yellow cottage where a woman in curlers had answered the door, smiled warmly at me, told me she'd be happy to donate a jar of her homemade plum jelly to the time capsule if I wanted it.

"Okay," I said.

Ronnie stepped aside so I could enter.

❖

Dead animals. That was the first thing I noticed about the inside of Ronnie's house. A deer head, a stuffed pheasant, a mounted trophy fish, their marble eyes staring through me.

Second was how his front room—the living room—was noticeably sloped down toward the bay window. The furniture looked well used, a copper-colored sofa worn shiny at the armrests, a green easy chair spread full out, like Ronnie'd hopped straight from it to answer the door. He had a book open on the chipped end table within reach of the chair. I couldn't read the title without being obvious. The little girl lay on her stomach in front of the television, which was off, the screen dark and deep. She was coloring, scribbling in one spot with a fat green crayon over and over again until the color showed up nearly black.

"That's Cathy," he said. "The twins are napping."

My eyes kept traveling to the animal carcasses displayed like trophies, which I supposed they were. He followed my gaze. "I'm the best hunter in the county," he said, misreading my attention. "I can field dress an animal before it hits the ground."

I nodded. It occurred to me then that it was the middle of a weekday. "What do you do for work, Mr. McSorley?"

He'd been about to head up the stairs and stopped, hand on the rail. He turned, a puzzled expression on his face. But then he wiped that off and smiled. "Ronnie, I told you to call me. Your mom didn't tell you what I do?"

I shook my head.

"I own a construction company. Hurt my back, so the doctor says to take it easy for a couple weeks."

"I'm sorry to hear that."

"Am I making you uncomfortable?"

The question jolted me. I realized I hadn't moved from the middle of the living room, and my body didn't want to walk up those stairs. What story had my face been telling without my knowledge? "No, sir."

"Because we can wait until Patty gets home to go upstairs, if that would make you feel better. She just ran to the grocery store."

Hearing that did ease me, though my feet still weren't moving. "I'd like to have a look at that newspaper."

Saying it, I knew I was on the edge of learning something about my dad, something true and solid and maybe bad from before I was born. But what was the alternative? I clutched at the backpack straps, stalling for time. "Ronnie, do you know if my dad was in the military?"

He tipped his head, a sad smile on his face. "Linda is as forthcoming at home as she is everywhere else, huh? Has she told you anything about Paul?"

I shook my head again, worried for a moment that I wouldn't be able to stop shaking it.

"Well, come on up, then. I'll tell you more than you ever wanted to know."

CHAPTER 23

"You know the old Engle Brewery downtown?"

"Yep." Of course I did.

"We used to have parties there, back in the day."

He'd led me to his and Patty's bedroom, which I didn't like because it smelled like hair and *people*, but the bed was made, the nubby cream-colored chenille bedspread pulled tight, and there were no clothes strewn on the floor or messes on the matching nightstands, so I supposed it was okay for a short visit. He popped into the closet and returned with two cardboard boxes, one balanced on the other. They appeared heavy, which surprised me since he'd said his back was hurt.

He set both boxes on the bed with a grunt. "The place is dangerous now and was dangerous then, all broken glass and leaning walls. I suspect that's one of the reasons your mom wants everyone to avoid the place. But she couldn't get enough of it when we were younger. Kids love that haunted-looking shit, excuse my French."

It sounded like he was now sticking me in the camp with children.

"We all hung out there. Me, your dad, your mom—boy, did she have the hots for him, it's like she was born loving Paul—Chief Mike, Theresa who has you working this crazy time capsule idea, and my Patty, though she was a Petoskey back then."

I tried to picture it, this man spending time with my dad, all of them young. I couldn't hold the image.

"And Darlene Richmond," he said. "You know her?"

"Does she live in the trailer park? Have a daughter named Dawn?"

"That's the one." He opened the top box, dug out photographs and yearbooks and trophies, piling them alongside it. "We were thick as thieves, the seven of us. The magnificent seven."

I'd heard the phrase before. I think it was a movie. "This was back in high school."

"Yep. We all grew up in the same neighborhood, more or less." He drew something small out of the box. It looked like a coil of yellow paper, and it fit into the palm of his hand. His whole face went squishy as he studied it. "Would you look at that? I'd forgotten your father left this in my car. Meant to return it to him, but I don't suppose he'd have wanted it any more than I did."

I was hungry to know what he was holding, but he shielded it from my view. "What is it?"

His eyes slid to me, then back to his hand. "Nothing."

It ached not to be able to see it, but I couldn't make him show me.

He tipped the now-empty box upside down, as if searching for a secret compartment. "Newspapers must be in the other one." He began returning the stack of memorabilia to its original container, tossing in the yellow coil he'd been holding.

"Yes, this was back in high school," he said, returning to my earlier question. "Paul, Mike, and me were on the football team. I know what you're thinking, with me and your dad being the size we are, but we were quick."

My dad, with his delicate hands, softly plucking flowers and labeling them. *On the football team.*

"Darlene, Linda, Patty, and Theresa were all cheerleaders, or at least they wanted to be. I can't remember the specifics." He closed the top of the first box and reached for the second, his face screwed up in thought. "I don't recall if I was dating Patty at the time. The seven of us took a while, deciding who we'd settle down with."

He glanced at me, and I tried smiling politely, mentally willing him to continue, craving more information about my dad.

My stiff grin must have worked, because he returned his attention to the box. "Anyhow, this particular summer day was going to be like any other. We were heading to the brewery to drink and throw pop bottles at rats. Except your dad had to bring his little brother along."

Another shot of electricity, the mention of Dad's brother. *Benny.* It was like having the characters in a TV show walk out of the set and begin to move around the room. Everything dusty taking life, Dad's past growing flesh and blood and bone.

This second box was sealed with tape. It squealed as Ronnie tore it off. "We all liked your uncle Benny." He stopped, a thick line between his brows. "Isn't that something? He was your uncle by blood, but he never reached his ninth birthday. What do you think about that, being older today than your uncle will ever be?"

I didn't know what to think, so I thought everything, my brain a blur, thoughts a big, fat green crayon scribbling to black. I couldn't have answered him if I wanted to, but he didn't seem to expect it.

"I can't remember who got the idea to head to the river to swim. It was a hot day." He'd been opening the box, but he paused and glanced off a thousand miles. "It was a scorching month. July, record-breaking temperatures. Reminds me of this summer."

I could feel it coming closer, the awful thing he was going to tell me. I was in an ecstasy of terror, a shivering animal stuck in a trap, not sure if the footsteps meant she was about to be set free or killed.

He shook the memory webs out of his head and returned to the box, yanking out newspapers, glancing at their dates, putting them aside. "We packed into my pickup truck—everyone could ride in the bed in the '60s, it was no problem, no cops getting into your business as long as we kept the beer out of sight. I parked at the trailer park. That place hasn't changed. If you've seen it now, you know what it looked like then and how close it is to the Minnesota River. There was a tire swing over the river back then, maybe still is now."

There was. I'd seen it the same day I'd spotted him chasing Cathy through the woods. I wrapped my arms across my belly, squeezing my elbows. The walls of Patty and Ronnie's bedroom felt like they were tilting in toward me.

"We were drinking and swinging on that tire into the water, laughing and roughhousing, I suppose. Benny was sitting by the truck. He was an oddball, not quite right in the head, if you know what I mean. He didn't know how to swim, but he loved your dad, followed him like a puppy. Paul usually kept a close eye on the kid, but he was having too good a time that day. Him and your mom disappeared to do their thing, and the rest of us broke off into whatever pairs we made back then, just like it happens."

But there were seven people. Seven people plus eight-year-old Benny made eight. How was that *pairs*?

"That's when Benny went to the river. We'll never know what made him jump in. Maybe he saw your dad do it? He copied everything Paul did. But Paul wasn't there to save him this time. He was drunk, we all were, and he got so busy with your mom, he forgot about Benny."

His words slammed into me. I wanted to scream at him, to make him stop talking, to leap through the air that had turned into concrete and strangle him so he would *shut up*. Mom had said it was an accident Benny drowned. An *accident*. No way had Dad been drunk. I'd never seen him take so much as a sip of a beer.

"It was a real tragedy. One you can't blame your dad for. He was just a kid himself, and kids make dumb mistakes." His eyes flicked to me. "They had to drag the river for Benny. I was there the day they pulled his body out. The whole town was. We wanted to do something, even when we knew it was too late. People are funny like that, you know?"

Help. That's the shape my mouth made. Ronnie didn't see it, or if he did, it didn't slow him down.

139

"Your granny screamed so loud when she saw the body, I bet they heard it on the moon. Your grandpa, *he* was the military man. Not your dad." His eyes skittered to the army knapsack slung over my shoulder.

"Your grandpa had been a regular at the bar before Benny's death. After, he might as well have moved in, he spent so much time in the bottle. And your dad disappeared inside himself, is the best way I can describe it. Can't blame him. Guilt like that will chew a person whole and digest them for as long as they let it. It took all of a month before your grandparents and Paul moved to Minneapolis to get away from the town that reminded them of what they'd lost."

I was hypnotized by Ronnie and his words, paralyzed.

He chuckled ruefully, his face bland, weathered. He was the same age as my dad, but he looked older, his hair graying at his temples. He reminded me of an anchorman, his voice calm as he delivered the most horrific news with regret and unassailable authority.

"I'm afraid this story doesn't have a happy ending for most of your relatives," he was saying. "Your grandfather drank himself to death, and your grandma soon followed. But at least your mom and dad got theirs. The story I heard was that they accidentally met up again at college a few years later, but Linda had always had her sights on Paul. I wouldn't be surprised to learn she'd hunted him down and that he'd married her out of shame. He'd let his brother die to go to her. Something good might as well come of it."

His mouth tipped up at the corners. "And I suspect that something good is you."

CHAPTER 24

My heart shriveled up like the part of the hermit crab you're not supposed to see.

The Paul Jubilee that Ronnie was describing wasn't my dad, not the man I'd known. My father had been gentle, and responsible, and only ever spoke in a soft voice. He brushed my hair until I fell asleep. He was the one who'd helped to make Paul's Angels such a success, driving us around so we could distribute advertising flyers.

June loved him. *Everyone* loved him.

He would never have gotten so drunk or so sex crazed that he'd forget about his little brother.

Never.

But even as those thoughts marched out, I remembered that I also had believed I'd never kill my own father.

Yet I had.

Ronnie was reading my face as best he could without knowing what I'd done in California. "Accidents happen," he said. "That's why they call them accidents."

He dug back into the box, pulled out a newspaper, read a headline, turned it to face me. "Here it is. I kept it with a bunch of stuff your father gave me when he left town."

I read the title: Local Boy Drowns in Minnesota River

I couldn't focus enough to read the article. The text was too small, my heart beating too loud. I didn't want to touch the newspaper, didn't want to feel its slick coolness, but he rolled it up and offered it to me like a baton, so I took it.

I yanked off the knapsack, not my dad's but my drunk old grandpa's, and I slid the rolled newspaper inside. "I'll give this to Theresa."

I wouldn't. That wasn't how this worked. I was to bring her ideas, not *things*, she'd been clear about that. But it was all I could do to breathe and blink, breathe and blink.

"I need to go," I said, my gut roiling.

"Sure, kid."

I was definitely housed in the child camp now. "Thank you," I said, unsure what else to say. I slipped back into the knapsack straps and felt for the doorknob. Had I closed the door behind me?

"Say, do you do any babysitting?"

I thought of that bit of yellow plastic that he'd said belonged to my dad, my heartbeat quickening. "You bet."

"Are you free tonight?"

"Yes, sir."

"Great. I'll pick you up at seven. It's me and Patty's anniversary. I wanna take her out for a nice dinner, and our regular sitter fell through."

"I can walk." That was the best I could do, the strongest stance I could take for myself.

"All right," he said, flashing me a small smile. "Since you're going to be in charge, you might as well get comfortable here and show yourself out."

CHAPTER 25

I was in such a swamp of disbelief leaving Ronnie's that I didn't immediately register I was being followed. I was tasked with visiting each house on Oak, and then a dozen more one block over, but my legs were on automatic, pumping me blindly away from the treacherous story I'd just heard. It was the heavier footsteps, right on top of mine and then a little bit off but so near, that finally pulled me out of my shock.

I stopped.

Turned.

Crane was ten feet behind me, wearing long pants even though it was a trillion and one degrees outside, hands shoved deep in his pockets. He'd stopped when I had.

"What do you want?"

He flinched.

I felt as bad as if I'd hit him. "I'm sorry," I said. "I don't know why I keep snapping at you."

He stood still, eyes glinting through his bangs. "It's this town."

That moved something off my chest. I took my first full breath since I'd dashed out of the McSorley house. "Yeah," I said. "Maybe. What're you doing?"

He shrugged. "Just out walking."

I shaded my eyes. "It's a hot day for it."

"What are *you* doing?" he asked, brushing his hair away from his eyes.

"Gathering ideas for the Litani time capsule." I thought about the last time we'd talked. "Hey, why didn't you tell me Dawn was Darlene's daughter before I went over there?"

That almost-smile danced across his face, and he moved closer to me. "She beat you up again?"

"No, I was just surprised." I crossed my arms. "It would have been good to know, is all."

"She's just a kid," he said. "She's had some bad knocks. It's not her fault, the way she is."

"You said that right after she beat me up," I said, running my fingers over the scratches on my arm. They'd scabbed up. "Whose fault is it?"

He grimaced, all trace of good humor erased. "What do you see when you look at Dawn?"

The question startled me. A drop of sweat rolled down my temple. I brushed it away. "A brat. A bully."

"You're just like them." His voice was sad.

I looked around. We were the only two people on the sidewalk. "Like who?"

"*Them.* The people who see what they want to see."

Now I was getting angry. "She beat me up, Crane. She stole my shoes and tried to take my dad's backpack the first time I met her!" But it hadn't been my dad's backpack. It had been my grandpa's. I realized I should take back the lie, but I was too mad. "What am I missing?"

He moved closer to me, hesitantly, hands still in pockets. "How little she is."

That melted a corner of my anger. She *was* a shrimp.

"That she's always wearing the same clothes, and her shoes have holes in them."

I thought back to the Garfiend shirt she'd been wearing both times I'd met her, and I cooled off some more.

He raised his eyebrows, I could tell by the way his bangs shifted. "And how easy it is to look mean when what you really are is scared."

That one hit close to home. "You talking about me?"

Finally, he grinned. His smile was still one of the best things I'd seen in Litani, twisted canines and all. "You *have* been touchy more times than not," he said.

"It's this town," I said, repeating what he'd said moments earlier.

He laughed. "I suppose it is."

That laugh filled me up to the top. "Crane, do you wanna be my friend?"

"It pay?" he asked, still smiling.

"Nope, and the hours are terrible. Plus, you have to help me knock on doors."

He stepped alongside me, and we began to walk down the street together. "I suppose I don't have anything better to do."

❖

We grew easy with each other as the day wore on, Crane and me, as comfortable as two people could get when one of them was as talkative as a rock. But that's what I liked about him. It reminded me of my dad. A steady quietness, the kind you didn't need to fill.

"Have you heard the story about a boy who drowned here twenty years ago?"

It felt good to ask it like that, distant from me, like a medical question almost. *Any word on that new flu bug going around?* I wasn't ready to come straight out and explain my connection to the story, the way us Jubilees killed our close relatives. But I figured if I came at it sideways, Crane might tell me more than if I came straight out and asked.

He grunted as a response. That was the downside to the Dad part of him.

"Well, did you or didn't you?"

We'd hit all the remaining houses on that day's list. Crane would wait on the boulevard in the shade of one of Litani's spindly elm trees while I knocked on doors. I don't know if anyone else really noticed him—he was good at blending in—but *I* knew he was there, and that settled me.

One more person recommended we put an Engle Brewery can in the time capsule, someone else a signed baseball from the year the Litani Lions won the state baseball tournament (that person happened to own the very thing they believed should go in the capsule, a pattern I'd noticed), and I got more suggestions for yearbooks and personal items. A nice man smoking a pipe with a yowling basset hound at his feet mentioned he was an amateur historian and said he'd donate the book he was writing about the town. I was left wondering what else had happened in Litani in years past that was worth writing about.

I'd split my lunch with Crane, keeping the apple for myself after he'd looked at it like I was offering him a wart, but sharing my ham, Miracle Whip, and lettuce sandwich on white bread, offering up the perfect triangle. I could say a lot of bad things about my mom, but she sure did make a good sandwich. The ham was square, so it perfectly reached the ends of the bread. The Miracle Whip was generous, its tangy deliciousness squirting out if I bit too fast or too hard, the bread soft as a cloud, the lettuce crisp and sweet.

The Shasta she'd packed paired perfectly with it, even if it was warm from being lugged around all day. I was grateful when Crane passed on sharing it. I didn't think I'd have been able to take it back after he'd had a chug.

We were now on our way back to the trailer park to update Theresa and pick up tomorrow's list. I hoped Crane would be joining me again.

"I wasn't alive back when that boy drowned," Crane said, after so long I'd almost forgotten what I'd asked him.

"I didn't ask if you were *around*. I'd asked if you'd heard about it."

"I suppose."

"You suppose?"

"Rumors, that's all. Some kids playing by the river, one of them drowned." He sounded irritated, walking ahead of me. "Why are you bugging me about it?"

"Sorry," I said to his back. "But you don't always do a great job answering questions."

We'd reached the trailer park. Crane was storming ahead of me, which meant he was actually mad about something I'd said. I wanted to meet his anger with my own, but I knew I'd messed up. I should have been honest about why I wanted to know, and on top of that, my apology had been terrible. Dad always said that only a butt gave an apology with a "but."

I was running ahead to do better when he stopped so quickly that I ran into his back with an *oof*. "You could give a girl a fair warning," I said mildly, rubbing my nose and stepping around to see what was up.

We'd stopped in front of Sly's trailer, but Sly and the blue pickup were nowhere in sight. There was an emerald-green sedan parked out front. A balding older man leaned against the open driver's side door, arms crossed over his bulging belly. A woman his same age was hauling a cardboard box from Red Owl out of the back seat, two runners of sweat racing down each side of her face. Her hair was dyed a startling black, the harsh color magnifying the deep lines etched around her mouth.

"Well, hello there," the man said around a toothpick, his eyes walking up my body like flies. He didn't even glance in Crane's direction.

"Help me close the door, Victor," the woman said, sounding irritated.

"You wanted to bring it, you can carry it," he said, still staring at me. "I told you there were already enough movies here. We didn't need to bring more."

It took all my will not to hide behind Crane, to protect myself from the man's hungry gaze.

The woman swore under her breath and then closed the door with her hip. She came around to stand next to him, her doughy arms visible in her sleeveless blouse and flowered pedal pushers. The Red Owl box she carried didn't appear heavy.

"What're you kids staring at?" she asked.

I glanced down immediately. Her calves were veiny, one long-nailed toe on each foot leaning out over the edge of her white sandals. I brought my gaze back to waist level.

"Nothing," Crane said, his voice crackly. "We're leaving."

He started to walk away, but the old man pushed himself off the car quicker than I would have expected, going from lazy to aggressive in a flash. He planted himself in front of Crane.

"I know you, don't I, boy?"

Crane kept his arms dangling at his side, every muscle poised, hands open like a gunslinger about to draw. "Move," he said, his voice a low, dangerous growl.

The violence in his posture scared me. Without thinking, I grabbed his hand. It felt like a block of ice. "We have an appointment we need to keep, sir."

"I surely do not know *you*," the man said to me, sliding the slippery toothpick to the other side of his mouth. "I'm Victor. Victor Vogler. That's my missus, Eula. Sly is our boy. You've met him?" He smiled, and I saw Sly in him.

"Yes, sir," I said, tugging at Crane, "but we really need to get going."

"Don't let me stop you," Victor said, his grin gone ugly. "If you're bored later, stop by. We're having a party."

"Victor!" Eula said, glaring at him. "You didn't even want to bring the movies, and now you're inviting people over?"

"Thanks, but we have other plans," I said firmly, dragging on Crane to get him moving.

I felt their sticky eyes on us the whole time we walked away.

CHAPTER 26

"What was that about?" I asked once we turned a corner and their creepy gaze wasn't crawling across my skin any longer.

"What?" Crane asked. I'd dropped his hand once he'd started moving on his own, but I could still feel the ice of it in my palm.

"You were so angry back there, out of nowhere."

"No I wasn't."

"You sure were. Angry and stuck in place, like a statue."

I regretted the words the minute they left my mouth, the icky feeling made worse as Crane turned a deep scarlet. We'd stopped in front of Theresa's trailer. Sarah was in the window watching us, not even trying to hide her interest.

"Are you going in or not?" Crane asked.

"I just need to drop these addresses off," I said, "and grab new ones for tomorrow. Will you wait for me?"

"Maybe."

He was mad again. Well, he had every right to be.

I hurried up the sidewalk, stayed on the front stoop while I filled in Theresa on how my day had gone—*fine, some good ideas, it's in the paperwork*—and handed over all the information I'd gotten except for the newspaper from Ronnie. I tried not to think too much about why I was keeping that.

"Here's your stuff for tomorrow," Theresa said, handing me a stack of questionnaires and addresses the same size as the previous batch. Her gaze traveled over my shoulder. "Crane helping you?"

Relief washed over me. He *was* waiting for me. "Yes, ma'am. Is that okay?"

"That's more than okay," she said, smiling and waving at him. I didn't need to turn around to know that he wouldn't wave back. "Would the two of you like to come inside for some juice? It's a hot one out there."

If I went inside and I showed her the newspaper—Theresa had been there that day, that's what Ronnie had said, and she'd been paired up with someone—would she reveal something even worse about my father, something more disturbing than the fact he'd let his brother drown? I didn't have the stomach to find out.

"Thanks," I said, "but it's been a long day. I should probably be heading home."

"All right."

I knew Crane well enough that I didn't say a word as I passed him. If he was walking home with me, he'd do it, and if he wasn't, he wouldn't. Nothing I could say would change his mind. Except, when we'd nearly reached his trailer, I was slammed by a wave of loneliness.

"Do you want to meet Wort?" I asked.

"I know what a kitten looks like," he said sullenly.

"Not my kitten."

He grunted.

"Crane, I don't want to be alone, that's all. Haven't you ever been lonely?"

He looked away, but not before I saw his expression soften. "Fine. I'll come meet your kitten."

"We could watch TV, too," I said, pushing my luck. "Mom said there's a Tombstone pizza in the freezer I could make if she's not home in time for supper. I have to leave to babysit before seven, but that gives us plenty of time."

We were nearing Sly's place. The green car was still parked out front. Crane's shoulders drew up toward his ears, and I kept talking to distract him.

"My friend June and I like to eat our Tombstone pizza a real specific way. First, we take the cheese layer off. We only ever buy the cheese kind because June became a vegetarian after she read that Corey Feldman is. She has the *biggest* crush on Corey Feldman. She said he was great in the last *Friday the 13th*, but Dad didn't let me watch horror movies. Anyhow, we remove the cheese layer, roll it up like a tube, and use it to scoop up the tomato sauce underneath. That sauce is the magic of a Tombstone. It's kind of sweet and has so much flavor it's like it borrows taste from a whole 'nother dimension. Then—"

"I'm fine," he said.

We'd passed beneath the Blue Waters sign. "What do you mean?"

"You can stop chattering. They don't bother me."

I was caught off guard by his awareness of what I'd been doing. I'd underestimated Crane pretty much every which way today. Score one for the awkward kid. "But they made you mad before."

"Yeah, they did, because I wasn't expecting them." He cleared his throat. "You probably won't believe me, but all three of the Voglers are bad business."

"Why wouldn't I believe you?"

He shot me a look through his curtain of hair. "Never mind. Avoid them if you can."

"No problemo, Crano," I said, punching him lightly on the arm, "'cuz they give me the creeps."

He nodded.

"Hey, you want to stop by the playground on the way to my house?"

"You told Theresa you needed to hurry home." His faint smile had returned.

"You were listening!"

He shrugged. "I think I'd rather meet Wort. And eat pizza. And watch TV."

The way he said it filled me up like sunshine and bubbles. I started talking again, jabbering all about Pasadena, and June, and our detective agency, and my favorite subjects in school. It was so much like being in the woods with Dad, minus the woods. Crane would answer with a syllable or two. Even though he was quiet, it was different from the first time we'd met. I could tell he was listening now. He even laughed a couple times.

We both got lost in the good feeling of it, the heat and color of a summer day, just two buds hanging out, and before I knew it, we'd turned the corner onto my street.

There was a police car parked in front of Mom's place.

This time both Crane and I stopped.

"That's my house," I said, pointing at it.

"What's your last name?" Crane asked, using a dusty voice I hadn't heard out of him before.

"Jubilee," I said.

He stiffened, his face unreadable. "I gotta go."

"Crane! Wait!"

But he'd taken off at a jog.

CHAPTER 27

I looked at his retreating back, and then the police car in front of my house, and then his retreating back. I wouldn't have been one bit surprised to hear Crane had run afoul of the law at least once. I could see him skipping school, for sure. Or maybe he just didn't want to talk to the cops. That was a sentiment I could get behind. After the crazy up and down of today, the last thing I felt like doing was talking to goober Chad, and it was 50/50 his was the car parked outside. I stared longingly in the direction of my bedroom window, wishing I'd left it unlocked so I could sneak inside and cuddle with Wort for comfort.

My best option was to kill time in the hopes that whichever officer was inside would leave. Remembering the wild catnip I'd spotted near the brewery, I headed back in that direction. I could collect a few sprigs, enough to feed one or two to Wort fresh and the rest to dry in my closet.

It was a twenty-minute walk back downtown. My feet were sore from a full day of walking, I had a headache from the heat, and it made my skin crawl to get so close to the brewery that I might as well be inside it. Still, when I found the catnip right where I remembered it, I felt a familiar soothing. *Plants.* I rubbed my thumb over the fuzzy leaves of the tallest shoot, inhaling its sweet peppermint flavor, admiring its white blossoms. I'd plucked the first branch—one overcrowded with leaves; pulling it would allow the rest of the plant to thrive—when a brown furball appeared out of the bushes ten feet away and dashed into one of the brewery's gaping doors.

I yelped in surprise and jumped back. Once I'd calmed myself, I took a few steps toward the brewery. That brown furball had looked *a lot* like Motherwort. Was it another kitten from her litter?

A car drove by slowly, a white two-door, the guy behind the wheel staring. I think. It was hard to know for sure because he was wearing sunglasses. A yell caught my attention, and I whirled toward the heart of downtown, where one man was clapping another on the back right outside Albert's Pourhouse. It was all very normal. For Litani, at least. I willed myself to relax. I was a scientist. Well, a levelheaded person, at least. I couldn't leave without checking in on the animal, not if there was a chance it was another kitten that needed rescuing. I would peek inside the brewery, just inside the first building. If I didn't find a kitten in a couple minutes, I'd head home with some fresh catnip for Motherwort.

No harm, no foul.

Steeling myself, I ignored the bright yellow No TRESPASSING sign nailed to the face of the smallest of the brewery's buildings and stepped through its yawning mouth, a doorway rimmed with rotting wood.

The coolness hit me first, the temperature of the murky interior a startling contrast to the furnace of summer. The smell came next, part rot and part damp, with something bitter laced through it, possibly a hops smell left over from the brewery days. Enough rippling light leaked in through the open door that I could see this used to be an office, with a battered desk still in the far corner. Tipped-over filing cabinets littered the floor like giant bones. A rustling sound quickened my heartbeat.

"Kitty?"

A shape darted out and disappeared through the open door at the far side of the room, into the belly of the factory. I wiped my clammy hands on my shorts. I didn't want to go any farther.

"Kitty? Please come out."

Only silence answered me. I glanced back at the rectangle of sunlight promising if not safety, at least familiarity. But Chad was likely still at my house, and a scared kitten might be just on the other side of that doorway.

I walked toward it, fear pressed like a hand to my throat. I sucked in a sharp breath as soon as I stepped through that second doorway. I knew from the outside that the factory's main building was the size of an airplane hangar, but that didn't prepare me for being inside such a massive space. It was cavernous, the vastness of it echoing, the slashing ribbons of sunlight from the broken windows mounted way up high no match for the jungle dark in its far corners. Shapes pushed through the gloom, giant silver vats and tubes and ladders leading to an overhead walkway.

It would be so easy to get lost in here.

I cowered instinctively when something—bird? rat?—scratched seventy-five feet above me, showering the air with glittering dust. I was taking a step backward, every cell in my body telling me to run home and not look back, when a kitten-size shape separated from the shadow to my left and skittered deeper into the darkness. I took a tentative step in that direction, careful to avoid the broken glass, crushed cans, and food wrappers. A couple more steps and I reached a table. A few more and I was alongside a crusty mattress. Stomach turning, I kept tiptoeing deeper into the dark, pausing as needed to let my eyes adjust. Every time I was almost on top of the creature, it would scurry ahead, just out of sight, just out of reach.

This is an abandoned building. Not haunted. I can leave anytime I want.

Those words and ten minutes of slow going got me all the way to the rear of the factory. It was cleaner, quiet, the vast machinery muffling any sound from the real world. There was also another room back there, its prefabricated walls dwarfed by the factory surrounding it, turning it into a block inside a giant's playroom.

A foreman's office?

That was the last thought I had before I noticed the enormous star inside the circle painted on the floor, white candles at each point of the star setting it apart from the gloom.

And then I heard a man's voice.

CHAPTER 28

Every hair on my body stood up as fear ripped through me. Instinctually, I dived toward the darkness at the center of the factory. It required me to hop over the pentagram, but I didn't care. I propelled myself into the first hiding place I saw, an opening no larger than a basement window at the base of one of the silver vats, grateful for the first time in my life that I was so small. Something squished beneath my knees as I crouched, and the sour smell of pee and feces was overwhelming.

From this angle, I could see the left half of the door the voice had come out of. A light flashed on the other side of it, and I drew back as far as I could.

"That's a good boy," the man was saying. "You're a superstar."

My hand flew to my mouth, covering the whimper. I recognized the voice. It was Sly. He stepped into view a moment later, ten feet away, a bulky black video camera in his right hand, bobbing light coming from the flashlight he held in his left.

Moments later, a boy I didn't recognize stepped into view. He was young, small, his head not much higher than Sly's wolf belt buckle. When Sly's flashlight caught the child's face, my stomach dropped.

Tears were running down his cheeks, but he wasn't crying. I knew that because I was looking right into his big, frightened eyes, and they looked like two wild animals that'd been dropped onto his face, desperate to escape, trapped.

I gasped.

"Someone there?" The yellow light flooded the opening I was trying desperately to hide in, passing over it. I slammed my eyes shut and held myself still.

"Musta been the rats," Sly said after a few moments.

I opened my eyes. The light had mercifully passed me and was now trained on the pentagram.

"That's some nice work," Sly said, his voice relaxed. "Don't you think it's some nice work, kid?"

The child didn't speak, didn't even nod. Something terrible had happened to him. I knew I should do something, should leap out, make a noise, run for help, but it was like someone had tossed a sleepy, heavy blanket of do-nothing over me.

And then, it got worse.

The rumble of a second male voice, one I didn't recognize, came from the abandoned office. How many were there?

"What?" Sly asked, turning toward the doorway.

The rumble again.

"Yeah, I'll make you a copy." Sly patted the boy's head. "See? Just like I said. You're a superstar. Now let's get outta here. This place gives me the creeps."

He turned the kid away from me, leading him out the way I'd come. Their movement scared the creature I'd followed in here. It raced away from them, scurrying across the pentagram and appearing right in front of my nose.

It was a chipmunk.

CHAPTER 29

It took every bit of self-discipline I possessed to sit still for a count of five hundred, watching the direction of the vacant doorway, which was so much darker now that Sly had taken the light away. No one moved, no light came on, no one else spoke.

I knew at least one more person was in there, though.

Finally, I couldn't stand it any longer. Slowly, quietly, muscles shrieking with cramps, I crawled out of the opening, afraid to stand upright but even more scared to remain a moment longer. I tiptoed through the center of the factory. I tried my best to move quietly, but when I tripped over a box and fell to the ground with a clatter, I tore off like a wild thing, weaving around garbage, leaping over tarps, trying not to see the splashes of darker color on the floor.

When I busted through into the sunlight, I didn't stop. I kept running, pushing through the stitch burning at my side, stopping only when a charley horse knotted up my leg right by the playground. I dropped to the ground, breath heavy, knees and hands covered in grime.

But there was no one at the playground to help me, no one at all.

Because kids didn't play outside by themselves in Litani.

I massaged the painful rock in my calf, caught my breath, limped the last two blocks. I was relieved the police car was still out front. I was going to demand they arrest Sly for whatever he'd done to that little boy.

Even though I'd expected an officer to be inside, I was surprised to discover Chad sitting on the couch when I walked in, like he'd been waiting for me.

"Hello, Francesca," he said, all formal, glancing at my dirty knees and then my face. I was struck again by how young he was, so young that I bet he couldn't have grown a mustache on that baby face of his if he'd tried. He looked uncomfortable, too, sitting on the couch in his uniform, and I didn't think it was the terrible sofa making him look that way.

"Where's my mom?"

"She'll be here soon. We're preparing to conduct interviews. In her office."

Chad was alone? In my house? "What kind of interviews?"

"We're going to talk to some kids from the trailer park. We've got new information. We think a few of them are . . . being hurt."

What he was telling me was so unexpected that, for a moment, I forgot what I'd dashed inside to tell him. "Why here?"

He nodded. "Prosecutor Jubilee figures they'll be more comfortable in a home setting than in a police department."

That made sense, so why did it sound so wrong? "I saw something," I said, surprised at the heat of shame those words brought. I hadn't done anything wrong.

Chad sat forward, his gun belt creaking. "What?"

I glanced nervously toward the door. I'd planned on Mom being here when I told Chief Mike or Chad what had happened. "Sly. In the brewery with a little boy. He had a camera. Sly, I mean."

Chad jumped to his feet. "When?"

"Just now."

"Wait here."

He hurried outside. I went to the screen door and watched him slide into his car, ripping the radio mouthpiece off his dashboard.

Whatever he was saying into it was upsetting him; I could tell by his angry movements and the looks he kept giving the house.

My muscles went weak with relief. He was taking me seriously. He would help the boy.

❖

"Francesca, will you come out here?"

Chad had told me to wait in my room until Mom got home, and I was more than happy to oblige. Twenty minutes later, I heard a commotion. Car doors slamming in the street, our front door opening and closing so many times I lost count, male voices and then Mom and then little-girl voices, and then suddenly, a sharp knock on my bedroom door.

I jumped off my bed and stuck Wort in the closet, then opened the door a crack. "Hi, Mom."

"I need you," she said.

My brain knew better, but my heart soared. "Really?"

"Yes. I want you to make these girls feel at home while I talk to Mike and Chad."

She didn't need *me*. She needed a hostess. Or babysitter. I couldn't say no, even though I desperately did *not* want to talk to girls who'd been hurt, not after what I'd witnessed at the brewery. I didn't know how old they'd be, what they'd look like, but I knew they'd be quivering, different, *contagious*. I was sure of it. I didn't know how I knew, but there it was, the truth of it vibrating just below my skin.

"I'm babysitting tonight. For Ronnie and Patty," I said, trying to find a way out.

"Great," she said, already walking down the hall, assuming my compliance. "This won't take more than an hour."

I let Wort out of the closet before slipping out of my room. She'd hardly made a peep since I'd brought her home, but she'd had the whole run of my bedroom. I couldn't have her meowing from the closet with Mom around. Petting and kissing her, I whispered in her ear to give me courage.

She swatted at my mouth.

I left her on the bed and slipped out the door. The hallway dragged on forever, the carpet thicker, more treacherous. I could hear Mom talking to one or both of the officers, their voices muted. They must have been in her office. The television wasn't on, and that was the first thing I would change when I reached the living room.

I turned the corner.

Dawn and Crystal, two of the original three who'd beaten me up, were sitting on the couch.

CHAPTER 30

It's not her fault, Crane had said about Dawn.

"Hello," I mumbled, my voice strangled. The painful lump in my throat made it impossible to utter anything else.

Dawn in her Garfiend T-shirt barely tossed me a glance before returning her glare to her feet, which were wearing my shoes. She had to point her toes to touch the floor. Ginger-haired Crystal's feet swung freely. She kept her eyes trained out the front window, even though there was nothing to see except two police cars cooking in the sun.

I coughed. I needed to keep the conversation going. If there was silence, I'd throw up or start crying. "Are either of you hungry?"

"Whuddyou got to eat?" Dawn asked.

What did they do to you? "Tombstone pizza. Pepperoni, I think. And I know how to make really good ham sandwiches. I'm pretty sure there's a tube of Pringles somewhere, too."

"Do you have Capri Sun?" Crystal asked.

"Naw," I said, "but we have orange juice and milk. And soda."

"Soda?" Dawn asked, scowling.

How were we talking about food like the whole world hadn't changed the rules on me, like I hadn't just learned that two kids I knew were being abused? "Yeah, Shasta. Orange and grape and lemon-lime."

"Oh, you mean pop. Grape, please," Crystal said. Then, in a heart-breakingly transparent way, she asked for food without really asking for it. "I've never tried Tombstone, but I sure like pizza."

"I'll take orange pop with mine," Dawn said, "and I want to watch television."

"Knock yourself out." I tilted my head toward the remote, not trusting my trembling hands to pick it up for her. "I'll preheat the oven and grab the so—grab the pop."

❖

Weeknight afternoons was smack dab in the middle of juicy reruns, *WKRP in Cincinnati* and *Little House on the Prairie* and *CHiPs* and *People's Court*. Crystal wanted to watch *Little House on the Prairie* so bad. Dawn said it was stupid *but whatever*. I pretended to watch, thankful the Summer Olympics hadn't yet begun. It would have hurt too much to see LA on TV.

I wasn't sure how to act with these two. It was somewhere between having friends and babysitting, plus they'd beaten me up. So forget the friends part. *Visitors.* The pizza had turned out so perfectly, golden brown on the cheese bubbles and the edge of the crust, that it belonged in a commercial. My mouth watered looking at it, but Crystal and Dawn were gobbling it down like, well, like Wort had first eaten when I'd brought her here.

"Thanks for the pizza," Crystal said, her mouth churning food like a cement mixer. I knew how hot Tombstone was straight out the oven. Like lava. She must have had a mouth of steel.

"You bet."

We sat like that for a while, *Little House* on the television, staring at it like zombies. Mom called each girl into her office, separately, for short interviews, and then sent them back to the couch. If they listened to the rising and falling voices coming out of Mom's office after, they didn't let on. Chad musta told Mom about what I'd seen in the brewery, too. There was going to be hell to pay in this town. I watched the girls out of the corners of my eyes, sad for them, wanting to ask so many questions, not wanting to know the answers.

Finally, when I couldn't stand it anymore: "Dawn?"

"Yeah?" She was laser-beaming on the TV.

"That game you asked me to play back when you"—I decided to be generous here—"when you first met me. Was that the same game that you told my mom some grown-ups made you play?"

Her bottom lip jutted out. "I wouldn'ta done it the same with you."

"But it'd be the same game?"

"The Game isn't just one thing," Crystal offered. "There's tag, and hide-and-go-seek, and duck duck gray duck."

"But those are real games!" I said, surprised. I'd been expecting something dark, terrible. Had Mom made a mistake?

"They're real, all right," Dawn said. Her blonde hair and button nose and pink mouth were baby-perfect, but her brown eyes looked about a million years old. "Just not the same way most kids play them."

Things were clicking into place, terrible, raw puzzle pieces lining up. What Dawn had said that day Michelle'd gone missing: *I think she's dead . . . I'm next. Me and then Crystal and the rest of the babysitting club.* Mom at the spaghetti party talking about *the children swearing that older men have invited them to play "a game."* That awful, awful inscription I'd seen in the *Your Body* book in Mom's bedroom: *DD, age 10, breasts and buttocks, penetration.* Crane's protection of these girls even while he was saving me from them.

I gripped the edge of the wicker chair so I didn't float away. I heard myself speaking from a great distance, my voice echoing down a tunnel, sounding so calm, so unfamiliar. "Did Michelle play the games?"

Crystal nodded and grabbed for the last piece of pizza. "But she was going to tell. That's why she's not here anymore."

That gutted me, but before I could ask any follow-up questions, Mom, Chad, and Chief Mike walked out of her office in that order. Mom looked flushed, Chad embarrassed, and Chief Mike exhausted.

We all three stood up.

"Oh, good, you girls got something to eat," Mom said.

The pizza cardboard was bare except for crumbs. I hadn't eaten a single piece.

Dawn burped.

"Chief Mike is going to bring you two to a safe home here in town to stay at while we figure out next steps. Would you like that? Staying in a safe home?"

If I didn't already know firsthand how terrible Mom was with kids, her question would have made that clear. Nobody likes being carted off to a stranger's house. I could testify to that to the moon and back.

Crystal nodded, though, and I could tell she was trying to make her mouth smile. Dawn maintained her surly expression, and I admired that. It was appropriate to the situation.

"Good," Mom said, as if she'd gotten exactly the reaction she'd wanted. "Chief Mike will drive you there. And thank you, girls, for being so forthright with me. It was the right thing to do."

Then, in a move I would have bet my own life against happening, she hugged them both.

Hugged them!

Crystal clutched my mom, Dawn rag-dolled the interaction, but that wasn't the point. *My mom was giving out hugs.* I remained as still as stone, waiting for mine. I was at the end of the line, nearest the kitchen. Three more feet and her arms would be around me. Would I like it? Would it be stiff, forced? Would it feel like home?

She smiled at both girls and turned to me. "Chad will give you a ride to the McSorleys'."

"I told them I'd walk," I said around the rocks in my mouth.

"Nonsense. It's no longer safe to walk at night."

I glanced out the window. It was still bright. There was no point in arguing, though. All I cared about was getting that hug. "All right," I said, still zapped to my spot.

She'd embraced these girls, these strangers, never me, not in seven years. It shouldn't matter, not compared to what Dawn and Crystal were living through; I should be worried for them and not thinking baby thoughts, but I couldn't help myself.

Hug me. Please.

"I have to go into work," she continued, cheeks still that warm cherry color, her eyes brighter than I'd ever seen them. "Today's a big day in Carver County, and your mom is going to make waves. I should be home when Ronnie drops you off tonight, though, so be sure to wake me up so I don't worry."

My chin started to quiver, so I covered it with my hand. It was a load of bull crap, her caring when I was home. She was doing that thing where she put on a show for her audience, and by their expressions, they couldn't have cared less. But I discovered I didn't care if she was acting. I desperately wanted her to hold me, however it had to happen. If it was fake, fine. If it was half-hearted, okay, just give it to me. I kept myself still, I smiled, I tried to look welcoming, lifting my hands up and toward her ever so slightly.

She stepped toward me.

And then she turned, grabbed her purse, and strode for the door, not saying goodbye to even one of us.

"Girls, we should be going," Chief Mike said. "Gather up your things."

"We don't have *things*," Dawn said disdainfully, tossing her hair.

My neck creaking, I turned from the door my mother had just disappeared through to the four people in the living room. Three of them were doing their best not to look at me, to not be party to my shame, a girl whose own mother wouldn't hug her.

Not Dawn, though. She was studying me with a strange look on her face.

I stared back.

To my surprise, she looked away first. She dropped down to one knee. She untied and slipped off my favorite shoes, the Converse sneakers just worn in enough they were molded to my feet but not so worn they looked trashy. She held them out to me.

"Thanks for letting me borrow these."

I blinked rapidly to keep the tears back and accepted the shoes. "You're welcome."

Dawn followed Chief Mike out the door, her back stiff, her bare feet dirty, Crystal on her heels.

CHAPTER 31

"If they're telling the truth," Chad said on the drive to Ronnie and Patty's house, glancing back at me in the rearview mirror, "what happened to those girls is terrible."

His tone of voice tugged me out of my deep thoughts. Dad'd used the same one when he really needed to get something off his chest. My brain automatically slipped into helper mode. "What do you mean?"

"The more I hear—and we're taking Sly Vogler in for questioning, by the way—well, it breaks my heart to think that someone would do something like that to . . . to kids. I don't want to believe these sorts of things happen." He grew quiet for a moment, and in that space, I realized that it wasn't just that he was young; it was also that he and I weren't so very far apart in age. "What do you think about it?"

I watched the trees crawl past. It would have been a fifteen-minute walk to the McSorleys'. The speed Chad drove, I didn't think the drive was going to be much quicker.

"I think the world is a dark place," I said. I didn't know where I'd heard that phrase before, but it sounded like an appropriate response.

"I bet you assumed small towns would be safe," he said, "at least compared to Los Angeles."

I'd had that same thought myself, but I didn't want to make him feel bad about his hometown. "There's a lot of murders in LA. At least that's what I heard. I lived in Pasadena, though. With my dad."

"Heard he was a real nice guy, your father."

This comment drew my attention from the mailboxes I'd been watching coming and going. "Who'd you hear that from?"

I saw his shrug from behind. "Around. Maybe your mom."

That seemed unlikely.

"He was amazing," I said, my voice unnecessarily defensive. Was I trying to convince myself? "He was kind, and smart, and everyone who met him loved him."

"Hold up, now," Chad said, lifting his hand. "I was saying he sounds like he was a good man. We're on the same team."

"There's the McSorley house," I said as we drove past it.

Chad slammed the brakes so hard that my head bonked into the back of his seat.

"Crap sandwich!" he said. "Mind was wandering. Here you go."

I hopped out, realizing I was back to feeling the same way about Chad as the first time he'd given me a ride: he was a putz. "Thanks for the lift."

He tipped his police cap at me. "Call me any time, ma'am."

He didn't drive away until I was inside the house. I hoped he was daydreaming, or studying the neighborhood for creeps, and not watching me walk away.

❖

It was weird being back inside the house where earlier today I'd learned the truth about my dad. Well, *a* truth. It was hard not to obsess about Ronnie and Patty's bedroom closet upstairs and what else was in those two boxes. Was there more about Dad, or even Mom? And specifically, what was that yellow strip that had so surprised Ronnie when he'd discovered it?

But I didn't have any time to peek, not when the kids were awake. Babysitting for the McSorleys was nothing like babysitting for Theresa, which had been a mix of boring and easy.

The McSorley children were a handful.

The six-year-old, Cathy, watched me warily at first, like she thought I might be there to steal something. It was clearly important to her to establish dominance, or her value. I couldn't tell which.

"John and Jerome don't like butter on their popcorn," she pronounced as I was making a snack for the twins according to Patty's instructions.

"Your mom said they do," I said.

She'd been telling me what John and Jerome liked and disliked since I'd arrived. As far as I could tell, they mostly enjoyed wrestling each other and watching a VHS tape of *Something Wicked This Way Comes* (which I didn't think of as a little-kid movie, but Cathy assured me it was their favorite, and the way they'd pause their wrestling every few minutes to yell out lines confirmed that), but Cathy had opinions about how they preferred to be spoken to, the temperature of water for their bath later (too warm and they'd cry, too cool and they'd pee), and now whether they liked butter on their popcorn.

"Don't burn it, either," she ordered as the kernels really started popping. "Our last babysitter did it that way. We didn't eat it."

"Look, Cathy," I said, taking the pan off the burner and turning, hands on my hips. "I know how to make popcorn."

Boy, did I. It had been Dad's favorite snack.

Cathy was scowling at me from a chair at the kitchen table, kneeling on it the wrong way, her elbows on the chair back. "You don't *either* know how to make popcorn. At least you don't know how to make it for John and Jerome."

She had me there. I decided to change tack. I'd never had a babysitter growing up because Dad never went out. It must have been uncomfortable to have a stranger in your house, telling you what to do. Maybe if I gave her some control, she'd stop badgering me. "Do you want to be my helper?"

Her expression shifted from bossy to terrified so fast it made my head spin. "I'm tired," she said quietly.

"I don't mean do any work," I said, totally baffled. What had I said that'd soured her mood? "I thought you could help me take care of John and Jerome, is all, since you know them so much better than I do. So like, with their food, you can just tell me everything right up front rather than after I start doing it. You can test the bathwater to make sure it's right, you can help choose the bedtime story, all of that. What do you think?"

"John likes butter on his saltines," she said, testing the boundaries of our new contract.

"See, that's good information to have beforehand," I said. "What else?"

"Jerome likes them plain."

"Thank you."

"You're welcome." She smiled, a small one, even though the set of her shoulders told me she was still suspicious. "I'm going to go watch the movie with them."

"All right," I said, relieved my plan had worked.

The rest of the night went much more smoothly. Snack time was messy, the bath even more so, but the boys settled in front of the television after that. I sat down on the floor in front of them and pulled out The Book, trying not to feel the vacant eyes of the mounted dead animals on me. The house was extra creepy without grown-ups in it, all shadowy hallways and too many doors. I'd kept the three of us to the kitchen, living room, and bathroom as much as possible and had all the lights on bright, even before the sun began to set.

Cathy had grown so sweet that I showed her The Book and invited her to help with the plant personality I'd been creating for Dawn, though I didn't tell her who it was for in case she knew her. She admired the pictures I'd drawn so far, though she screwed up her nose when I showed her Dawn's.

"But that's a weed," she said. "A bad one."

"That's what I thought, too," I said, and began filling in the sketch.

CHOOSE YOUR OWN PLANT PERSONALITY
YOU'RE CAPTAIN OF YOUR OWN DESTINY!
WHICH PLANT PERSONALITY DO YOU CHOOSE?

BULL THISTLE
You grow in soil that's been left unattended, and you'll replicate
quickly if not mended. If we mess with you, purple-headed bull, we get
the horns. But every bit of you has value if we see past the thorns.

I was pleased with the results.

I'd research more later, but I knew enough about the plant to know it was perfect for Dawn. First, bull thistle benefited the plants around it because its deep roots broke up the soil. Second, the plant had real medicinal value, particularly for those who suffered from arthritis or bad joints. Finally, when it came to nutrition, I remembered from a lecture of Dad's that the fresh peeled roots were packed with nutrition and tasted like a woody Jerusalem artichoke, and the juicy, peeled leaf-stalks provided water if you were in a bind.

The boys were getting bored with the television right about the same time I finished Dawn's page. They agreed to a game of Chutes and Ladders followed by four readings of *The Monster at the End of This*

Book. ("One mo' time!" Jerome or John—I couldn't tell them apart—kept yelling.) The fourth reading finally mellowed everyone out.

"That's it," I said. The clock read 10:00 p.m., but I felt like I'd been there for three days rather than three hours. Kids were a lot of work. "Lights out."

"We have to play tunnel first," Cathy said softly. Her main-floor bedroom was across the hall from the boys', but she'd joined us for story time.

"Tunnel!" both boys yelled, only it sounded like *ton-oh.*

"It's bedtime," I protested. I hadn't had supper yet, just some popcorn, and I'd spotted a bag of frozen cookies in the freezer that I wanted to dig into. That, and I was desperate to sneak into Ronnie's closet. I had to know what he'd been hiding in his palm.

"It doesn't take very long," Cathy protested. "You told me I was your helper, to tell you what we do here. We always play tunnel before bed."

"You should have said something earlier," I said, but I was already giving in, and they saw it on my face. The boys jumped out of bed and dashed toward the door in their Spider-Man Underoos, followed closely by Cathy.

"Only for five minutes!" I yelled after them.

I stepped out of the boys' bedroom just in time to see all three of them disappear into the bathroom where the boys had taken their "perfect temperature" bath an hour earlier. That surprised me plus made me kind of uneasy. I'd pictured a fort with blankets or hiding under furniture. What game could possibly be played in the bathroom?

My worry grew as I neared the bathroom door they'd closed behind them. "Knock knock," I said. "May I come in?"

There was no answer. I pasted my ear to the door. I was greeted by complete silence on the other side. The first time it had been quiet for more than two seconds since I'd arrived. Dread pressed its cold hand to the back of my neck.

"I'm coming in, you guys."

I opened the door.

The bathroom was empty.

CHAPTER 32

"Cathy!" I yelled, ripping back the shower curtain to reveal an empty bathtub. I tore open the closet door and found only towels and medicine and spare toilet paper. My heart raced so fast I was dizzy. "John! Jerome!"

The bathroom was large, but it was still a bathroom: bathtub with shower, closet, toilet, sink, and vanity. No way could they all fit inside the vanity, the only place I had yet to look. I opened that door anyway. Inside were three empty walls, nothing else except for a towel spread across the bottom.

The air screamed out of me. "Cathy!"

I'd lost three children in a bathroom. Had a black hole opened? I didn't believe in Satan or demons. Had that been my fatal mistake? I stumbled backward. I needed to call the police.

I was out the door and halfway to the hallway phone when I heard it.

A giggling, so soft it was barely audible over my thudding heartbeat. It was coming from behind the door next to the bathroom, which I'd assumed led to a linen closet.

"Cathy?" I walked shakily toward the door and opened it slowly, not sure if I was more scared of seeing something in there or *not* seeing something in there. I stayed as far back from the door as I could while still being able to turn the knob.

The giggling grew louder the wider the door swung.

Inside was a linen closet, an unusually deep one, and all three children were clustered in the far corner. Cathy's little hands covered John's and Jerome's mouths, leaving nothing free to silence her own giggles.

"You found us!" Cathy crowed.

I dropped to my knees, sick with relief. "How'd you get in there?"

"Tunnel!" Jerome and John crowed.

"See?" Cathy said proudly, pulling back a piece of plywood to reveal a rectangular hole that led directly into the vanity, whose door I'd left open in my fright. I could peer through it right into the bathroom.

"You sneaks!" I said.

This brought a fresh wave of giggling. I couldn't be mad, though. I was too grateful I hadn't lost three kids to Satan on my first night babysitting them.

"And this leads to the candy room," Cathy said, sliding away a square of wood immediately behind where they'd been hiding.

"What?" I asked, my scalp suddenly crawling.

"Can-dee!" John and Jerome shouted, tumbling out of the closet to make room for me.

"Come see," Cathy said, her smile overbright.

I kneeled and crawled forward. I paused at the hole in the back of the closet. It was about the same size as the opening I'd hidden in at the brewery. "What's in there?"

"Candy," she said simply.

The opening was lighter than the rest of the closet. Either there was a light or a window in the space it led to. I ducked my head so I could look in without *going* in.

A room the size of a small bedroom was on the other side, the walls bare, the floor empty except for a single bowl in the middle. A small window on the far wall let in bleak moonlight. It must have been Ronnie's gun room, minus guns, or a remodeling project gone wrong, or a half-finished addition that was serving as a playroom until Ronnie's back got better.

"I'll take your word for it," I told Cathy. "It's bedtime. Help me close this up."

But she didn't need my help. She slid back the piece of plywood separating the closet from the candy room and then the closet from the bathroom while John and Jerome wrestled in the hallway. I carried them into bed and tucked them in, thinking about how scary this twisty-turny house would be once I was the only one awake in it.

"Are there any other tunnels like that in your house?" I asked Cathy, following her into her room and helping her into bed.

"Uh-unh," she said, still looking far too pleased with herself. "Just that one."

"You scared my pants off," I said.

"I know," she said, smiling drowsily.

I kissed her head. I didn't know her very well, but it felt like the right thing to do.

❖

Ronnie and Patty had said they'd be home by midnight, but that didn't mean they couldn't show up earlier. Was I really going to sneak in their closet? Despite my fear of going upstairs alone, I was surprised to learn the answer was *yes*. If I wanted to learn more about Dad, I had no choice.

Still, it was a risk, and a scary one.

I walked to the front window and peeked out. Darkness was full, the neighborhood quiet, though televisions flickered in a few windows. I decided to leave the McSorley TV on. That way, if Patty and Ronnie came home prematurely, I could dash downstairs and say I'd just had to use the bathroom. They might wonder why I wasn't using the main-floor one, but if I hurried down fast enough, they wouldn't even know I'd been upstairs.

The dark-alley footsteps of my heartbeat drowned out every other sound as I scurried up the stairs. When I'd followed Ronnie up here, I'd been so jumpy, I now realized that I hadn't taken in much around me. I was probably even more nervous this time, but it was a different kind of nervousness. I was scared, but I was also exhilarated, like when me and June were getting close to solving a case.

The second story of the house was smaller than the first, a long hallway with two doors to the right and two to the left. I knew the first led to the master bedroom. The second must have been a spare room, maybe a sewing room, and the others were likely a bathroom and a closet. It might be good to find which one was the bathroom in case I needed quick cover, but I was too hopped up on adrenaline.

I made straight for Ronnie and Patty's bedroom.

I couldn't turn on the light because if they pulled up, I was dead. I'd need to drag the box out to the window.

In the dimness, their room looked much like it had earlier except for all the dresses now piled on the floor. Patty must have tried on quite a few before selecting the pretty orange-and-yellow chevron-patterned one that she'd been wearing when I showed up. I waded through the clothes on the floor, the smell of bodies—hair and skin and sweat—amplified by the darkness.

When I tried the closet knob, it wouldn't turn at first. In a panic, I wondered if it was locked. Maybe this was where Ronnie kept his guns. But I twisted harder, and the door opened. My breath caught at the sight of the dark shape leering down at me before my eyes adjusted to the deeper level of gloom.

It was just a coat on a hook.

I slid a chair over and balanced on it to reach the boxes, which were exactly where Ronnie had left them. I grabbed the top one, half expecting it to be booby-trapped, but it came down without a hitch. It was heavy but manageable.

"Come to Mama," I said, stepping carefully off the chair. I tiptoed around the obstacles, toward the window, and was grateful to discover it was open. I'd for sure be able to hear a car pulling in. I set the box down with a grunt.

No turning back now.

I undid the top, taking care to remember which corner had gone in first and what order the items it contained were stored in. Ronnie probably hadn't noticed those details when he put it away, but better safe than sorry.

A football trophy rested on top, **MVP** tattooed into the brass plaque on its base. He'd pulled it out earlier, but I hadn't been able to read any of the details.

Paul, Mike, and me were on the football team. I know what you're thinking, with me and your dad being the size we were, but we were quick.

Beneath that were some track medals, a bowling trophy from last year with his and Patty's names on it above **Mixed Doubles Champions**, a bunch of papers that looked like a mixture of high school records and grown-up stuff, and there, on the bottom, the yellow strip of paper or plastic that had fit in the palm of Ronnie's hand.

When I held it toward the window, I saw it wasn't paper at all.

It was a hospital bracelet, cut off near the button and yellowed with age.

I read it, the words twisting my stomach, turning my tongue into boiled meat.

Paul Jubilee. DOB 02/24/48. Psych. Invol. Comm.

I was staring out the window when the headlights pierced the night. Ronnie and Patty were home.

CHAPTER 33

"You're still up!" Patty said, her voice slurred, her pretty orange-and-yellow dress stained at the hem, a dark-brown blotch, or was it maroon?

"Yes, ma'am," I said, the words scraping like broken glass across my tongue, trying not to look at Patty's dress.

I'd crammed it all back in the box, not caring what order it went in, closed the top haphazardly, shoved it back on the closet shelf, returned the chair more or less to the spot where I'd found it, slammed the closet and then the bedroom door, sped down the stairs, and thrown myself on the couch just as the front door had opened.

I was trying to keep my chest from visibly heaving, and not just because of the race to put everything back. I was broken into a million quivering pieces, my heart and brain and guts all vibrating, floating, an exploded girl.

Ronnie and Patty didn't seem to notice.

"How were the kids?" Ronnie said, his moves liquid, relaxed, exactly like he'd been after a few drinks at Clara's. Except, why was he looking at me so strangely? He couldn't possibly know what I'd done.

Could he?

"Great," I said. "Cathy was a big help."

Ronnie snorted. "I'll just bet. She's got ideas on what everyone should be doing."

"She didn't give you too hard a time?" Patty asked.

"No, ma'am." It was hard to speak normally. I didn't have enough air. Had I closed the closet door after me? "How was dinner?"

"Good," Patty said, holding up a doggie bag. "Broasted chicken and steak! Are you hungry?"

"No," I lied.

Patty wiped the back of her hand across her forehead. "My word, it's hot in here. We should have put a fan out for you. Ronnie, go grab that box fan from upstairs."

"That's okay!" I jumped to my feet. "I should be getting home."

Ronnie twirled his key ring on his fingers until the keys landed in his palm with a metal thud. "I've got the car all warmed up."

"I can walk." I grabbed my knapsack, making sure the Jubilee patch was turned away from Ronnie. I needed to escape this house.

"Your mom'll kill us if we let you walk home," Patty said. "It's not safe."

"Patty, we trusted her enough to watch our children. We can certainly let her make up her own mind about walking," Ronnie said, turning his attention to me. "But I'm happy to give you a ride if you want. It's no problem."

"I'm okay walking," I said.

I wanted to blast my way outside, to run and never stop, but they both stood planted in front of the door. If they didn't move soon, I was going to launch myself through the window.

My dad was in a psych ward.

Involuntarily committed.

I was familiar with the term. There'd been a whole episode devoted to it on *Days of Our Lives*, the soap opera June's mom planned her summer afternoons around. One of the main characters had been attacked by a violent stranger. It shattered her whole world, and her husband (who was no great shakes, to be honest) had her involuntarily committed. I'd been doing my homework while the episode played. I'd caught most of it.

Involuntarily committed.

I realized the wristband hadn't stated *when* my dad was there. I assumed it was after Benny drowned. What else would have sent him into a mental hospital?

I swallowed. "You know what? I guess I'll take that ride after all."

"That's my girl," Ronnie said, tapping his head with one hand and reaching for his wallet with the other. "You're a smart one. I can see it on your face. You look like your dad, you know."

Patty was watching me, nodding. "She sure does."

"Five sound good?" Ronnie asked.

I reached for the bill. He yanked it back, startling me. He laughed when I jumped. "Just joshing. Here you go."

I reached for it again, and he yanked it back one more time. This was a game, one I couldn't win.

"Ronnie, give her the damn money."

"I'm trying," he said with mock innocence, but this time he let me take it. If he hadn't, I would have walked out without it. He must have read that in my eyes, too, because he shot me a lopsided grin before leading the way outdoors.

I followed tentatively.

I'd never ridden in a man's car before, not in the front seat right next to him, not with any guy except my dad. It was uncomfortable, too close, the fake leather seats clammy against my bare legs, the radio playing some unfamiliar country song.

I gripped the interior door lever and swallowed loudly as he pulled out of the driveway. "Ronnie, do you know if my dad was ever in the hospital?"

I was studying him out of the corner of my eye, watching like a hawk, so I saw when his Adam's apple dropped like an elevator and then charged its way back up. "I'm not sure I should be the one to tell you," he said, his earlier goofiness all gone.

"Tell me what?"

He started to turn his head toward me but kept his eyes on the road. "That's for you to ask your mother."

"But you already told me about the drowning."

He snorted. "You've got a smart mouth."

Except I didn't. It had taken everything I had to ask Ronnie the question. I couldn't bear to ask again, to straight-out demand to know why my dad had been hospitalized against his will. It must have been that he let his brother die, right? It must have made him go crazy for a while.

That would be understandable.

But it wasn't just for a while, was it?

I knew that from the unraveling.

The memory dragged me back in time, to the day Dad told me he was being laid off, him looking crazy and sad at the same time, plucking the berries off the plant he'd brought into the kitchen.

"Already got my next job figured out," he'd said, his hands working at that plant. "I've been meaning to do this for a while, actually, but my teaching kept me too busy. The school owned any discoveries I made, in any case. But what do you say to getting rich?"

I remember trying to smile, but I was terrified. I'd never seen that side of Dad. "Sounds good to me."

"That's my girl. Grab me the tincture kit, will you?"

As I gathered the vodka, sterilized jar, tear dropper, and the boiling pan, he explained his plan. The plant he'd brought home wasn't a currant, like I'd first thought. It was hawthorn, and while the blossoms had stronger medicinal properties than the berries, the bark and the leaves were what you really wanted.

"For what?" My blood pumped with hope and fear.

"For hearts!" he said, holding a ruby-colored berry between his thumb and pointer finger. The sun caught it just right, illuminating its heart shape and blood color, illustrating the rule that nature always showed us how to harvest its treasures. Walnuts, shaped like a brain, were exceptional for cerebral health. Slice a carrot crossway and what did you see? An eye, and there was no vegetable better suited to improving sight. Avocadoes worked wonders on the uterus, celery on the bones, grapefruit on the breasts.

And this ruby berry, apparently, was a miracle cure for hearts.

"Does anyone else know about hawthorn?" I asked, struggling to keep up. It had been only that morning when we'd pulled into the parking lot of the Red Box Picnic Area, everything normal, exploring until we located the creeping Charlie and pineapple weed. Now Dad was racing around the kitchen like a fiend, talking too fast, scraping over the fact that he was about to be unemployed, talking about chemicals and futures and breakthroughs like a mad scientist.

"Sure," he said, "but they don't have my secret ingredients."

He fished a Tupperware container of white powder out of the sack.

"What's that?" I asked.

"I told you," he said, smiling, looking more and more like himself as he began to process the hawthorn, removing leaf from stem, bark from branch. He was smiling his soft smile, his brown eyes twinkling. "It's a secret."

But we didn't have secrets, Dad and me.

As if reading my mind, he said, "It's been a long day, honey. I want to get a batch of this mixed up, and then test it out—" He held out his hand at the look on my face. "I'm a scientist, Frankie. I'd never mix plants without knowing exactly how they'll interact, and I'd never ingest them if they weren't completely safe. I'm a perfect candidate for the tests, though. With my heart, there's no one better. Worst-case scenario, I won't have to take the beta-blockers anymore. Best case, we get rich. Sound good?"

I nodded. None of this sounded good, but we'd get through it. Together.

He turned his back on me. He didn't want me in the kitchen anymore. It stung, but I could help him other ways. I hurried to his bedroom, located his best dress shirt, ironed it, and put it out with his one suit. I typed a résumé. It was short—he'd had only the one job that I knew of—but I used a lot of adjectives (best teacher, smartest scientist, nicest man) to pad it. I polished the windows and vacuumed the floor. The whole time I worked, so did Dad, mixing and blending and boiling, filling the house with sweet and acrid smells, until he had three separate amber jars swelled with liquid, each sporting a different label.

"You did it!" I said when he called me into the kitchen.

He looked tired. "I did. Now to sample." He took an eyedropper out of the first bottle and squirted liquid on his tongue. He screwed up his face. "Tastes nasty. That's how you know it's working."

I smiled. That's what he'd told me when I tried my first cough medicine at age six and told him it tasted like cherry poison. "That's how you know it's working" had been a running joke with us ever since.

It'd be a little over a week until June finally came for the sleepover. A little over a week until I killed him.

Ronnie lurched the car to an abrupt stop, wrenching me back to the present. I looked up, startled. We were in front of Mom's house. It felt like only moments ago we'd taken off from Ronnie and Patty's.

I needed to dig into that newspaper story, scour it for details.

"Thanks for the ride, Mr. McSorley."

"Ronnie," he corrected, his eyes black.

CHAPTER 34

"Mom?" I leaned against her closed bedroom door. It was warm to the touch, the inside of the house stifling. The McSorley house had been just as stuffy, but I'd been too busy managing the kids and thinking about what was hiding in Ronnie's closet to dwell on it.

A fan was shushing inside Mom's room, but otherwise, the house was as quiet as a tomb. She'd told me to let her know when I was home. She'd done it for show, I was sure of it, but that didn't mean I could defy a direct order.

It was funny. I'd been so comfortable in my dad's bedroom, bringing him medicine, picking up, washing his sheets, returning his cleaned and ironed clothes, waking him up when he overslept. But the thought of opening my mom's bedroom door and seeing her sleeping, vulnerable, even though she'd asked me to check in?

It made me queasy.

I didn't know her, not like I knew my dad, but then, in light of what I'd learned today, I wondered if a person ever knew their parents at all.

"I'm home," I whispered to the door before scurrying to my room.

Wort was curled up on my bed but stretched when she saw me, the kitten version of a big welcome-home grin. "How was your day, baby girl?"

She purred as I pet her, a rich, crackling rumble. In the few days I'd had her, her belly and face had filled out, her fur had glossed up, and her purr had grown to where it sounded much larger than she was.

"It's stinky in here, isn't it?"

And hot. I glanced at the window. It sure would have been nice to open it, but as long as there might be someone lurking—and I'd seen too many shapes and shadows out there to discount that fear, not to mention what Sarah and Kyle had said about a man at their window, on top of Sly and that boy in the brewery—I wasn't going to be stupid. Instead, I double-checked the window lock before cleaning out the litter box and sneaking an ice cube for Wort's water, careful to be quiet.

"You'll have the run of the house tomorrow, when Mom's not here," I said.

Once I'd gotten Motherwort settled, I dug out the newspaper Ronnie had given me. I'd taken my time tending to Wort because I was hesitant to read the article about Benny's drowning even though I knew I must, but it was the middle of the night, and I was tired, and I decided I might as well get it done and over with.

I flattened the newspaper across my elephant bedspread.

Local Boy Drowns in Minnesota River

July 11, 1966. Tragedy has struck the sleepy town of Litani, Minnesota, where a boy has drowned in the Minnesota River. Benjamin Jubilee, 7, grew up a mile from the river but according to his mother had never been taught to swim. At his age and with no training, he would have been no match for the river's current.

"He never should have gone in," his mother, Mrs. Charles Jubilee, said.

Benjamin was enjoying a summer day in the company of his brother, Paul Jubilee, 18, and a group of Paul's friends. Paul was not available for comment, but according to Ronald McSorley, 18, one of the friends who was present, "We told Benny not to go in the water. We told him those currents weren't safe. But he went in anyhow."

"He was such a sweet boy," according to Mrs. Jubilee. "Teachers said he was polite. He never talked back. Everyone liked him."

Rescue officials were alerted just after 5:00 p.m., and members of the Carver County Fire Department located the boy's body beneath the Litani Railroad Bridge a few hours later.

Other agencies involved in the search included Minn. Water Patrol, state police and Litani police. Townspeople describe Litani as otherwise peaceful. Authorities say funeral arrangements are pending.

The article was short, and it broke my heart.

My poor, poor father. The man who would pick only flowers and plants that were abundant. Science, he could justify. Medicine. Food. But not if it would cost the plant too much. He live-trapped and released rodents rather than kill them, including the mouse that was eating our cereal and peeing in our crackers. Even mosquitoes he'd flick off rather than smack.

Drunk or not, it must have destroyed him when his brother drowned.

Or driven him to insanity.

My eyes traveled to my bedroom door. I so wished I had a mom I could ask questions of. Just walk out of my room and into hers, tell her I needed her to hold me, to start out explaining what had happened to Benny, then to her and my dad, then her and me, and then this whole haunted town.

But that's not who I was, and it *definitely* wasn't who she was.

I did have her office, though.

Her files.

If she woke up and found me snooping, she'd be furious. I could guess that much. Maybe so furious she'd kick me out on the streets.

But I still had to try. How could I sleep without answers?

I let myself into the hall clutching my pen flashlight and pressed my ear against her door. Still only the shushing of the fan. I wished she were a snorer. What if she wasn't even in there? I stood, frozen in indecision for a moment, when it occurred to me I should look for her car in the garage.

Which was where I found it.

She was home.

I needed to make this quick.

Her office was neat, as expected. I marched straight to the first cabinet, the best bet for finding a file on my dad, as Jubilee fell in the front half of the alphabet. I depressed the button on the middle drawer and slid it open slowly, the whisking noise it made barely a whisper in the quiet house. I thumbed through the files, searching for the *J*s.

I located the file labeled **JUBILEE** and slid it out. When I read the full name on it, my arm hairs turned into exclamation points.

Francesca Jubilee.

The first Jubilee file was mine.

The moonlight was bright enough to allow me to locate it but did not provide enough light to read it. I took a chance and clicked on the flashlight, dropped to the floor cross-legged, and opened the file, blood thudding in my ears.

Inside was my birth certificate, my tiny black footprints taking up one whole corner. A pink bracelet not much larger than a bottle cap was taped to it, its beads spelling FRANCESCA. My full name, Francesca Vera Jubilee, was typed out above my weight: 6 pounds, 2 ounces. The folder also contained a letter written from my mom to her parents, presumably never sent. It was dated on my birthday, like, the actual day I was born, June 3, 1970, and it explained how wonderful the birth had been, how miraculous my ten fingers and toes were, how much she loved my squishy red face.

That was it. The whole of my file. Not a single picture.

Feeling oddly empty, I tucked the papers back inside and stood to return it to the slot just ahead of the file marked **Paul Jubilee** before pulling that one out. I discovered a lot more information in his than mine. Photos of Mom and Dad in high school, looking happy and young. They were rarely in the same photograph, and when they were, they were not side by side. I recognized a young Chief Mike, Ronnie and Patty, baby-faced Darlene looking as innocent as summer rain, chubby and smiling Theresa. There were other people I didn't know in a few of them, but mostly, each photo was a different version of the magnificent seven. I wished the photographs had writing on the backs, names or dates or locations, but they didn't.

Mom and Dad's divorce papers were beneath the pictures. They'd gotten their divorce in California in 1975. Irreconcilable differences. Those were the words on the front of the thick document. I read a few pages past that, but the language seemed designed to confuse, all legal terms that didn't tell me what I'd wanted to know: What had the irreconcilable differences been?

I put down the divorce papers and picked up the copy of their marriage certificate. They'd gotten married on April 16, 1968, in the Carver County courthouse. Chief Mike and Theresa White—likely Theresa Buckle's maiden name—had been the witnesses. The document didn't tell me if anyone else had been present, but I suspected not.

There was nothing else in Dad's file. I even shook the divorce packet to see if anything slipped out. I put everything back in the same order I'd found it and returned the file. There was only one other file I was interested in.

The Zloduk case.

I knew it would be disturbing to read, but somehow it was all connected; I felt the truth of that covering me like skin. Benny's death, Dad's time in the hospital, the Zloduk case, and now the other kids getting hurt. I padded over to the farthest file cabinet.

I slid open the bottom drawer.

I searched the rear of it.

And then I searched all of the bottom drawer, just to be sure.

There was no Zloduk file.

CHAPTER 35

The next morning followed the pattern of the previous ones. Mom was gone when I awoke, despite my best efforts to see her. She'd left my lunch on the counter with a note that she wouldn't be home until late and I should make the Banquet fried chicken in the freezer for dinner.

It ended with, *I need to talk to you when I get back. —Mom*

Well, I needed to talk to her, too.

If I could work up the nerve.

So the day started crunchy and didn't improve from there. Wort had diarrhea—from what I couldn't imagine, as nothing in her diet had changed. I boiled up a batch of rice and hamburger to feed her in the hopes that would take care of the problem. Once I had that in order, I stepped outside to discover the sun shining as bright and hot as an interrogation light. There was no breeze to deter the gnats sliding in the sweat that rolled down my neck. La Brea Sweat Pits for bugs.

I hurried past Sly's trailer on the way to Theresa's. I was relieved he wasn't out front. I was hoping the opposite would be true of Crane, but he, too, didn't appear to be home, which meant he wouldn't be joining me today.

And even worse, Theresa's husband, Tom, answered the door. At least that's who it must have been. He was wearing a loose T-shirt and boxer shorts. Sarah and Kyle were arguing in the background, Sarah's resentment at shriek level.

"Hi," he said, his glance dropping momentarily downward. "Sorry about the shorts. This heat is miserable. You must be Frankie. You here for the time capsule stuff?"

"Yes, sir." I had to raise my voice to be heard over Sarah. Something about it being *my turn you promised I hate you.* "Is Theresa around?"

He rubbed the back of his neck, smiling ruefully. "I wish. Something happening over at the church that required her expert input. I'm in charge of the little monsters until she gets back. She said to give you this."

I averted my eyes as he turned toward the kitchen table. I sure wished he'd put pants on before answering the door. Sarah hopped out onto the front stoop, still wearing her pajamas as well, her face swollen with crying.

"Kyle's being mean," she told me.

"Tell him to stop. And you shouldn't be outside in your sleep clothes."

She stuck her tongue out and went back in.

That was right in line with how my day had gone so far.

After seeing Theresa's name on my parents' marriage certificate last night, I'd made up my mind to come straight to her and ask all the things I couldn't ask my mom. So of course she wasn't home. Of course Sarah stuck her tongue out at me. Of course I was standing in the blooming heat waiting for a man I'd only just met to hand over some papers while wearing his underwear.

"Here you go," Tom said, pulling my attention back to the inside of the house.

"Thank you." I took the packet he handed me. "Theresa will be home this afternoon?"

"God willing, earlier than that," he said, looking exhausted and it wasn't even ten in the morning. By the time he closed the door, the power had shifted in the house and Kyle was now screaming at Sarah.

Why anyone would ever have kids was lost on me.

I'd planned to keep on trucking past Crane's trailer on the way out, but I realized I really wanted to see him. I walked up and knocked before I could talk myself out of it.

He answered almost before my knuckles met the door.

"What do you want?" he asked. I could tell he meant to sound angry, but he was failing. It didn't help his act that one of his eyes was visible.

"I wanna know why you ran yesterday when you found out my last name."

"It wasn't just that. You had a cop car out front."

"That doesn't help your case."

He leaned against the doorjamb. "Cops aren't always the good guys."

"I know that."

But I didn't, not really. Or at least it had never before occurred to me that that might be true. I thought about Chad, and Chief Mike. In their uniforms, I assumed they were on my side. In casual clothing, they were just men, though, and men I didn't particularly like, one of them being weaselly and the other too gruff. I supposed they could be bad at their jobs like anyone else. Putting on a uniform didn't change someone's fundamental makeup.

"And your mom has a reputation," he said, watching my face with that one eye.

This perked me right up. "What is it?"

He lifted his shoulders and dropped them.

"Are you going to help me with the time capsule project today?" I asked.

"Is the pay the same as yesterday?"

I grinned. "Even less."

❖

"Crane, what grade are you in?"

He'd been pretty quiet the whole day, and I'd let him, but after a few hours of boring door-to-door, we'd made our way to the playground. We were resting on our own swings, floating lazily back and forth, dragging our feet in the sand as we each ate a half of Mom's latest sandwich. She might have been a cold fish, but no one could argue her magnificent sack lunch skills. Today she'd packed me an egg salad sandwich flecked with tuna, which would normally be a gamble on a hot day, but she'd taped two Mr. Freeze pops to it, one orange and one grape, and they still had some slush left in them.

The firm tuna gave a nice contrast to the creaminess of the egg, and diced pickles provided a salty pop of flavor. It was overall a delight to eat with the syrup-sweet Mr. Freezes to wash it down.

"It's summer," he said. "I'm not in any grade."

"You know what I mean."

He had a chunk of egg stuck to his lip and took the napkin I handed him. "I dropped out last spring, at the end of my junior year," he said, wiping his mouth. "Waste of time."

"What?" I'd watched after-school specials about kids who quit school. They turned to drugs and prostitution almost *immediately*. Like, the dealers and the pimps were waiting outside the school for them. "You're not going to graduate?"

"I can make more money working."

"But you *don't* work," I said. "Not since I've met you. And you're smart. I bet you have dreams."

He kicked at the sand, scattering a spray of it across the grass. "You don't know everything."

"Crane!" I jumped out of my swing and faced him. It might have been the poor night's sleep or the agony of moving here and everything I'd found out since, but I'd had enough. "You need to stop being so sneaky and start talking plain."

"You first," he said, but his voice was gentler than before.

His hair was completely covering his eyes, shutting him out, but he was right. I couldn't ask him to do for me what I hadn't done for him.

Fine. I squared my shoulders. "I did something terrible to my dad."

Crane stopped his swing.

I continued, the words spewing out hot and inevitable. "Him and my mom divorced when I was five, and my dad kept me. My mom didn't even want me. The one chance I had to make her love me, I blew it, and so my dad was all I had, my whole world, and my best friend. And I . . ." I couldn't bring myself to say the words, to admit to killing him. "I let him down, and now he's dead, and I have to live in this awful town, where my mom and dad grew up and where everyone seems to have secrets and no one's talking."

I choked in air, wishing I could calm my racing heart. I was standing in front of Crane but staring at my sneakers because I couldn't bear to witness him judging me.

I didn't want to keep talking, but it was too late to stop. "And I just found out that I didn't know my dad at all, that everything I thought I knew about him was a lie. In real life, he let his little brother drown, back when he was in high school. He was supposed to be watching him, but he got drunk and made out with my mom instead, and Benny died. My dad was hospitalized before or after that because he flipped his wig. I can't ask my mom for the specifics because she hates me so much that she can't even stand to be in the house with me."

Far away, someone hollered at someone else. A flock of birds took off from a nearby tree, startled by something.

But Crane made no noise.

When I couldn't stand it any longer, I lifted my head slowly, expecting an emotional blow. I was shocked to meet both Crane's eyes, blue and sincere and bare to the world.

"I'm really sorry, Frankie," he said.

I gripped my elbows.

"I'm sorry your dad didn't tell you everything bad that ever happened to him, but that doesn't make what he *did* tell you a lie. Did he tell you he loved you?"

"Yeah." I sniffled.

"I bet that was true. Did he stick around?"

"For sure."

"That's true, too."

We were both silent for a while. I liked that Crane didn't try and touch me and make things weird.

"We should get back to work," he said, waiting until I stepped back to get off his swing.

"Sounds good." I began packing our trash into the knapsack.

"Your mom makes good sandwiches."

"I know," I said, tucking the sticky Mr. Freeze tubes into the sandwich bag.

"That's what I mean by 'you don't know everything,'" he said, his voice so firm, so serious for a discussion of sandwiches, which I thought was what we'd been talking about. "For example, you don't know that love comes in different packages."

I scowled at him, then at the sandwich bag, slimy inside with egg salad residue. "You're saying this is how my mom is telling me she loves me?"

He shrugged. "Might be all she has to offer."

❖

"You didn't tell me anything about yourself," I said to Crane.

We were finishing up the last house on my list. Most of the people I'd tried had not been home. Of those who had, a bunch carried either no opinion about what should go into the time capsule or a very clear opinion *about* the time capsule, specifically that it was a waste of money and a snipe hunt meant to distract from the "Satan worshippers taking over the town."

"What?" Crane asked. He was staring at an old Victorian mansion across the street, his voice so distant that I didn't know if his question was directed at me or the house. It was a huge building with a porch the length of it, painted white with dark-green trim.

"I told you about my dad, and you didn't spill anything about yourself," I said, standing next to him, shading my eyes so I could study the house. A face was in the bay window. "Is that Dawn?"

Crane turned abruptly and began walking quickly in the direction of the trailer park.

"Is that the foster home where she and Crystal are staying?" I asked.

He kept striding so fast that I had to jog to keep up. When I put my hand on his arm, he whirled. I was shocked to see him crying.

"Yeah," he said. "That's the foster home. It's not just Dawn and Crystal in there. It's all the kids who've been hurt this last round."

"*All* the kids?" I asked, swaying. "This *last* round?"

"Yeah." He swiped at his eyes and started walking again but slower so I could keep up. "There's at least a dozen in there."

"That can't be right," I said, stumbling as I looked over my shoulder at the house. A shiver ran through me. "That's a whole baseball team."

"It sure is."

I stopped, awareness hitting like an asteroid. "Then none of us are safe."

"Not in Litani," he said.

I ran up and grabbed his arm. "Crane, we have to help. We have to figure out who's hurting the kids."

"Everybody knows, and I mean *everybody*. The trick is getting the people in charge to care."

"My mom cares."

He grunted. "Does she? If there isn't an audience?"

His words hit like a slap, but I couldn't help recognizing some truth in them. I wondered in what capacity he'd met her. I assumed from the way he'd taken off when he'd seen the police car outside my house that he'd been on the wrong side of the law. Had he faced her for shoplifting?

Vandalism? "Sure she cares. I heard her talking to Chief Mike about it just a couple days ago. Dawn and Crystal were at our house. She said she was bringing them to the foster home to keep them safe."

"Then why hasn't anyone been arrested?"

I felt myself getting angry. "Because she doesn't have enough evidence!"

"A dozen kids isn't enough evidence?" Crane asked. "Or not enough of an audience?"

"What do you even mean by that?" I asked, exasperated.

"The Zloduk case. She drew that out longer than she needed to, kept it going until the press showed up."

"What do you know about the Zloduk case?"

"Plenty," he said. "I might know your mom better than you do."

"Doubt it," I said because it made me mad, not because I wasn't beginning to believe it. "How could you?"

He glanced my way. I thought he was going to argue because that was the mood I was in. The pain in his eyes shocked me. "You never asked me my last name," he said.

I couldn't pivot out of anger that quickly. "So what?"

"I have to go," he said, hurrying away, his voice agony.

"Crane!"

He stopped. Turned. "Promise me something."

"What?"

"Don't throw me away."

His words peeled me clean. "What's going on?"

He shook his head and took off toward the trailer park faster than I could follow.

CHAPTER 36

I assumed Crane was camped out inside his trailer when I walked past. His single-wide was dark inside, the front door shut, but it always was. I strode by without stopping. I told myself it was because Crane clearly wanted time to himself, but I was afraid it was something else. He'd unsettled me, accusing my mom of being some sort of ghoul who wanted to stop child molesters only when it made her look good. He didn't know how the law worked. I didn't, either, but the thought of having a mom who would do that was too much to bear.

Because if that were true—my mom cared about attention more than kids in danger—on top of my dad having killed his brother through negligence, than what kind of person did that make me, the product of those two?

But I already knew.

It made me a murderer.

There'd been times, mostly when I was petting Wort or hanging with Crane, where I saw my actions in a softer light, could justify them. But when I stacked them right next to a plain view of who Linda and Paul Jubilee were? I was an apple crouching so close to the tree that I might as well have never dropped.

Realizing that triggered a memory.

Despite his temporary excitement that night over the hawthorn, Dad collapsed into himself the week after he lost his grant. I tried to cheer him up, to tell him he'd land another teaching job soon, but his interview suit with its ironed shirt hung, untouched, on the outside of his closet door. The résumé I'd typed up for him lay next to the typewriter. He was sleeping in late and moving slower when he bothered to get out of bed. Some days, when I returned home from school, I discovered he hadn't left his bed at all.

I loved him, but I wished he would do more. I understood, though. His job had been his life. His job and me. Now it was just me, and I didn't know how to carry all that. It bled into every area of my life. I'd been too embarrassed to tell June Dad had lost his job, so she thought I was being crabby because of something she'd done. I missed more homework than I turned in. It got so bad that the school must have called Dad, but he either hadn't answered or forgot to talk to me about it.

Dad didn't have any close friends, no real family except me and Aunt Edna, who'd give me a stiff, powder-scented hug and a handful of butterscotch disks at the end of our courtesy visits. I was at the end of my rope, had my mind made up to finally call Mom, when out of the blue Dad pulled himself out of his hole.

We were eating Campbell's Chicken and Stars soup—the only food he was able to tolerate—when he sat up straight, as if he'd just thought of something. "You should invite June over for a movie watch," he said. "Get some smiles back in this house. You shouldn't be babysitting me all the time. I want you to be a kid."

I glanced at him, wary. June hadn't been over since that last time when he'd peeked in on us, doing his dorky Dad thing. He'd been so much healthier then. If she came now, she'd see how he'd changed. I wouldn't be able to hide it from her anymore. That, and she might wear him out with her natural boppiness.

"You sure?"

It was a Friday, so she and I could stay up late. But I had so much homework piled up. And Dad hadn't showered in days and looked so weak. I was about to make up some reason she probably couldn't come when he rested his spoon on the table.

"Please?"

I had wondered every day since how my life would have been different if I had said no, every day up until this one. That day, I realized it wouldn't have mattered. I was destined to turn out rotten no matter what. Just look at my parents.

I shook my head, willing myself back into the present. I'd walked myself all the way to Theresa's trailer.

"Frankie!" she called from the other side of her screen door, where she was fanning herself. "You're back early."

"A lot of people weren't home," I said, dragging myself up her front steps, through air so hot it was solid. I was glad to see her, not only because she was an improvement over her husband but also because it meant I could finally ask her some questions . . . if I could gather the courage.

"Or were too hot to answer the door. How can you stand to be outside in this humidity?"

I didn't tell her that I wasn't aware I had a choice. I slid my knapsack off my damp shoulders and was about to pull out the papers when she ushered me into her house.

"Not out in the sun, child! Come inside. I've got icy-cold lemonade."

"That'd be nice."

Sarah was lying on the couch, swaying two knockoff Barbies arm in arm like they were slow dancing. Kyle was nowhere in sight.

"Did Mr. Buckle go to work?" I asked.

"He's taking a nap," she said, laughing. "Watching the kids for two hours tuckered the poor man out. Parenting isn't for the weak."

I accepted a glass of lemonade as well as a chair at the kitchen table. The battered window air conditioner was doing its best to keep out the heat, but it was making more noise than cool air. Theresa had placed a bowl of ice in front of a round circulating fan and was flapping a handheld accordion fan in front of her slick face.

"Tell me everything you learned today."

I pulled out the paperwork and went over it with her, my attention traveling to Sarah. I wanted her to go to her room so I could ask Theresa about Benny's drowning. I saw she'd done me one better and fallen asleep, the dolls slumped across her chest.

"Theresa," I said, interrupting her just as she was telling me about the church crisis she'd had to intervene on, something about a mix-up in who was bringing which hotdish to this Sunday's fellowship that spun out of control when it came to light that one of the women was cheating with the other's husband, "can I ask you something about my dad?"

Her fan, which had been as constant as a hummingbird's wings since I'd entered her house, paused midair. "What is it, dear?"

"I heard about the drowning. That day at the river, with Benny? I heard that you were there, too. I guess . . . I guess I just want to know what really happened."

"Lord, I was worried you were going to ask me about that." Theresa shook her head so fast that her cheeks jiggled, and then she patted her red hair and drained her lemonade, the ice cubes crammed against her mouth. When she put down her glass, she was no longer meeting my eyes. "Why don't you tell me what you heard."

I shared a shortened version of what Ronnie had told me while she watched a spot above my shoulder, her fan fluttering away. When I stopped talking, she rested her hand on my arm.

"Honey, it wasn't like that. Not exactly."

My hopes sat up, but I shoved them down.

"Your father hadn't been drinking, first of all," she said. "I'd never seen him take a drop in his life, before or after that day."

I let out a breath I didn't know I'd been holding.

She continued. "He'd seen what liquor did to his own parents. And he wasn't interested in Linda back then, either. He liked Darlene, for goodness' sakes, who was just as sweet and pretty as a girl could be. They were dating, as I recall."

She snapped her fan closed and rested it against her chin. "It was so long ago, but I can't see how he would have broken off from the group to go anywhere with your mom, certainly not to 'make out'—that last part I can guarantee."

She opened her fan back up and held it in front of her face, hiding everything but her eyes—sparkling with regret or amusement, I couldn't be sure—and her glorious red hair. "I have to confess that I had questionable morals back then. I hadn't met Tom yet, and Chief Mike—he was regular old Mike the quarterback at the time—and I were a bit of a thing. Just some high school love. We'd snuck off for some harmless kissing when Benny went into the river."

Her eyes got a faraway look, but I needed her here. "You *sure* my dad hadn't been drinking?" I asked.

She dropped back into the moment. "No, and not only because he never had a taste for liquor," she said firmly. "Paul was as responsible as the day was long. No way on God's green earth would he drink when he was watching Benny."

My heart grew so big it about popped. "So the drowning wasn't his fault?"

A shadow passed across her eyes. "Your mother would have a better idea of whose fault it was, but your father didn't do a thing wrong that day. He loved Benny. Sure, Benny annoyed him sometimes like only a little brother can, but those two were as close as two peas in a pod. Had to be with the parents they had."

She snapped the fan closed again and tapped her mouth with it. "I'm sorry. I shouldn't speak ill of the dead, especially when they were your grandparents."

"It's okay," I said. "I didn't know them."

"You're not missing anything." She leaned forward as if to whisper, but her voice came out regular. "Your grandpa was mean and your grandma sad. Depressed, they'd call it today, but back then we just thought of her as moody. They'd started drinking themselves to the grave even before Benny drowned. His passing just hurried up the process. A tragedy all around."

"I also heard . . ." I didn't want to say that I knew my dad had lost his marbles. She'd given me a tremendous gift already. Why give her a reason to take it away? But I had to know. "I heard he went crazy. Dad. After Benny."

Her eyes narrowed. She was fanning herself again, wisps of hair taking off from her face before returning. "Who told you that?"

"I saw his hospital bracelet. It said he was involuntarily committed."

Her face crumpled, real misery showing in her eyes. She didn't speak for a few beats. "I'd forgotten about that."

I waited for her to say more. She'd grown silent again. A clock ticked, and Sarah snored lightly. Finally, Theresa continued.

"He wasn't crazy, that's for sure. He was brokenhearted, which was the most understandable thing in the world. He'd lost his best friend. That damn river swallowed the child right up. Your dad felt alone in the world after that."

But he had me, I almost said, but of course he didn't, not then.

"Paul needed to rest and recuperate, that's all. And that's what he got in the hospital. He was fine after that, as fine as he could be." She closed her fan and used it to pat my cheek. "Who's filling your head with all these stories?"

I shrugged. "Just stuff that I picked up here and there."

She studied me down the length of her nose. "All right, child. You can keep that bit to yourself. But your dad was a good man, and don't let anyone tell you different."

Her words were bittersweet. It confirmed what I'd so wanted to believe but made what I'd done to him that much worse.

"A lot of lives were destroyed that day," she murmured.

"The day Benny drowned?"

She nodded. "The bad stuff that's happened since can be traced back to that. To the day innocence died in Litani."

Crane had said something similar. "You mean what's being done to kids here?"

"You either pay the devil now or you pay him later, but he always collects," she said, her expression closed off for the first time since I'd met her.

When she grew silent again, the air heavy between us, I cleared my throat to ask her my final question. "What's Crane's last name?"

"Zloduk," she said, absentmindedly. "Would you like some more lemonade?"

CHAPTER 37

Mom walked through the door, resting her purse on the corner table and tugging off her pumps with a sigh. When she spotted me sitting silently on the couch, she fell back, hand over heart.

I'd wandered home after talking to Theresa, played with Wort, tried to read, played with Wort some more, picked up around the house, microwaved the Banquet chicken, tasted only salt and gristle as I chewed it, and then sat myself on the couch, waiting for Mom, reeling.

Crane was a Zloduk.

Had he been a victim or a predator?

"Hi, Mom," I said. I was clutching my own hands, worrying at my fingernails.

She flicked her wrist to read her watch. She held herself as if she'd run a marathon, heavy bags under her eyes, skin gray with exhaustion. "It's after ten. What are you doing up?"

"I wanted to talk to you."

She sighed and slowly removed one gold earring and then the other. They made a tinkling noise as she rested them near her purse. "I know my note said I wanted to speak with you, but can it wait until tomorrow? It's been a long day."

You bet it has. A long month, as a matter of fact.

"No," I said, proud of how strong my voice sounded. "It needs to be now."

She stared longingly at the kitchen. If she was having any loving thoughts about that Banquet meal, I could save her the heartache.

"The chicken tastes like salted cardboard."

She whirled on me, eyebrows forming an angry vee, sudden fury in her voice. "Are you saying I'm a bad mother?"

"What?" This was not the direction I'd expected the conversation to take.

"I prepare your lunch every day, which is more than my own mother did for me." Her voice was quivering. "I'm sorry I can't also cook your dinner from scratch."

"Why are you so mad?"

"Why are you so ungrateful?"

The target was moving too fast for me to keep up. "I hardly see you."

"That's not my fault. Somebody has to pay the bills."

I was melting on the couch, her words kicking me, but she wasn't even looking at me anymore.

"Mom?"

She jumped as if she'd just realized I was in the room. "Oh, Jesus. Frankie. I'm sorry." She dragged herself over to a wicker chair and dropped into it as if her legs had given out beneath her. The hardness in her face had left as quickly as it'd come.

She'd called me Frankie.

"I don't know where that crazy shit came from, honey. Some old tape playing in my head. But I need to ask you something, and I suppose now is as good a time as ever." She leaned toward me, her eyes completely focused and over-wide, showing the whites. Our knees were nearly touching. She took a deep breath. "Did your dad ever touch you?"

I opened my mouth. Closed it.

"I shouldn't even ask, but I have to. After what I've learned today." She crossed her legs, her loose foot jittering. She looked beat and wound up at the same time.

"I know you and Officer Wendt talked about what's happening here. Kids are getting abused, Frankie. Litani kids, people doing the same thing to them that your grandfather did to me."

Her words hit my ears like battery acid. This was the start of the rest of the story, the one she'd begun to tell me on the ride back from Clara's spaghetti party.

"I will send every monster to prison, no matter what it takes." She grabbed my wrist. Her touch shocked me. "That's why I've stored them at the same house, you know. The children. So I can teach them to speak properly. Otherwise they'll sound poor, and none of those fuckers ever believe poor people."

I was so past the point of shock that her swearbomb hardly even registered. But did this mean that Crane was wrong and my mom really did care about the kids?

She shook my wrist, which she hadn't yet released. "You have to bend the law sometimes, do you understand? You must make decisions to protect your town. That's your true family. Your community. They'll never abandon you, and that comes at a price. We all must do our part."

"Mom?" I was terrified by her energy, her words, the way fire seemed to be leaping off her.

"What is it?"

The words popped out. I hadn't planned them, couldn't stop them any more than I could stop the sun from rising. "I think someone's been peeking in my window."

That's when she saw me.

She *really saw me.*

A heaviness lifted from my shoulders.

She hopped over to sit next to me on the couch. "Tell me everything."

Suddenly, for the first time since I'd wrecked everything seven years earlier, I was inside her bubble. It felt like ink and stars and magic, and I never wanted it to end. I told her about the knocking the first night here, the cigarette butt I'd found outside. I moved my description of the night in her office (when I thought I'd seen a demon at the window) to my own bedroom. Even though I was sure Chad already had, I also told her about Sly and the boy and the man I hadn't seen in the brewery. Then I connected it all, telling her my hunch that Sly was the one lurking outside my window.

She hung on every word.

When I was done, when I had no more stories to tell, she flew off the couch. "I'm going to call Mike right now."

Watching her whirl the dial on the phone, I felt shame and pride in equal measure. Shame because I'd kept from her that I'd been in her office that night, pride because . . . well, because it felt like Mom and I were finally on the same team. It made no difference that I'd never actually seen a lurker, only cigarette butts and shadows. There *had* been someone out there. I knew it. It didn't matter if it was Sly or not. Whoever it was, I wanted them caught.

She hung up the phone after a flurry of tight words and turned to me, her cheeks flushed, her voice returned to its county-prosecutor cool. "Don't worry, Francesca. If there's someone outside your window, we'll catch them."

I swallowed hard. I was back to being Francesca.

"Mom, you said you heard awful things today. What were they?"

She stared down the hall—longingly, I thought—toward her bedroom. But she faced me, her expression sad, and she answered, tired as she was. "At least two dozen children have been molested."

My breath hooked. That was a whole classroom of kids. In a town this size, probably a whole *grade*.

"We've uncovered a sex ring. They prey on children. Their own, others. Make them play games to get their clothes off, and then they molest them." Her eyes darted to me. "Of course you already know one of the players. He lives at the trailer park, just like Ronnie guessed."

Hornets buzzed in my chest. *Please don't say it's Crane. Please please please.*

"It's Sly Vogler. The same man you believe is lurking outside your window."

I could have wept with relief. Not Crane. "But if you already knew about Sly, why'd you call Chief Mike just now?"

She ran her hands through her hair, sighed. "Everything I told you just now is confidential. We were holding off arresting Sly until we had all our ducks in a row. But if he's coming to my house, we might need to move quicker than planned."

She glanced at her watch again before continuing. "We think he's at the center of the ring. He picks up women at AA meetings. Broken women trying to heal, like Darlene, Dawn's mom. He seduces them, offers to watch their children. He's got a record, though the women don't know this. He's been twice convicted of child sexual assault, first time when he was stationed in the service in South Carolina and second time when he was living out in California."

She was talking to me as if I were an adult, a friend, a confidante. I'd told her it was okay, but it wasn't. I didn't want to know any of this.

"We're going to arrest Sly," she said, arms crossed, a soft smile on her face. "And that's just the beginning. *We're going to get them all.*"

I wasn't really even listening any longer. The adrenaline that had kept me pumping through this conversation had drained, leaving me wrung out. I wanted to go to bed, to cuddle with Wort, to wake up in a different world. I'd actually started to fade when she said it.

"Crane Zloduk, too."

"What?" I asked, alert now, my heart sick-hammering.

"He's going to be the next to go down. After Sly. They're working together. I just need to prove it."

Somehow, my mouth formed the words. "How do you know?"

She walked over to the table to grab her earrings. She was going to bed. This was the end of the conversation for her. "He was one of the victims in the Zloduk case, a cousin to the main victims, but he refused to testify. His not testifying protected Sly, the only perp in that case I wasn't able to bring to justice. Best-case scenario, it's Crane's fault we couldn't arrest Sly along with the Zloduks, which allowed him to start this new wave of abuse. Worst case, and I believe this to be true, Crane is in on it now, probably the mastermind. Kids who were damaged grow up to be predators themselves. I see it all the time."

She disappeared down the hallway.

CHAPTER 38

Mom's scream woke me from a dead sleep. It was so piercing that it brought me to my feet before I was fully awake. At first I didn't recognize my surroundings. Then I realized I'd crashed on the torture device of a couch, not intending to but too bone-tired to drag myself to my room after Mom's big reveal.

"What is it?" I called, battling dizziness from standing too quickly. I steadied myself. Tangerine-tinted sunlight was streaming through the front window. Mom hadn't drawn the drapes as she usually did.

How had I slept all night on wicker?

"You tell me," Mom said, appearing from the shadowy hallway, her hair wild looking. She appeared strangely vulnerable, her thin bathrobe tied around her waist, face pale, sleep still in her eyes.

Until I noticed what she was clutching.

My heart sank.

"Wort!" I leaped forward to snatch the kitten from her. I knew momma cats held their babies by the scruff of their necks, but the way my mom did it was hurting Wort. The kitty was so frightened that she scratched at me, hissing, and twisted free before taking off toward my bedroom.

"Filthy animal," Mom said, looking down at me as I sucked on my bleeding fingers. "I saw the food and the litter. I know you've been hiding him from me. I thought we were *friends*."

My eyes felt hot. "What were you doing in my room?"

"Would you believe I was coming to ask you if you wanted pancakes for breakfast?"

I blinked away the hair falling into my eyes.

She was glaring. "Your little fiend leaped at me. How long have you been hiding it?"

There was no point in lying. "I found her the first day I came. I was going to tell you about it, but—" Mom planted her hands on her hips, and I knew there was only one way to finish that sentence. "But I didn't. And I should have. I'm sorry."

She cocked her pointer finger and thumb like a gun and aimed it at me. "I can abide a lot of things, but sneakiness isn't one of them. It's a terrible quality, Francesca. I've lost all trust in you."

I nodded, miserable. "I'm sorry," I repeated.

"We'll deal with that later. After you get that creature out of my house. Animals are not meant to live indoors."

"What should I do with her?" I asked, already heartsick. I couldn't bear the thought of Wort on her own in the wild, but I didn't know what they'd do with her at the pound. Put her down?

"I don't care," she said, heading to the kitchen. "As long as it's not here."

❖

"Is that a cat?"

Wort was huddled in my arms. She'd calmed down after Mom's yelling but gotten riled up all over again on the walk over. I'd run straight to Crane's house, the army knapsack over my shoulder, Wort in my arms, tears streaming down my face. Crane had answered my frantic knocking immediately even though it was not yet 8:00 a.m.

"Yeah. The one I showed you the sketch of. Motherwort."

He held out his hand as if to pet her, and then he yanked it back. "He looks nice."

"She. Can you keep her?" I didn't believe what Mom had told me about Crane. He wasn't hurting kids. Besides, I had nowhere else to turn.

He stepped aside to let me into his trailer, offering me a seat at his small Formica table with its old-style gold metal chairs. He began pacing rather than sitting himself, his nervous movement in the tight space drawing attention to how large he was. His place appeared exactly like the last time I had been there. Neat but run-down, with some orange crates used as bookcases next to a couch covered with a faded Indian blanket.

"I don't need a cat," Crane said. But he said it in a way that gave me hope, and he'd brushed his hair out of his eyes.

"It's just for a little bit," I said. "Until I find a permanent home for her."

I held Motherwort out to Crane. She was shivering. He reached for her tentatively, cradled her. The kitten looked tiny inside his big paw. He stroked her forehead with a single finger, and she immediately began purring.

"She likes you!"

Crane smiled before he could catch himself, showing me his beautiful twisted teeth. "Can you show me the sketch again?"

I slid the knapsack off my shoulder, pulled out The Book from where I'd nestled it between the box of cat food and bag of litter and food and water dishes, and flipped through it.

"Who's that?" he asked, pointing to a page I'd just passed.

"Dawn." I turned back to her page, showing him the purple-headed thistle.

He studied it, his expression growing sad. "Have you drawn one of me?"

The question made me feel shy. "Not yet."

He nodded. "I'd probably be a weed, too."

"One person's weed is another's flower," I said. "That's something my dad always said. If someone thinks it's worthless, it's because they're not looking hard enough."

"At the plant?"

"Sure," I said.

He appeared thoughtful. "Have you drawn any other new ones?"

I nodded. Deliberately skipping over the Sly page, I held The Book open to him so he could see the sketch of Darlene I'd done after Theresa had told me Dad and Darlene had dated in high school. I'd been waiting for Mom to come home and trying to picture it. I'd had the hardest time wrapping my brain around that image, but to be fair, I couldn't imagine my dad dating anyone.

Crane gently placed Wort on the floor so he could hold The Book and give it his full attention. I could see he wanted to keep her in his hands, so I appreciated his focus extra much.

CHOOSE YOUR OWN PLANT PERSONALITY

YOU'RE CAPTAIN OF YOUR OWN DESTINY!
WHICH PLANT PERSONALITY DO YOU CHOOSE?

DANDELION

You persevere. They can pluck, spray, mow, and curse you. But do not forget. You persevere.

He stopped just short of touching the sketch. "She looks so sad."

I studied him, the gentle giant, Wort purring at his ankles, hoping to be picked up again, not even noticing me anymore now that she'd met him. "Crane, have you been hanging out outside my window?"

His face snapped shut exactly at the same time he closed The Book. "Why do you think that?"

"I've been seeing shapes and shadows." I was worrying at a strip of loose skin alongside my thumbnail. "It's okay if it's you, Crane."

"No," he said, his voice deep and full of anguish. "It's definitely not okay. No one should be outside your window."

I leaned over to pull the cat food, litter, and a shallow aluminum pan from my knapsack, deliberately looking away from him so I couldn't see his face and chicken out. "What happened to you, Crane?"

"What do you mean?"

I poured litter into the pan. "I know you're a Zloduk."

I'd expected him to be evasive. Everyone else had been so far, me included, so it caught me off guard when he spoke plainly. "If you know the name, you know what happened to me."

I waited, still kneeling over the pan, still not looking at him.

"I didn't get it as bad as some of my cousins, the ones who lived on my grandparents' farm, but it was bad enough." His voice was still so deep, a bottomless pool of cold water. "What's happening now in Litani is the same thing."

I risked a glance at him. His hair was completely covering his eyes. I stood slowly. "Because Sly is still out there?"

He jolted, like someone had stuck a knife into him. "All the adult Zloduks were arrested, but that doesn't mean all the evil was put away. The ones they trained are doing to others what was done to them."

"Who?" I asked, pushing it. I was painfully aware that Crane hadn't named Sly just now when I'd given him a chance, was saying the same thing my mom had. *Kids who were damaged grow up to be predators themselves.* Was he confessing?

When a car door slammed outside his trailer, I realized both he and I had been standing within inches of each other, our bodies taut. A walkie-talkie crackled. Crane's eyes flashed with fear and darted around the room.

"You shouldn't be here," he said, his voice hoarse. "I'll get in trouble if they find you in my trailer. You need to hide."

His panic was sudden and contagious. "Where?" I whispered.

He pointed at a narrow closet alongside the refrigerator. I grabbed Wort and jumped toward it, ripping open the door. A broom with a dustpan clipped to it was inside, balanced on top of a case of Shasta. I squeezed myself in just as the knock landed on the front door.

"Crane Zloduk!" I recognized Chief Mike's voice.

"What do you want?" Crane sounded terrified.

"I want you to come down to the station. I have some questions for you."

I moaned, quiet like a ghost. Was my mother following through on her threat to arrest Crane?

"Do you have a warrant?" Crane asked.

"Not right now," Chief Mike said, his voice calm, authoritative. "You want me to get one and come back? Because it's going to look bad for you if you make me do that."

"You said it's just to answer questions?" Crane asked. "I have responsibilities. A cat. I need to be back tonight."

That's when I knew beyond a shadow of a doubt that Crane lived here alone. I'd suspected it before, but he'd just confirmed it. He was seventeen years old; he should have been a senior in high school, and he was on his own.

"You'll be back tonight," Chief Mike said. "You have my word."

"All right," Crane said. I heard shuffling noises, probably him putting on his shoes, then grabbing his wallet. The front door and then car doors opened and closed, and an engine hummed to life. I counted to a hundred before stepping out of the closet. When I hurried to the window, they were gone.

It felt bad to be in Crane's trailer without him. I made sure all the hallway doors were closed tightly so that Wort couldn't get into trouble, filled her water and food dishes, pet her, and promised that I'd be back as soon as I could. Then I locked the front door behind me.

It was another hot day, one coming after another, strung together like lava beads, this whole July in Litani just one big, uncomfortable mistake. But maybe there was hope. If Crane was innocent, there was nothing for me to worry about. But my life had been nothing but anxiety for weeks, and now didn't feel like a good time to give that up. If they'd arrested Sly like Mom said they planned to, he would tell them that Crane wasn't involved. Then Mom and Chief Mike could leave Crane alone. Right?

I walked toward Sly's trailer on trembling legs. I didn't know what I was expecting. A confession spray-painted on the side? The equivalent of a smoking gun in the bushes by his front door? Whatever it was, I didn't find it. I walked around his trailer twice, kicking at the ground, turning up nothing but garbage and cigarette butts. I was about to head home when, on impulse, I stuck my face up to the glass, cupping my eyes with my hands.

A face stared back at me.

I shrieked and jumped away from the trailer.

Moments later, the front door opened, and Victor, Sly's father, strode out. He was laughing, an ugly rasping sound. "Scared you straight, didn't I?"

"Yessir," I said. I was backing away. He was even scarier without his wife. His skin was yellowish, and there was a brown stain near his lip. Waves of sourness rolled off him. "Sorry to have bothered you. I shouldn't be here. I was looking for Sly."

"Haven't seen him for over a day, so good luck with that."

Victor took a step toward me. I stumbled back, fell to the ground.

"Are you scared of me, girl?" His only hair, a white wisp over each ear, was in disarray, pointing toward the sky like horns. His smile was sharp.

"No, sir," I said, my quavering voice belying my words. "It's just that I have to be going."

Except my body was not listening to my mouth, because I couldn't figure out how to stand up.

He got a thoughtful expression on his face. "How well do you know my boy?" he asked.

"Not well at all," I said truthfully.

Victor scratched at his bristly neck. "Maybe you could help me. You know that Red Owl box my wife was carrying in here the other day? It had some movies and pictures in it. Do you know what happened to them? Been looking high and low, but they seem to have grown legs and walked off."

"Like I said, sir, I don't really know Sly."

"I heard you the first time." His beady eyes narrowed. His face was mapped with exploding red veins. "Since you're here, you want to be neighborly, come in and help an old man search? At my age, we get tuckered out pretty easily, and you look like you have all the energy in the world. Whaddya say?"

He reached out to me.

I watched his hand slither toward me, the long yellowed fingernails nearing, but I was frozen, a fly trapped in his web.

CHAPTER 39

"Leave that girl alone, Victor."

Victor turned toward the tired voice, and once he was no longer staring at me, I was free. I leaped to my feet and raced toward Darlene, so grateful I could cry.

She looked like she hadn't slept in a year. Her dirty blonde hair was greasy, and her eyes had their own bags packed. But I could have hugged her.

"Hey now, Darlene, why don't you remember your place." Victor hooked his thumbs through his belt loops, a gesture I recognized from Sly. I guessed it was supposed to seem relaxed, but it just made him appear coiled, like a snake winding up to strike. "The girl and me were just having a friendly talk. That's none of your business, now is it?"

"I know how your talks go," Darlene said, but there was no bite to her words. She carried a black plastic bag in each hand. By the rotten-cheese smell they were giving off, I assumed they contained garbage.

"Can I help you with those?" I asked.

She glanced down at the bags as if surprised to find them there. "The city stopped picking up my trash. Isn't that the shits?"

"It sure is."

I glanced over at Victor, who was looking angry enough to swallow his own tongue. I didn't want to spend another second near him. I took one bag from Darlene and followed her as she walked toward the owl-map office building. There was a dumpster next to it with a sign clearly stating residents were not to throw their trash in. If she saw the sign, she ignored it. She tossed in the bag she was holding and then did the same with the one I'd been carrying.

I risked another glance behind me. Sly's trailer was still visible, but Victor wasn't.

"How's your cat doing?" Darlene asked, pausing to light a cigarette.

"Really well." The lie sat heavy on my chest. "That's not true. Mom said the kitten can't live with us, so I had to drop her off at Crane's just now."

"Your mom's a real ballbuster," she said agreeably, sucking smoke out of her mouth and up her nostrils. She reminded me of a worn-out dragon.

"You knew her when she was young," I said, a statement of fact.

Her eyes slid to me. "Sure. It's a small town."

"The same way you knew my dad."

She started striding away. I hurried to keep up, steering clear of Sly's trailer as we walked past. Still no Victor, but since his green sedan hadn't been out front earlier, he was likely inside, waiting for a ride.

"I read about my uncle drowning. Benjamin. You were there, weren't you?"

"If you read about it, you know I was there." She didn't sound angry, only bone-weary. A breeze kicked up and blew her scent toward me. Now that she wasn't holding trash bags any longer, I could smell the liquor on her. She was drunk in broad daylight.

"I used to be pretty," she said out of the blue. She glanced over at me and took a big drag from her cigarette, still walking toward her trailer. "Back then they used to call me Sunny, I was so full of sunshine. Happy all the time." She chuckled her emery-board laugh. "Can you believe it? Me. Happy. A cheerleader. Knew right from wrong."

Looking at her now, knowing her daughter was in a foster home, did make it hard to believe. But I'd drawn her as a dandelion, and that meant something. Dandelions were known as the elixir of life. Every part of them was edible—flower, stem, leaf, and root—and they were one of the most nutritional plants known to humans, containing fiber, protein, antioxidants, vitamins, and minerals. Although dandelion tea was good for nearly everything that ailed you, the most powerful benefit of dandelions was that if properly processed, their leaf and root extract fought the growth of cancer cells.

But most people saw them only as an invasive weed.

"That all changed the day Benny drowned," she said. "Things haven't been the same since, not for anyone." She shrugged so slowly that it looked like the weight of the world truly lay on her shoulders. "Dawn's dad was the best I could do after that, a trucker who stayed around just long enough to get me pregnant. When Sly showed up, gave me a little attention, it felt good. Something different from the grind of working at the gas station. Anyhow, I thought I deserved a little fun."

She paused, then sighed, a wet, hitched sound. "We all just get by to get by, and then we die," she said.

The finality in her words flipped on my argue button. "It was an accident, right? Benny's death. It wasn't anyone's fault. Accidents happen."

"We never meant to hurt him," she said, her voice broken, empty, as we turned the last corner before her trailer. "That I can tell you for sure."

I was about to ask her for an explanation when she stopped cold.

"Aw, shit," she said, the lit cigarette falling out of her hand. I watched where it landed, still glowing, then looked toward her trailer. A cop car was parked out front, Chad standing alongside it.

"It's time, Darlene," he called out.

She made an angry noise. "That bitch promised that if I snitched, I wouldn't get arrested. She's a damn liar on top of everything else."

Chad stepped around his car and walked toward us. "You can come peaceably. No need to make a scene in front of the girl."

I could tell by the way his hands were open and hovering near his handcuffs on one hip and the gun at the other that he was scared. The acrid scent of burning grass crawled up my nose. Darlene's dropped cigarette. I ground it out with my shoe.

"I'll come with you," Darlene said, her voice defeated. "Without Dawn, it doesn't matter where I end up. Might as well be somewhere I don't have to pay rent. Can I grab my smokes first? I just snagged a new carton."

"That'll be fine," Chad said, visibly relieved. "Just make it quick."

CHAPTER 40

I didn't want to see Darlene get in the cop car, so I hoofed it back toward Crane's. I sat on his lonely steps for an hour, wishing I hadn't locked the door. When I couldn't stand the stares of people passing by or the sound of Wort meowing for me inside any longer, I took off toward the forest.

With the kids at the foster home and all eyes on Sly, I figured it was safe enough.

I hadn't been back since Dawn and her girl gang had roughed me up. That felt like a whole lifetime ago, and it hadn't even been a week. I absently noted the plants as I walked past them, thought about what my dad would say, imagined him with me as I traveled toward the river where he'd lost his brother. I found my way back to the tire swing, considered tiptoeing across the log where I'd first stuck my feet in the cooling water, then realized that Benny likely had drowned right here.

I kept walking, staying near the flowing river, skirting poison ivy at the edge of the woods, strolling past blackberry brambles. The river followed me as much as I followed it, licking and winking its silvery smile. If the July Benny'd drowned had been as hot as this one, like Ronnie had said, it made sense how the water would look like an invitation, even to a kid who didn't know how to swim.

I carried The Book with me and so couldn't go swimming even if I wanted to, but I had no intention of touching that graveyard water.

But still I shadowed it in the general direction of my house, needing to be outside, craving the comfort of nature. At one point, the river veered away from town and led me toward a train bridge. I crawled up onto the tracks. They seemed to go on forever, cutting through sighing corn plants on the other side of the bridge, narrowing to a pencil scratch in the distance. I closed my eyes and spread my arms, imagining what it would feel like to follow the tracks, simply walking until I couldn't walk anymore. If someone stopped for me, I'd tell them I was an orphan. Maybe I'd end up in a foster home just like the two dozen Litani kids. It couldn't have been any worse than where I was now.

But that wasn't an option. I was responsible for Wort, and I couldn't leave until I knew she was permanently safe. I also had to ensure Crane made it back home and that Dawn and Crystal were protected.

I stepped off the bridge, heartened when a breeze rippled the water and blew a burst of relief in my direction. But then I paused. It'd brought something else, too, something rotten. The scent of death goose-pimpled my flesh. That's when I noticed the sign attached to the cement arch.

LITANI RAILROAD BRIDGE

Where Benny's body had been found, according to the newspaper article.

I started to back away in quick, jerky steps. I'd made it only a few feet when a sound beneath the bridge caught my attention. It was coming from behind the fieldstone pylon nearest me, not more than twenty feet away. I stiffened.

The noise repeated. I recognized it as the scraping of rock. I was poised to run when a body stumbled backward out of the pylon's shadow.

A child.

Michelle.

I gasped and ran toward her. "Michelle!" I screamed.

She whirled, falling in the process. She'd lost her glasses, had cockle-burs in her hair, and her bare arms and legs were swollen with bugbites and sunburn. Her eyes were wild, and this close, I could see that she still had part of a single braid tied with a ribbon, though the rest of her hair was a mad tangle. But she was whole, and alive.

She fell and crab-walked backward to get away from me.

I stepped closer. "Michelle, it's me! Frankie." But that was not the name I'd given her that day. "Francesca, I mean. You beat me up a few days ago!"

Her face didn't show recognition, but there must have been some-thing in my voice, because she stopped trying to escape and charged at me, wrapping one skinny arm around my waist. The other she used to point into the murky dark under the bridge, toward where the smell was the strongest.

I turned in that direction, and I could see what had escaped my view earlier, when I'd stuck to the high ground so I could walk onto the bridge. But from this angle, there was no missing it: jean-clad legs, a heavy bronze belt buckle catching the sun.

If I walked closer, I bet I would have seen a wolf carved on that belt buckle, and if I let my eyes travel up, past the bare belly spattered with reddish muck, toward whatever was left of the dark, terrible troll under the bridge, I'd never sleep again.

CHAPTER 41

I don't remember much of the walk back to the trailer park, only that we didn't make it even close before someone recognized Michelle and called for Chief Mike. An ambulance showed up and whisked Michelle away. I don't remember describing what I saw under the bridge, but I heard the police cars screaming in that direction and then there was Mom, smiling brittlely in her white work blouse and brown skirt with matching brown sandals.

She hustled me into her car.

I could tell she was aching to drive to the bridge, to claim her front row seat.

But she didn't. She drove me home, wrapped a blanket around me and set me up on the couch, and began puttering in the kitchen. Was it lunchtime? Dinner? How could there be food after what I'd seen?

When the phone rang, she leaped at it, had it cradled to her ear before the echo of the first ring faded. She stretched the cord to its limit to take the call in her bedroom, but I could hear her excited whispers.

When she came out much later, her face was grim, determined. "Michelle is insisting she ran away. She said she came across Sly's body accidentally and that he was already good and dead. The coroner is doing a full exam. It'll be difficult to be certain in this heat, but his best guess right now is that Sly's been dead for less than twenty-four hours."

When I didn't respond, she made an irritated noise and returned to the kitchen, clanking pots and pans, running water. "Not that you asked, but Michelle is going to be fine," she called out. "Malnourished and dehydrated, but we'll get her up to snuff and then really start asking the questions."

But I'd seen Michelle's eyes. She was not going to be fine, not that quickly—if ever. I heard the rattle of a cupboard being opened and closed, followed by the sound of a lid popping. I stood and walked to the kitchen.

"I hope you're hungry!" she said, catching sight of me. She was pouring a jar of white sauce into a pan. "We're having chicken Alfredo."

She was acting like a normal mother. A TV mom.

"Crane Zloduk is my friend."

Her mask slipped for a moment, but she stapled it right back into place. "He's dangerous," she said, her smile stiff but intact. "Even more so now that Sly's out of the picture."

"Crane isn't dangerous. It's not fair to say that when you don't even know him." My voice started out as a low buzz, but it was growing. "You can't punish *everyone*, you know. You're not God."

Her face blazed for a moment, and then in a shocking move, she hurled the half-empty Alfredo sauce jar at the wall. It exploded a few feet from my head, glops of white trailing down the wall. "Don't ever tell me what I can do."

I'd thrown up my hands to shield my face. I dropped them, balling them into fists.

I'd raised my voice before—from the sidelines of a soccer game, when June and I were singing as loud as we could, to catch Dad's attention when he was almost in his car and I realized he'd forgotten his lunch.

But I'd never *yelled* at someone.

I hollered now, advancing on Mom as I did. "Don't have a cat. Don't have a friend. Don't care when your mom rips a tooth out of your head. Don't feel like a piece of crap when your mom doesn't want to see you for seven years!"

Spit flew out of my mouth, flecking her face, and I didn't care. My throat burned, and I wasn't done. "Did you even think about me all this time? Really *think* of what I was going through? Having to take care of Dad all by myself? Getting two lousy cards a year from you? Not having a mom?"

My chest was heaving. I wanted to keep yelling but couldn't think of anything more to say.

Mom wiped some spit off her cheek and spoke calmly through tight lips. "What was I supposed to do? You asked to live with your dad. You always liked him best."

"What?"

She leaned against the counter but misjudged the distance, falling off balance for a moment. She was trying to appear in charge, but I'd rattled her. Good. Except, I suddenly felt jittery and empty at the same time. I squeezed my hands into fists to hide their shaking. I'd done it again, the thing I'd been desperate not to do. I'd made my mom so mad that she was going to kick me out, and this time I had nowhere else to go.

"Your dad and I sat you down during the divorce and asked you who you wanted to live with. You said your dad. You didn't even pause."

My forehead furrowed. I didn't remember that conversation, but even if I had, who lets a five-year-old make those sorts of decisions? "You could have invited me here for summers."

She pushed off the counter, jabbing her finger in my face. "But I couldn't. Because you told me you hated me that day when I pulled your tooth."

I shook my head and stared at the yellow linoleum floor, trying to peer through the clouds of time. I'd been smelling my perm, thinking of Barbie doll pee, eating my Cookie Crisp. She'd shown up, yanked the tooth, my mouth had filled with blood.

"I want my dad!" I'd screamed.

She'd backed away, right up toward the kitchen sink she stood in front of now.

"I'm sorry." Had her voice quavered?

And then it came flooding back, what I'd said next.

"I hate you!" I'd screamed. *"I hate it here! I want to go home!"*

Recalling the whole memory carved me raw. "I was a *little kid*," I said.

"Yes, well," she said, pressing her lips together tightly.

She wasn't going to apologize. She certainly wasn't going to hug me, because she couldn't do for me what no one had done for her.

"I killed him," I said, my voice a hundred years old.

She'd been turning toward the sink. She whirled back. "What?"

"Dad. I killed him."

A look of discomfort traveled across her face, like she'd felt a cramp. She tossed her head to shake it off. "You didn't. It was his heart defect. It finally caught up with him. I read the medical report."

That's what everyone thought. I rubbed my face. I'd tried. "May I go to my room?"

"Of course," she said, her voice overwarm. "Don't worry. I'll clean up the mess."

I nodded and walked out of the kitchen. I'd forgotten for a moment that Wort wouldn't be waiting for me in my bedroom. Being reminded broke my heart all over again.

CHAPTER 42

I must have fallen asleep, because the next thing I knew, it was dark and my stomach was growling. I blinked at the dimness of my room, trying to get my bearings. What had woken me? Then I heard it, Mom's voice, raised. I stood, rubbing my eyes with the pads of my thumbs, and stepped out of my bedroom.

"*None* of it?" she shrieked into the phone. "*No* visual evidence? The photos? Movies? All gone?"

She grew quiet while the person on the other end of the line spoke. Her next sentence sliced through the air, serrated, each word frighteningly enunciated. "What about the cascading arrests, then?"

Her shoulders relaxed as she heard something that must have made her happy. "Good. At least you didn't goat-rope that."

She jabbed the hang-up button without saying goodbye and dialed another number immediately. "News desk, please," she said. A few seconds of silence, then: "Whoever's working the night shift. This is Carver County prosecutor Linda Jubilee."

Pause, forced chuckle. "Yes, I'll hold."

She hummed while she waited. We stood like that for a few minutes, her rocking and making music under her breath, me lurking in the hallway and trying to keep my empty stomach from exposing me. Finally, someone must have picked up on the other end.

"In the flesh," she said in response to them. "And I have a doozy of a story." Pause. "No, better than that." Her good mood was back, and then some. "Not exclusive, no. That wouldn't be fair. But if a scandal that'll make the McMartin case in California look like a walk in the park interests you, then you'll want to listen up."

My gasp drew her attention. She turned, eyes narrowing as she spotted me down the hall. "I'll have to call you back, Sam."

She hung up the phone. "You slept through dinner. I worked hard on it."

"I'm sorry," I said. We wouldn't be talking about the fight, then. "I didn't mean to."

"You'll have to heat it up, but it won't be very good. Not after it's gone cold."

I couldn't think of anything to say except to apologize again, so I kept my lips pressed together.

She switched topics. "I need you to dress up tomorrow. Your best clothes. The cords and blouse you wore to dinner at Clara's should work. Be ready by eight a.m."

The idea of wearing long pants in this heat made me miserable in advance. "Where are we going?"

"Nowhere," she said, her smile returning. "They're coming to us."

"Who?"

But I knew.

She'd called reporters.

Crane had been right about everything.

"Never you mind. I need to go back to the office for a bit," she said, reaching for a slip of paper near the telephone. "Don't wait up. And don't go out at night. There are still monsters hiding out there."

I nodded, but watching her grab her purse and head into the garage, a bright smile lighting her jack-o'-lantern face, I knew monsters lived out in the open. They lived right inside our homes.

CHAPTER 43

The next morning, seven reporters gathered in the yard, hanging on Mom's every word as she thanked them for coming and then launched into a recap of the Zloduk case, angling to establish her credibility. The reporters' outfits reminded me of California clothes. It wasn't a completely different animal from what people wore in Litani—a shirt is a shirt, and slacks are slacks—but was different enough. The colors were brighter, the cuts trendier.

Two of the reporters held tape recorders in one hand and huge microphones in the other, thrusting them toward Mom's mouth. The other five scribbled on notepads. I stood next to Mom, feeling like a big scab in my stiff clothes. She had her arm around me. I was the prop.

I'd been silent, but when I ran my hand under my nose, the only female reporter smiled warmly at me.

"Mrs. Jubilee," she said to Mom, who'd paused for a breath, "your daughter is beautiful. What's her name?"

"Francesca," Mom said. She squeezed my shoulder and smiled down at me. I wanted to tell these people that I did not even know her. That I wished I were living with my father, but I'd killed him, so here I was under a roof with a woman who thought it a good idea to hold a press conference on her lawn while people were hurting children.

But I was a microscopic bug clutching a tiny leaf in a massive storm, and all I could do was hang on.

"Do you think the child should hear this?" a reporter wearing a baseball cap asked. I decided I liked him.

"Isn't that part of the problem?" Mom asked sharply. "That we don't talk honestly with our children? They need to know what they're up against. We should give children the same respect we give adults, and we should *always* believe them."

The hypocrisy was staggering. I wouldn't in a million years have said something, but I couldn't help myself from coughing. Mom squeezed my shoulder again, but as a warning this time.

"Then let's get to it," a reporter wearing aviator sunglasses said.

"Yes, let's," Mom said, her eyes glittering. "The Litani Police Department and Carver County Prosecutor's Office have worked in tandem to uncover an unfortunate and widespread outbreak of Satan worshipping and child sexual abuse in Litani. It's no secret that one of the alleged perpetrators is dead—"

"Murder or suicide?" the sunglassed man asked, interrupting.

Mom's eyebrows arched. "We're awaiting autopsy results. As of now we have seventeen children in a safe house—"

The female reporter's eyes went wide, and a few of the men blanched.

"And five adults have been arrested."

"Including Victor and Eula Vogler this morning?" one of the reporters asked.

The reporter wearing the baseball cap turned on him. "Where'd you hear that?"

"I guess *People* magazine hasn't cornered the market on scoops," he said, grinning. "I got pictures of the arrest, too."

People magazine? Here in Litani? Mom's button must have been busting with pride, having orchestrated all this. She'd mentioned cascading arrests on the phone last night. The Voglers being put in custody was surely part of it. Pure spectacle.

"This seems to be shaping itself into another Zloduk case," the *People* reporter said. "Is that what you're suggesting?"

"Even worse," Mom said. A couple of the reporters flinched, but she didn't notice. "This is not contained to a family. It stretches to the farthest reaches of this town. We expect another half dozen arrests in the next few days."

She aimed her next words toward the largest camera. "We are absolutely heartbroken here in Litani. But given the potential reach of the abuse, the police are now going door-to-door to question children to see who else has been molested."

Just like I'd gone door-to-door for the time capsule. I rubbed my neck, which was already damp from the humidity. Today was going to be another relentlessly hot day. When would this weather break?

"It's horrifying, awful, and it's moving fast," Mom said. "We believe the Blue Waters trailer park is the epicenter of the abuse."

"Eradicate it," one of the reporters said.

Mom nodded.

My throat grew tight. Crane lived at the trailer park. And Theresa and her husband and kids. The trailer park wasn't the problem.

A lot more questions were tossed at Mom, and she caught each one of them and lobbed a few back. She said she couldn't comment on specifics but that there was a scourge in Litani, a terrible plague that no one was safe from.

"This town is my family," she said dramatically, repeating a version of what she'd said to me last night. Maybe she'd been rehearsing. "I am not going to rest until every child is safe."

"How *are* you protecting the children?" the female reporter asked, interrupting Mom for the second time. The men had cut off Mom, too, but it seemed to burn her extra hard when the lady did it. "The ones who've been abused as well as the ones who haven't."

Mom was scowling. "The children who've been hurt have all been moved to foster homes. As to the town, we have a curfew in place."

Again, news to me.

"That's one thing I'd like you to spread the word about," Mom said, finding her pace again. "Evening patrols will travel through town to enforce the curfew. But it's important to note that what we're dealing with isn't strangers snatching children. If it was, I'd never let my daughter out of my sight. What we have here is parents and friends of the family abusing their own kids under their own roofs. We believe we know all the people involved and so the problem is finally contained. I will be releasing names soon."

As I watched her, I wondered if anyone in real life had parents who did the right thing. Maybe we were all pretending. There were more questions and my mom's responses in her almost gloating attitude, but nothing new popped up. Litani was hell. The adults who were supposed to protect us were the ones hurting us. That was the gist.

"When are you going to trial?" the *People* reporter asked Mom.

"You know me," she said, too casually, like we were a group of friends talking about a high school football game. "I never go to court until I have the case locked up. We're gathering the last of the evidence, and once we have that, I'll push for the trials to start immediately. I'm happy to report, however, that we have a witness who can connect what's happening now to the previous Zloduk case."

Alarm crawled across my skin. Was the new person Crane? If so, what had my mom said or done to get him to agree to testify now when he wouldn't before? I needed to ask him myself.

The reporters were beginning to shift, talking to each other, dispersing the attention away from Mom. The press conference had been going on for over twenty minutes, and Mom hadn't really trotted out any specifics.

"I'm also in contact with the FBI," she said, clearly relishing this bit she'd saved for last. "We're going to see about dragging the river for bodies."

That got the reporters buzzing, a new round of questions shoved at her.

For a disorienting moment, I'd thought she was talking about Benny, but then she clarified.

"Several of the children who've been abused claim to have seen a child murdered and tossed in the river as part of a game they were forced to play. While there are no Litani children missing"—*anymore,* I thought to myself—"we plan to search the river out of an abundance of caution."

Once she had their attention again, Mom reiterated that at this point they still had no hard evidence of children being murdered, only accusations, and she was not going to file charges until they did, but those hedges didn't matter. The journalists were already talking about booking motel rooms to ride this out. When Mom called her show to a close, they couldn't hurry away fast enough. I assumed they were going to call in with the news they had so far.

My guts felt like they'd been pickled. "Excuse me, ma'am?" I said to my mom, playing my role of dutiful child even though the reporters were out of earshot. I hadn't used my voice yet this morning, and it was scratchy.

"Yes, dear?" She was still in Fake Mom mode.

"I'd like to get right back on it with the time capsule work. I think it's important that we keep things on a positive note as all this is happening." Sometimes it's okay to play somebody else's game if you're doing it to protect someone. Like yourself. And I needed to get away from Mom and check in on Crane in equal measure.

"Fine," she said, glancing toward the retreating reporters. She was probably wishing she could call them back so they could hear my suggestion, proving how much community spirit we had. But they were too far away. "Just be home for supper."

"I will."

CHAPTER 44

I found Crane at his trailer, but he refused to talk about when exactly he'd been released and what had happened to him at the police station. He didn't want to talk at all and just kept stroking Wort, his face sealed as tight as an envelope.

The next week felt like living inside an extended funeral. Whispering. Chaos. Frayed nerves. Everyone being *extra nice*, no one sure of the rules. Crane didn't want to canvass with me anymore, and when I dropped by to visit him and Wort before or after, he was as talkative as a potato. The only bright spot in either of our days was the kitten, who I was jealous to admit loved living with Crane. She had free rein of the whole place.

The time capsule gig wasn't going well, and not only because I had to do it alone. I hadn't exactly been popular before, but people wouldn't even crack the door for me now. I could see them peeking from behind their drapes and then letting them drop when they recognized me. I didn't take it too hard, but it made it difficult to gather information. I was tempted to fill out the surveys myself, but that would have been dishonest.

And boring.

The only time I took it personal was when I spotted Patty at the grocery store. When she saw me coming, she turned as pale as a root and beat cheeks in the other direction. She knew me firsthand, and I thought I'd done a good job sitting Cathy and the twins. Maybe it was just that nobody wanted to be caught with a kid anymore, and especially a kid related to Linda Jubilee. They were too worried she'd have them arrested.

When I wasn't gathering data for the time capsule or playing with Wort while Crane ignored me, I was at Theresa's, where things were halfway normal. It grew to where I didn't even mind her kids so much. It just felt good to be around someone who acted like a mom. She fed me cookies and Kool-Aid and chattered about all sorts of things— harmless gossip, her dream of opening a hair salon, stuff of that flavor— everything but what was happening in Litani. The closest she came to mentioning Mom's growing case was when she talked about how hard it was to find parking downtown with all the reporters descended like locusts.

And then another time when she told me she was worried for Crane.

"Your mom is out to get that boy," she said, cutting sugar cookie circles from the tube. "He's the one who messed up her perfect record when he wouldn't testify."

I was gnawing on a ball of cookie dough she'd given me. "That sounds like something she'd definitely be mad about."

❖

I took a bag of those cinnamon-sugar-dusted cookies to Crane's with the intention of playing with Wort. I'd hoped that today would finally be the day Crane would open up to me again, but he wasn't home when I arrived. His absence reminded me how little I knew about him. Was he emancipated, like a high school boy June and I knew who supposedly had his own apartment, or was I the only one who knew he didn't have a grown-up living with him? If he worked, where, and why had I never seen a car? If he didn't work, where'd he spend his days when he wasn't home?

He had given me a key to his place, at least, after making me promise to use it only to visit Wort when he wasn't around. When I unlocked the door and stepped in, she charged up to me, and if there's something that makes you happier than a kitty bouncing sideways at you, I didn't know it. I played with her until she fell asleep, and then I checked her water and food. Full. Her litter box, empty. Where was Crane?

I wasn't yet ready to wander home, so I pulled out The Book and the botany text I'd also packed. The way I saw it, there were two people in my life really crying out to have their plant personalities sketched: Crane and my mom.

I checked my mood: crabby, uneasy.

I would sketch my mom.

I'd known since that press conference what her plant personality was, but I'd held off on creating it in case I was being unfair. My surroundings had changed, but her plant personality hadn't, so I figured I might as well get to it.

The plant I had in mind was legendary in the botany community, spoken of in hushed whispers. Dad said it was one of those plants whose worst effects were also its strongest benefits. Specifically, the xanthotoxin found in its edible roots treated skin disorders, but the same toxin in the sap caused an allergic reaction on the cellular level, resulting in temporary but excruciatingly painful photosensitivity in any mammal it touched.

Sounded right to me.

CHOOSE YOUR OWN PLANT PERSONALITY
YOU'RE CAPTAIN OF YOUR OWN DESTINY!
WHICH PLANT PERSONALITY DO YOU CHOOSE?

WILD PARSNIP

Your roots are deep and sweet, but they're not worth the pain.
Because the slightest brush against you, changes someone's DNA.

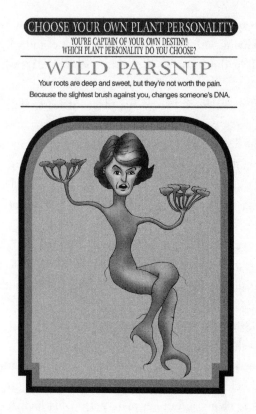

It wasn't very generous, but science was about making facts, not friends, which was *not* something my dad used to say, but I was sure he'd agree. When I'd put the finishing touches on Mom's plant personality and Crane still hadn't returned, I figured it was time to head home. I locked up and took my time, scraping my feet along the sidewalk, lost in memories of my old life. That's why I didn't immediately notice the handful of reporters outside Mom's house.

"Francesca Jubilee!"

I whipped my head up. I thought it was one of the male reporters from the press conference Mom'd held last week, but from fifty feet away they all looked alike.

"Is that Linda Jubilee's daughter?"

242

"It sure is," the guy said, striding toward me. He was definitely the *People* magazine reporter.

I cringed.

Another journalist ran up to me, hoisting one of those big old microphones, bigger than a banana, and shoved it in my face, a cameraman on his heels. "What can you tell us about the latest news? Have you heard the mayor is being arrested for hosting satanic parties?"

I couldn't collect myself fast enough. Mom was arresting spaghetti-dinner Clara? My face showed shock, and they jumped all over it.

"Who is your mom going to arrest next?" asked the same female reporter from before.

I wished I could give her an answer, not only for her but for me.

"Is it true what they're saying about the elementary school principal?"

I dropped my head and raced into the house.

The phone was ringing when I stepped inside, which was a rarity. Sure, Mom was always calling people, but people rarely called our house. Its relentless vibration reminded me of a ticking bomb. I couldn't stand for it to continue shrieking, so I snatched it up.

"Hello?"

"Frankie! What is going on up there? My mom said she heard about your mom on the news!"

"June?" It was disorienting hearing her voice in the middle of all this craziness. She sounded so normal. "You heard about Litani all the way in California?"

"Are there really Satan worshippers murdering kids there?"

Her voice had an eagerness that I didn't like. "I haven't seen any."

"You must be terrified, Frankie. It's even worse than you said."

"I can't talk right now," I told her. "There's reporters outside." While true, I'd said it in a way that made her think they wanted to talk to me. Which I suppose they did, but I'd said it as an excuse to get off the phone. The chasm between my past life and my current one was officially too wide, and I didn't belong in either of them.

"You can call me anytime. You know that, don't you?"

"Thanks, June."

I rested the phone in the cradle and looked around. Mom wasn't home, of course. I wasn't hungry, either. I strode into her office. I didn't even bother sneaking this time. What else could she take away from me? She'd gotten rid of Motherwort, and it wouldn't be long until she arrested Crane for good, if she hadn't already.

But once inside her office, I looked at the neat file cabinets and realized I didn't care about any of her work files. I wanted to know the personal stuff. I stormed into her bedroom. Her bed was unmade, clothes dashed over the furniture, shoes out of the closet, dirty dishes by her bedside. She was prim perfect on the exterior, but I was finally looking at her behind the scenes.

For the first time, I wondered what it must have been like to have a daughter dropped on her. Her perfect life upset. Somebody always at her house, somebody she needed to worry about.

Well, at least somebody she *should* worry about.

I trailed my fingers over the spines on the bookshelf, pausing at the framed photo of her and my dad and the third woman I now recognized as Darlene. I grabbed it off the shelf, touching my cheek to the image of my father, a lump forming in my throat. Then I flipped it over to check for a date. One of the fasteners was loose. I pushed it and removed the backing. There was a letter inside. It was dated August 1, 1975. The year my parents had divorced. The smear on the front and its ghost-blue color told me it was a carbon copy. The letter was short.

> Dear Paul: if you contest the divorce, or worse, if you
> tell people I was cheating, I will tell people you abused
> Frankie. Don't test me.

It was unsigned, but that made no difference. Only my mother would write a letter like that and hang on to a copy.

I wasn't safe anywhere.

CHAPTER 45

I didn't stop by Theresa's to pick up my paperwork the next morning. There didn't seem to be any point, since the few people who'd answer their door had dwindled down to zero. I might drop by later to visit with her, but for now, I had a different mission, one I'd woken up with: I needed to talk to Dawn.

Anxiety plucked at my nerves as I neared the Victorian house. It was imposing from the outside. Who knew what lay inside? An adult who wouldn't let me pass, who would snitch to my mom that I'd come by? Broken children, weeping and rocking themselves?

I steeled my spine and walked up the steps. The front porch was clean, not a toy or a plant in sight. I knocked on the front door for a full two minutes, hearing voices inside. When no one answered, I gathered my nerve and walked in like I belonged.

"Frankie Jubilee!" Dawn hollered. She stood in the middle of a great room, high atop an ottoman, holding a broomstick like a scepter, a cape-blanket tied around her neck. She was surrounded by a bunch of kids, maybe a dozen, all of them pretending she was their queen. Some stood in a line behind her, others were bowing near her feet, still others were offering her trays of Ritz crackers.

I had to admire her style. The kid was a natural-born leader.

"What are you doing here?" Michelle asked from a nearby couch, pushing her thick glasses up. Other than peeling skin on her nose and a few healing scratches on her crossed legs, you couldn't tell from looking what a horrible ordeal she'd been through. Crystal was braiding Michelle's hair. Along with Dawn, they were the only kids I recognized.

I rubbed my arms, my flesh goose-pimpling despite the heat. Each kid in the room had been abused.

"I came to talk to Dawn."

"I'll tell you what I told the reporters," Dawn declared from atop her dais. "About the murders, and the blood we drank in the name of Satan."

"All hail Satan," the other kids chimed in, some of them giggling.

I might not have been good with kids, but I knew enough to recognize when they were playing. What else would a houseful of children left to their own devices do? Speaking of . . . "Whose house is this?"

"Her name is Grandma Jenny," Dawn said, flipping her cape over a shoulder like a superhero. "She went to the grocery store. She'll be back any minute, and she will *not* like that you're here."

Then I'd better hurry. "So there really were murders?"

"Murders and eating babies," a blond boy no older than seven called out.

"And they made me kick my dog!" another boy said.

"They sold my sister to devil worshippers," hollered a third.

All the kids were nodding, talking over each other, trying to tell me the worst thing possible. It hurt to hear, even though I could tell a lot of it was made up, each of them trying to outdo the others. It couldn't have been good to have all of them housed together like this.

I was growing dizzy trying to take it all in.

"That's enough, my loyal subjects!" Dawn proclaimed. "Bring me my holy smokes. I must speak with Princess Frankie alone."

A lighter appeared, followed by a pack of Eve Slims. Dawn took both, stepped imperiously off her throne, and led the way outside. She closed the door behind us after ordering the kids to leave us alone, then flopped down on the porch swing and lit up.

"How's it hanging?" she asked. Her hair was unusually clean and glossy, her eyes clear, but there was pain behind them. Or maybe it was fear. I kept forgetting she was only ten years old.

"How much of that was true?" I jabbed my thumb toward the house. "About the murders? And Satan?"

She shrugged and took a puff that didn't travel far down her lungs. "Hard to know. Some of us had to have sex a bunch of times. Other kids just got touched. Mostly now, though, we're letting off some steam. The reporters love that crap, the wilder the better. Stories for smokes. One of them even took my picture and told me I'm going to be in the *National Enquirer*! Well, they're going to blot out my face, but I'll know it's me. Can you believe it?"

"You shouldn't lie to them."

She snorted. "Oh, so you tell the truth all the time? What does that get you exactly? Anyway, I told the truth about Sly, and look how that turned out. I have to live in a house with a bunch of booger eaters and some old lady who's always at church or cooking us slop. I don't even get to see my mom."

I thought of the Darlene dandelion sketch.

"Did she know what Sly was doing to you?" I asked softly.

Dawn slumped, her neck turtling into her shoulders. "How about we talk about *your* mom? Why hasn't she arrested all the people who did this?"

"Are you being serious? She's arrested half the town."

Dawn sucked angrily at her cigarette, and the smoke must have reached the tender part of her because she started coughing. "Not the one who's running it," she said, swiping cough-tears from her eyes. "The one who made those movies with us in the brewery before the police started searching back there."

"Sly's dead," I said.

"Duh," she responded, rolling her eyes. "I'm not talking about him."

"Victor and Eula, then?" I asked. "Because they were arrested a week ago."

"Naw, not Victor and Eula."

"Then who?" This was the information I'd come for, but I didn't know if I could bear to hear the answer.

"You'll have to ask your mom, cuz I'm not telling. He's still out there. I don't want him popping me like he did Sly if I start flapping my gums."

"Please," I said, my voice cracking.

She stared at me. "You really don't know?"

I swallowed a piece of myself. "Is it Crane?"

She squinted at me, Eve Slim halfway to her mouth. "What?"

"Is Crane the leader? Is he . . . hurting kids?"

The sun was cooking the grass on the other side of the porch railing, making the air hurt to breathe, making it impossible to hide. Dawn's silence was unbearable. She was staring at me, expression unreadable.

Finally, to my unspeakable relief, she guffawed. "No way. That pansy ass? He wouldn't hurt a mosquito. He's the one who tried to keep Sly and the rest off us, but it's like chasing water because they just came back."

I nodded, my relief so great that I was unable to speak. *Crane's goodness was real.*

"Frankie?"

I'd gotten deep in my own head and almost forgotten Dawn was there. "Yeah?"

"Will you still be my friend? Even though I played The Game?"

I looked into her wide brown eyes, her face so close that I could see those dusty freckles on her button nose. Her words reminded me of what Crane had said.

Don't throw me away.

Well, I'd come prepared. I held up the paper sack I'd brought. I reached inside and pulled out my favorite pair of Converse. "Yep. And these are yours now. Forever."

CHAPTER 46

I had passed the Litani library on my way to the grocery store the day I'd found Wort, then a bunch of times canvassing for the time capsule. I'd first meant to research my dad there, but after what Mom and the others had told me, I'd lost my stomach for it.

I wasn't going to hide from the details anymore.

The library was nearly empty as I walked in. The elderly, sour-faced librarian glanced at me and then returned to reading the book she had open on the counter. There'd been something in her eyes, something tight, but she'd averted them before I could name it. I strolled to the newspaper rack first, seven different papers hanging from wooden poles like laundry on a line. The Litani paper was nearest, and its front-page headline screamed at me.

Witch Hunt Underway, No One in Town Is Safe

I plucked the paper off the rack and skimmed it. Clara Swenson, town mayor and the woman whose bacon bits had so intimidated Chad, had indeed been taken in for questioning. Same with four people identified as teachers and two more referred to as "administrative members of Litani Elementary and Middle School." Some of the people questioned had been released, some of them not. I returned the newspaper to the rack, my chest heavy, and gripped the *Star and Tribune*. That headline was much darker.

Satan Worshippers Take Over Bedroom Community

That seemed like a poor choice of words, but then again, I wasn't sure what a bedroom community was. The *Chicago Tribune* reported something similar. Probably every newspaper headline in the country did. But as timely as that information was, it wasn't what I'd come for. I put the newspapers back and approached the librarian's desk.

I made what I hoped was a polite *hmm hmm* sound. She kept reading for a bit longer, for what felt like a whole year, before glancing at me over the top of her glasses.

"Yes?" she asked.

"Can I please have the microfiche for the Litani newspaper archives?"

"What years?"

I hadn't been prepared for that. I hadn't thought there would be more than one. "All of them?"

She sniffed disapprovingly and then disappeared into the back room, returning with two small canisters. I hardly thought that was enough to earn a huffy noise, but I had bigger fish to fry.

"Thank you," I said. "Where are the microfiche machines?"

Her eyes pointed to the far window, her mouth as tight as a coin purse. There were bookshelves hiding whatever was back there, but given that the library was a single room, I was confident I could figure it out.

Sure enough, a single microfiche machine rested on a table kitty-corner from the front desk. No one was at it, either. I'd read the canister labels on the way over. One was marked LITANI FREE PRESS **1932–1959**, the other LITANI FREE PRESS **1960–CURRENT**.

I was primarily here to learn about what my grandpa had done to my mom, not from her mouth but from an unbiased source. I figured the only way out of this mess was to get to the beginning of the thread and start unknotting it there. My mother had been born in 1948, same as my dad. If my grandpa had hurt her as she'd said, and it happened before 1960, she would've been twelve. Might as well try that route first, even though it was a long shot.

I popped the canister open and threaded the microfiche into the machine. Dad and I had visited the UC library plenty of times, him hot on the trail of plant information, me his loyal assistant, so I was familiar with how it worked. I began by searching for Mom's maiden name in the index. I knew it was Rosewood from the divorce papers. While I wasn't feeling particularly lucky these days, I was grateful that it wasn't something like Hansen or Johnson.

Unfortunately, there were no Rosewoods indexed in the first reel. On a hunch, I tried Zloduk. I got two matches right away, both referring to Zloduk Construction. I skimmed the articles, each about a new project the construction company was going to undertake. The first project was the remodel of the brewery, which must've fallen through since the 1954 announcement. The second article exclaimed the wonderful news that Zloduk Construction had won the bid to build the very library I stood inside right now.

Reading that gave me the willies, like maybe there was still a ghost here.

More interesting than the text of either article, though, was the image accompanying the brewery piece. Looking at it brought a cold sweat. The photo featured Wagner Zloduk, front and center. The image was a fuzzy black-and-white, but he was an ordinary-looking man, one with a too-big nose. He had his arm draped around Josiah Rosewood, according to the caption. Given his age, and the way he was short like me and my mom, plus how he had her deep-set eyes, Josiah Rosewood was most certainly my grandpa. In addition to their names, the caption provided a glowing sentence about how their two construction firms were uniting on this project, though Josiah Rosewood's involvement hadn't been enough to warrant mention beyond the caption, which must not have been indexed.

My grandpa knew Wagner Zloduk.

Knew him well, judging by their body language in the photo, the two men leaning on each other and grinning like old friends. I pulled out a clean notebook I'd brought—no way was I going to tarnish The Book with the information I uncovered here—and scribbled down this new fact.

Once I got my bearings, I returned to the *Litani Free Press* 1932–1959 index. I didn't find anything else that looked promising. Even so, I skimmed the whole reel, going as fast as I could while still being able to read the headlines, even though the speed gave me vertigo. Nothing of interest.

I clicked that reel out and inserted the one starting at 1960. This one contained three Rosewood mentions. From the cross-indexing, it appeared the first was about Josiah Rosewood's construction business closing and the third about Linda Jubilee (née Rosewood) becoming the Carver County prosecutor.

The second knocked the wind out of me.

Community Scion Josiah Rosewood Accused of Raping His Daughter

"Hurt" and "abuse" were bad, but they were vague. "Rape" was real clear.

My grandpa had raped my mom.

The article was mostly an interview with Mom where she revealed the abuse had started when she was five and continued until she went to the police at age eighteen with "incontrovertible evidence." I was almost glad not to know what that was. As a result of Mom's testimony, Josiah was successfully tried and sent away to prison in Stillwater. For all I knew, he was still there.

I felt a surge of pride in my mom for putting him away. It was quickly replaced by fear for what it had driven her to do since. I needed to deal with this like a scientist, though: look at the facts, form a hypothesis. I wrote down the new information and returned to the index for my secondary search, this for any appearance of the names McSorley, Petoskey, Jubilee, Sickhaus, or White, the last names besides Rosewood that I knew had been at the river the day Benny drowned.

Two popped up.

The first was about the drowning, and I'd expected that. Ronnie had handed me a copy of that article himself. The second was dated two years before Benny's death. The headline was innocuous enough.

Zloduk Hires Local Teenagers to Construct City Library

Below that was a picture of a baby-faced Mike Sickhaus and Ronnie McSorley digging ground for the library. They were both wearing hard hats, grinning, hamming it up for the photo. The article talked about Mike's dream of being in law enforcement, but Ronnie thought a future in construction might be just the ticket for him. And how about that, both of their dreams had come true. But what deal with the devil had they made in the years between this article and today?

There was no mention of the Voglers in the index, and I was fine with that. I'd found what I'd come for. Ronnie and Chief Mike had worked with Wagner Zloduk, as had my grandpa. My grandpa had raped my mom, and it sounded like he had been after her all through high school, which meant she was in the thick of the abuse even that day by the river when Benny had drowned. Then, when she turned eighteen, something gave her the courage to testify against her dad and put him away.

My hypothesis was beginning to take shape.

The only thing left to do was find out what I could about Satan.

It was such a foolish thought to have and an even sillier thing to search for that I glanced around to make sure no one was watching. Dad had been an agnostic, which meant I was too. You couldn't believe in Satan if you didn't believe in God. But if Satan was making actual headlines, the scariest of them pointing toward Litani, Minnesota, then the scientist in me said it was necessary to research.

I discovered two mentions of Satan—one name, like Cher, or Sting—in the index. The first was an article printed a month before Benny's death. It said that "Satan-worshipping materials" had been found in the abandoned Engle Brewery. The police chief at the time assumed it was kids acting out, burning candles and sketching pentagrams and the like, as a result of too much exposure to "reefer and un-Christian movies."

The next article was more recent. It'd been published three weeks before I'd moved to Litani and was eerily similar in content to the first. It appeared that again, pentagrams, candles, scissors, and knives were turning up in the old brewery.

"That stuff isn't for kids."

I hopped up so fast that I cracked my knee on the underside of the table. The librarian was standing behind me with crossed arms, her gray bun looking so tight from my angle that it appeared carved from plastic. Someone should have told her she was a stereotype, that she didn't have to embody it, that all the other librarians I'd met had been cool.

"What?" I asked.

She tapped her foot. "Reading about Satan isn't for children," she said. "Kids should hang on to their innocence."

"Then grown-ups should let us." I grabbed my notebook and my knapsack and stormed out of the library without returning the microfiche or thanking her for her time. It felt like a tremendous act of rebellion.

I was still humming from the experience, so at first I didn't let the sight of a police car or the clot of reporters outside my house get me down. Not until the journalists turned from their conversations and raced at me like a pack of hyenas.

"Francesca Jubilee," the nearest reporter called out, his voice breathy with excitement. "What do you know about Theresa Buckle getting arrested for abusing her own children as well as her Sunday school pupils?"

CHAPTER 47

I flew like a rocket into the house. I ripped open the door and charged into Mom's office. With the police car out front, I was not surprised to discover Chief Mike with her. I was shocked he was holding her, though. His mouth was near her neck, his arms wrapped around her waist. When he spotted me, he released her like a bag of toads and stumbled back.

"What are you doing?" I yelled.

Chief Mike had the good grace to blush. Mom looked like she'd been crying, though.

"The chief was comforting me," she said.

"That's not what I meant." My voice was high and shrill, and I knew I sounded like a little kid and that made me even madder. "How could you have arrested Theresa? You're a monster. You have to stop."

To my surprise, she answered with weariness, running a hand through her immaculate hair. "You might be right. None of the hard evidence we were promised has materialized."

"Hard evidence?"

"Movies, pictures, blood, dead bodies. The things the kids in our custody swear happened but apparently left no trace. They said the Voglers had all the visual evidence, but that idiot, Officer Chad, gave Eula and Victor a twenty-four-hour head start before he searched their trailer and Sly's."

"Couldn't get in without a search warrant faster than that," Chief Mike said tightly.

I studied him real close, this man who worked with my mom, who was apparently dating her, if that's what it could be called, who'd been there the day Benny drowned. He was normal looking, possessing the kind of face that would melt into any background. That fuzzy Mr. Kotter hair and sideburns. Blue eyes. An impressive nose, normal lips. A man who carried a gun.

A man who a kid would be scared to tell on.

Mom kept going as if Chief Mike hadn't interrupted her. "The children's stories keep changing. One day it's Satan and abuse, the next day they tell us they were forced to make porn flicks and offer up blood sacrifices. There's no proof of any of it. What if it's all a lie?" Her voice broke.

I'd never seen her like this. Vulnerable.

"We'll find something," Chief Mike said. He reached out to touch her but dropped his arm just shy.

"What if we don't?" she asked, her face etched in despair. "Might as well go tell the press now what a fool I am. I couldn't even find a goddamned tunnel."

My heart beat loudly in my ears. "What?"

Mom and Chief Mike exchanged a look. It was quick and sharp enough to cut paper.

"A few of the kids who were abused said they were blindfolded, driven to a house, and led through a tunnel," Mom said. "We searched Sly's trailer as well as Eula and Victor's place out in the country. No tunnel."

I knew my mouth was open, but I couldn't close it.

"Chief Mike searched every inch of both homes. He even brought out an archaeological X-ray machine. Nothing."

She said some more after that, but I couldn't hear it over the crashing of my blood. I knew who the leader of all this was, the man who'd been in the back room of the factory with Sly and the boy, the man who'd likely murdered Sly.

I'm the best hunter in the county. I can field dress an animal before it hits the ground.

"If you find the tunnel, will you let Theresa go?" I asked, my voice hoarse. "And leave Crane alone?"

"Didn't you hear me?" Mom said, shaking her head. "Chief Mike took a fine-toothed comb to their homes. There are no tunnels beneath them."

"The tunnel isn't underneath a house. It's *inside* one."

❖

After I explained the tunnel's exact location off the McSorley bathroom, Mom and Chief Mike charged out the door, past the reporters, whose questions they ignored, and peeled away with sirens blazing. A few of the quicker journalists took off toward their own vehicles, probably to follow the police car. The ones who stayed behind gazed longingly at the house with me inside, but they didn't dare knock.

I was past tired. I was empty.

I crawled into bed even though it was only late afternoon. I fell asleep wondering about Mom and Chief Mike. Had he been the one she'd been having an affair with, back when she lived in California with Dad and me? It seemed unlikely. I ended up dreaming of long-lashed weasels crawling through underground tubes.

When later I was shaken awake by Mom, the inky blackness outside my window told me I'd been asleep for hours. I was embarrassed that my immediate thought upon waking was that she was there to hug me.

She wasn't.

"We found the tunnel," she said, her voice quick. "Exactly where you said it would be."

"You're going to arrest Patty and Ronnie?" I needed that much at least for Dawn.

She was sitting on the edge of my bed, vibrating with energy. "As soon as we find them. They've taken off with their kids. They won't get far."

"Are you going to let Theresa go?"

Her eyes were so wide that the whites glowed all around her pupils. "We can't let anyone go, not now. If Ronnie and Patty were involved, that means the whole town might be. The *whole town*. I can finally make Litani safe." She swallowed, the noise loud and juicy, and squeezed my leg. "I want to thank you. You're finally on my team. I need to get some sleep now. We'll talk more about it tomorrow, okay?"

I didn't have an answer, but it didn't matter, because she didn't wait for one.

I cried myself back to sleep, not waking up again until the man crawled in through my window and slid one hand over my mouth and the other across my throat.

CHAPTER 48

Ronnie's rough hands around my neck woke me up long enough for me to see his furious, shadowed face, and then the night exploded in silver stars before sliding into black.

I floated in and out of consciousness, noting shapes and colors and muffled bumping and buzzing noises, not sure if they were happening inside my head or out. He'd choked off whatever part of me felt fear, and for that I was grateful. Otherwise, I would have died of terror when we neared what was unmistakably the ruined Engle Brewery.

The buildings loomed so tall they nearly blocked out the moon. He brought me inside like a husband carries a new wife over the doorstep. I stared right up at his face. I could blink all I wanted, but the channel never changed: it was Ronnie.

Once inside the vast factory floor of the brewery, he flicked on a flashlight. He was holding it with the same hand that was near my head, so the light wobbled. He glanced down and spotted my open eyes. He grinned, and for a moment, I saw a demon's mask superimposed over his features.

"They're coming for you," I said. My voice was surprisingly strong.

"I know," he said. Violence pulsed just under his skin, and he was breathing heavily. He'd carried me out of my bedroom, past the playground, through neighborhoods. I hadn't seen a single car or heard a solitary voice.

"If you set me free, they might go easy on you."

What movie had I heard that from? It didn't matter.

He made a quick sound, like a knife sinking into a tire. "They're going to keep me forever once they find those movies; nothing can change that. I'm not sure who has them right now, but it's only a matter of time. Might as well enjoy some fun with the prosecutor's daughter while I'm waiting." He winked at me. "I've had my eye on you for a while. I like 'em snack size."

Amazingly, I still wasn't panicking. I'd read an article in *Scientific American* about how fear is a biological response designed to increase the chance of survival by provoking fight-or-flight instincts. If an animal has no chance of making it, however, fear becomes a negative response, using up the blood and breath needed to prolong the creature's final moments.

So, no fear = no chance.

"Did you hurt kids with the Zloduks?" My voice echoed. He was hauling me toward the rear of the factory. *Where the movies were made.* I could see only as far as the circle of light that surrounded us like a lurid halo. The nighttime intensified the dank, fresh-dug-grave smell.

"Naw," he said, sweat beading at his forehead. It had to have been a lot of work to carry a kid in the sweltering heat. "My dad worked for Wagner. That's where the poison started in this town, with that man. Wagner Zloduk was an honest-to-god Satan worshipper. The real deal."

Honest-to-*god* Satan worshipper. I almost laughed. Had his choking me given me brain damage? "What about my uncle Benny? Did you drown him?"

He ducked, and suddenly the dark surrounding his flashlight intensified, amplifying the smell of salt and fear and urine. We'd entered the office, the manufactured room in the back of the factory that I'd seen Sly walk out of with that poor scared boy. Ronnie dropped me unceremoniously onto the ground. I braced for impact, but something soft caught me.

When he flashed the light on the ground around his feet, I saw it was a dirty mattress surrounded by beer cans and wine cooler bottles, a naked doll lying on its face, condom wrappers. That's when I felt the first tinge of it, an icy terror slithering forward to devour me slowly, from the feet on up.

"Sly fancied himself a Satan worshipper, too," Ronnie said, leaning down. I heard the click of a button followed by the warm yellow glow of a camping lantern. "Brought too much attention to our recreational activities. That on top of losing our movies was enough for me."

He was looming over me, the lantern stretching his shadow.

"Ready or not," he said, leering, his hand going to his belt buckle.

I was drowning now, the lie of shock stepping aside to make way for an ocean of terror. "I miss my dad," I cried. "And I'm the one who killed him."

He'd been reaching for me, but that stopped him cold. His face was slashed with shadow.

"I poisoned him," I said, my hair hanging in my face. It was the truth. I'd killed my dad, and so what was about to happen was my fault. Now that I'd said it out loud, I had nothing left with which to hold back the final, awful memory of what had happened that day.

Total recall came flooding in.

When June showed up that night for a slumber party at Dad's request, she immediately knew something was wrong. I'd kept her at arm's length since the unraveling, keeping secret how bad Dad was getting, but once she saw him, there was no hiding it.

Dad lay on the couch, wrapped in blankets, ashen, his first burst of energy in over a week depleted once I'd assured him I'd invite June over.

She hurried to him, stopping a few feet away. "Are you okay, Mr. Jubilee?"

He smiled his crooked grin. "I am now that you're here, June Bug. Frankie's been doing nothing but taking care of me for days. It'd make this dad feel good if the two of you could watch a movie, pop some of that delicious buttered popcorn you girls make. Be kids. Whaddya say?"

June glanced at me, her voice tight. "You didn't tell me your dad was sick."

"It's not contagious," I said, misreading her concern.

"Dummy." She backed up far enough that she could punch my arm. "That explains why you've been so weird at school. You should have just let me in."

Just like that, I was crying. I glanced over at Dad, but he'd drifted off. June followed my eyes, and then she hugged me.

"It's been so hard." I explained it all, quietly, so as not to wake Dad. She listened to every ugly word. Suddenly things didn't seem so bad.

"We need to get him to the hospital," she said when I'd finished.

"He won't go," I said. "He might visit a regular doctor, though."

"I don't think regular doctors are open this late," she said. "But we could go first thing in the morning. My mom can drive us all."

It felt so good to not be in this alone. "Thanks. You still want to watch a movie tonight?"

She moved her shoulders like her shirt was itching her. "Your dad is sleeping on the couch."

"He usually goes to bed about this time," I lied. The whole day was his bedtime. Having June there put the weirdness since Dad had been laid off into perspective. He'd always been eccentric, but now he was just lost. And worse, seriously sick. Now that June knew, though, it was going to get better. All we had to do was make it through that night, and in the morning we'd bring him to the doctor.

"Really?" June asked.

"You bet," I said, sticking to the lie. I needed it, her being there, us pretending it was normal. He'd been bad for so long, don't you see? I didn't know that night would be different. I didn't know it was his last night. "You hang out in my room while I make sure he's all tucked in. Then we can pop some corn and watch *The Twilight Zone*."

"I'm in," June said, smiling and bouncing into my bedroom.

I closed my door behind her, feeling better than I had since Dad had lost his job. I was no longer alone on struggle island.

Dad was still sleeping. I nudged his shoulder, gently. He was cold.

"Dad," I whispered, the ground opening up to swallow me. "Dad, wake up."

He stirred. "Frankie?"

The whites of his eyes were yellow, the bags beneath them green, his skin so pale it had turned gray. He'd looked like this for days, but with June over, I saw how serious it was. I couldn't wait for tomorrow.

"I'm going to call an ambulance."

He gripped my wrist, his hand cold and dry. "I can't go to the hospital."

"Dad," I said. It came out as a cry.

"One more night," he whispered. "If I'm not feeling better tomorrow . . ."

He trailed off. I shook his shoulder gently.

His eyes flickered. "I just need my medicine, Frankie. That'll get me through the night, and then tomorrow we'll see a doctor."

I felt the tiniest blossom of hope. It would be so much better if he agreed to go in, if we didn't need to force him. "You promise?"

He nodded, weakly.

"Which medicine?"

But he'd slipped back into whatever grayness held him. I ran to the bathroom and found his prescription pills. I'd had to smash them up before and slip them into his mouth, and I would do it again. I had grabbed the mortar and pestle and was grinding the pill into powder when I had a thought. What if he had meant the hawthorn tincture? He'd been ingesting both daily, his beta-blocker in the morning and the tincture at night. Had he taken the tincture yet? June coming over had confused our routine.

June. She was waiting for me.

I so desperately wanted to not worry about Dad for a few hours.

But he needed his medicine. I carried the powder-filled mortar into the kitchen, my breath catching. His favorite tincture bottle had a few drops of hawthorn extract left. Which should I give him? Before I could talk myself out of it, I droppered the extract over the powder and mixed it up into a paste, then dashed into the living room and fed it to Dad.

He woke up halfway through. He smiled and swallowed. "I love you, Frankie Bean."

"I love you too, Dad," I said, tossing worried glances to my bedroom door. What would June think if she walked out and saw how we lived?

Dad's color returned almost immediately, and he stirred enough that I could guide him to bed. This had been our routine nearly every night for over a week. Tonight was the last time I'd have to do it alone, though. Dad had as good as said so, and tomorrow, June's mom would help.

I felt so hopeful as I kissed his head and tucked him in.

June and I watched *Strange Brew* on television. I remember her laughing and me feeling jealous at how easy it was for her. I tried to lose myself in the movie, but I was distracted the whole time, one ear aimed at Dad's bedroom. I was grateful when it was over and June said how tired she was, too sleepy to watch another movie. The sooner we went to bed, the sooner we could wake up and bring Dad to the doctor. I let her have my twin and rolled out a sleeping bag on my floor alongside.

I didn't really sleep, just tossed until my clock read 5:00 a.m. I couldn't stand it any longer. I was going to get June's mom over here, and she'd help bring Dad in. It'd be embarrassing and awkward, and I didn't care anymore. Once Dad was healthy, we'd land him another teaching job, and he and I could return to the woods, and my grades would shoot back up, and maybe I could finally talk him into getting me that retainer.

His room smelled sour when I entered. I would realize later—days later, when fragile bits of my memory started to return—that the odor was vomit.

In the end, an ambulance was called, but not by me.

My screams had woken June.

"So that's how Paul finally went out," Ronnie said, whistling as I finished my story. "That's some twisted shit."

"It was an accident." I squeezed myself. The words were coming out hot and green, an infection being purged. I'd never in a million years imagined Ronnie McSorley would be the one who'd hear my awful tale, but I supposed there was poetic justice, one awful person confessing to another. "Dad was the last person on earth I wanted to die."

Ronnie's arms flexed, the motion made enormous by the lantern. "You killed your old man," he said, his voice scraping like a shovel through gravel. "You're a father killer."

I'd thought that at least a hundred times since I'd found him dead. But hearing Ronnie confirm my worst fear, right then in that horror dungeon, broke something in me, something that burned silver and bright.

I hadn't asked for any of this, not one bit. Not my parents forcing me to choose between them at age five, or my mom rejecting me for life because seven-year-old me overreacted to her pulling my tooth, or even my sweet father making me care for him rather than checking himself into a hospital he was surely too scared to go to because of what happened to him after Benny died.

And I *definitely* hadn't asked to be here, in Litani, Minnesota.

I found myself leaping at Ronnie, pummeling his chest, kicking him. I'd been breathing in guilt, swimming in it, rolling in it, with only enough room left over for fear and grief. How dare he prey on that?

But I might as well have been kicking a rock for how much damage I inflicted.

Ronnie trapped my arms at my side and held me against him. I bit his shoulder, the nearest chunk of flesh. He tossed me toward the doorway, away from the mattress. I landed hard, my teeth clamping on the edge of my tongue. My mouth erupted with the hot penny taste of blood.

"You little bitch," he said. "If you're gonna be like that, we're not wasting time with chitchat." He finished unbuckling his belt and pulled it out with a violent flourish.

I swallowed the blood gushing from my tongue as fear finally, completely found me. I couldn't survive if Ronnie did to me what he'd done to the other kids. I wasn't strong enough. My only option was to die right now. I needed to make him mad enough to kill me so I wouldn't be alive when he did his evil.

I was tightening all my muscles, preparing to leap at his eyes, when his face lit up. He was staring over my shoulder, squinting into the darkness, focusing his light at a space just behind me.

"So nice of you to join us," he said to whoever stood behind me. "You're late, so you're gonna have to wait your turn."

CHAPTER 49

I didn't want to tear my eyes off Ronnie, so I scrabbled to the side and twisted just enough to see who he was talking to.

It was . . . Crane.

The only friend I'd thought I had in town stood, arms limp at his sides, holding a flashlight that wasn't turned on. He stared at Ronnie, his mouth slack.

I moaned. I'd been wrong. About everything.

But then Dawn appeared from behind Crane, moonlight from a high window striping the lollipop stick poking out of her mouth.

"Told you he'd come here." She popped the sucker out and used it to point at me. "*She's* a surprise."

"Get up, Frankie," Crane said, his voice a rasp, his eyes still locked on Ronnie. "Get up, grab Dawn, run as hard as you can, and don't look back. If I don't walk out of here tonight, I left Wort's food under the bed, and you're the only one who can find it. Second door on the right going down the hall."

Relief flooded my veins like mercury, thick and cold. I leaped to my feet and ran toward Crane. I wanted to hug him, but he pushed me and Dawn behind him, not taking his eyes off Ronnie.

"The police are coming," Crane told Ronnie.

"That's some bullshit," Ronnie said. "The only person less likely than me to call the police is you."

"I called them," Dawn said helpfully, peeking around Crane despite his effort to shield her.

"They come and I'm still here, I'll give them those movies of you," Ronnie spat at Crane. "You want that? You want everyone seeing what your family did to you?"

"You don't have them," Crane said. "Not anymore."

That stopped Ronnie cold. "How do you know?"

Crane didn't answer.

"You dumb shit," Ronnie roared, lunging toward him.

Crane was ready. He had five inches and fifty pounds on Ronnie, but Ronnie was strong and he was quick and he fought dirty. My legs were two noodles, and I was so scared I couldn't draw a full breath, but I'd be danged if I'd let Crane fight alone. I lunged toward a woodpile in the shadows, grabbed a hunk of two-by-four, and charged back to the struggle, swinging at Ronnie every chance I could.

Dawn stayed back and watched. The few times I caught a glimpse of her face, I was chilled by the naked hate.

I couldn't get many good hits in. Crane and Ronnie were punching and grunting. It looked like Ronnie was winning, but if Crane and Dawn had been telling the truth about calling the police, it didn't matter. We just had to keep Ronnie occupied until they arrived.

I heard a siren keening from far away. We had a chance! At least that's what I thought right up until Ronnie got in a nasty punch under Crane's chin.

He knocked Crane out cold.

My friend fell with a sickening thud and my heart shuddered.

Ronnie turned to me, crazy in his eyes. "I don't need much time."

He lurched toward me.

I grasped my chunk of wood like a baseball bat. Just then, a banshee flew from Ronnie's right. It was Dawn clutching a rock the size of a baking potato. She brought it down on Ronnie's head with all her weight and fury. If he'd seen her coming, he'd have easily blocked the attack, taken a glancing blow at best. But he had all his attention trained on me. He took the hit clean on.

The force and impact knocked him to his knees, where he shook his head as if to clear his vision. Before he could get his bearings, Dawn shrieked and came at him again, tears streaming down her face as she bashed him a second time with the rock.

And then a third. And a fourth.

He made a bad sound from his gut, the one a dog makes when it's working on a throw up, and keeled over. She was kicking his pulpy face with my favorite shoes when the police pulled up, their lights flashing into the brewery's cavernous interior.

I saw no reason to stop her.

CHAPTER 50

Crane didn't go home that night, but it wasn't because Ronnie got him. It was because once he regained consciousness, Chief Mike told him he needed to go to the hospital to get checked out and that once he was well enough, he was going to jail.

I screamed it over and over again: *Crane saved me.*

But it didn't matter.

Chief Mike didn't listen, not really. He said if Crane was innocent, he wouldn't be in jail for long. I looked at Dawn for help, frantic, but she wasn't talking, her face as closed off as a coffin. She'd already helped herself to the only justice a kid like her or Crane was likely to get.

Chief Mike ordered us to wait in the back seat of Chad's car until Mom showed up. He tossed us a couple scratchy blankets—the last thing we needed in this heat—and returned to the ambulance to talk to the medic who was taking Crane's pulse. Even from that distance, I could see how scared and doomed Crane looked.

My helplessness was suffocating. When I realized Dawn was shivering next to me in the back seat, I tossed my arm around her. That's why we'd been given blankets—shock.

"How'd you and Crane know to come here?" I asked.

She glanced up at me, her eyes reflecting in the moonlight. "Crane's been worried about you since you came to town. He figured Sly or

Ronnie might come for you, either because of your size or to piss off your mom."

She dragged in a breath. "Crane had been staking out your place to make sure they didn't get you, just like he'd sometimes do outside my place, or Michelle's or Crystal's. Now that we're in the home, I guess he's spent most of his time looking out for you. Tonight he fell asleep on his watch. Woke up just in time to see your window was open and you weren't in your room. With Sly dead, he knew it was Ronnie, so he came and got me and asked me where I thought Ronnie'd take you." She swung her arm toward the brewery like a game show hostess revealing a prize.

I ducked so I could look through the open cop car door at the full moon shining down on the brewery, and on Crane, and on Ronnie, whose twitching body was being carried out on a stretcher and guided into a second ambulance. The paramedics said his vitals were fine and that he was going to make it, which was a pity.

Mike and Chad were heading back into the brewery, their flashlights bobbing.

"Dawn?"

"Yeah," she said, her voice quiet.

"You want to put an end to this?"

She slipped her warm hand in mine, and we slid out the door Mike had left open and melted into the evening. We flew like nightbirds through the dark blue all the way to Crane's house. I found the spare key and let us in. While Dawn played with Wort, I went to exactly where he'd directed me to go: under the bed behind the second door on the right in the short hallway.

I knew in the way that he'd said it—*you're the only one who can find it*—that I'd discover something important, so I wasn't surprised to see the Red Owl box Eula Vogler had been carrying the day I met her. It was filled with pictures and movies, some of the cassettes labeled "Zloduk," some "Vogler," even a couple with "Rosewood" scribbled on them.

From what Ronnie'd said, Crane was in some of these videos, but he wouldn't have directed me here if he didn't want the truth to come out.

I couldn't hand the box over to Mom. I didn't trust her.

I knew just the person, though.

Dawn helped me get Wort ready for what might be a few days alone, setting out several bowls of water and a whole cake pan of food. Then we each took one handle of the Red Owl box and made our way to Litani's only motel. Across town, we could hear the echoes of a commotion and see the steady flash of cop car cherries beating against the purpling dawn. We ignored it, letting ourselves into the motel lobby, where we convinced the puffy-eyed night clerk to tell us which room the female reporter was in.

The sun was just beginning to show its forehead when she answered her door.

After me and Dawn gave her the lay of the land, she first drove us to McDonald's because we were starving, and then she took us to the office of a Hennepin County judge she trusted. It was intimidating being in his chambers with their dark-paneled walls covered in bookshelves and diplomas. Dawn kept twisting her shirt. We were both filthy and battered, little hoboes in his rich office. It didn't feel real.

He seemed nice. He took the tapes.

Then the reporter drove us to my mom's house.

Mom wasn't home when we arrived. I let Dawn have the shower first and gave her underpants, shorts, and a shirt to wear. They'd be big on her, but they were clean. She was asleep in my bed when I finished my turn in the shower. I crawled in next to her, my back to hers, and fell asleep almost before my head hit the pillow.

Mom woke us up later that day. She'd raced to the brewery looking for me and was furious we'd run away. I didn't even tell her about the tapes.

I figured she'd find out soon enough.

CHAPTER 51

Mom drove Dawn back to the foster home.

She returned later that afternoon to tell me that both Crane and Ronnie were being kept in the hospital under observation. She said Ronnie was headed straight to jail from there. She wasn't sure about Crane.

Then the strangest thing happened: she stayed home that night and had dinner with me, an honest-to-god sit-down meal. It hadn't even been twenty-four hours since Ronnie'd abducted me. We didn't talk much, me and Mom. I think we were both grateful when the phone rang.

The videotapes had been copied, duplicates sent to Mom's offices as well as to the office of a Carver County judge.

Things moved pretty quickly after that.

By the next morning, everyone but Ronnie and Patty, Eula and Victor, Darlene, and Michelle's mom, Karen, had been released. Mom was gone when I woke, so I heard the good news from Chad, who'd stopped by to tell me. I ran straight to Theresa's trailer when I heard she was free. She held me for so long, both of us crying. I'd been worried she'd be mad at me because Mom'd had her arrested. She was worried I'd been hurt.

Unfortunately, according to Theresa, the press had somehow also gotten their hands on a copy of at least two of the videotapes. I chose to believe the female reporter had nothing to do with that. In any case, I avoided reading about it or watching the news. If I was going to hear the story of any of the kids on those tapes, I was going to hear it from them. This was especially true of Crane, who had been moved to jail. Me and Theresa cried about that, too.

I checked on Wort on my way back to my mom's. She was fine, playful, happy to see me. It hurt being in Crane's house while he was locked up, though.

Mom still wasn't home when I returned.

Her absence wasn't unexpected. If the breathless phone call I'd received from June before I'd left for Theresa's was any indication, the eyes of the nation were on my mom, waiting to see what she'd do now that she had these tapes featuring the actual perpetrators. Would she apologize to the people she'd wrongly accused? Or would she double down on the murder charges?

Me, I didn't care about the case. I was only worried about Crane.

I fell asleep that night cradling The Book, thinking about what plant my friend would be.

I woke up the next morning, astonished to find Mom in the kitchen.

"What are you doing here?" I asked. I hadn't meant it to be mean. It was an honest question. I'd assumed the supper we'd eaten together two nights before had been a one-off, something she'd done so she could keep up her public image of being a caring mom.

She looked up from where she sat at the kitchen table. She was dressed for work. She had dry toast and a cup of whitened coffee in front of her, was reading the newspaper. Her smile was sad. "I suppose I deserved that."

I rubbed the back of my neck. This didn't seem like my mom at all. I backed up so I could glance out the front window. It was still early, the rising sun spilling its watercolor paints across the horizon.

"No reporters," she said. "I told Chief Mike to take care of them. I thought I'd take a day off of work. Just you and me."

For a split second I was seven all over again, excited that my mom with her important job was making time for me. But reality crashed quickly down. My throat was bruised from being strangled by Ronnie. I walked with a limp from him throwing me to the ground. Dawn was in foster care. Crane in jail.

My mother cared only about herself.

So I regarded her suspiciously. She'd either lost her ever-loving mind, or she was playing a trick.

She pursed her lips, studying me. "I suppose I deserve that look, too. Want to take a walk?"

I almost said "yes, ma'am," but I bit my tongue just in time. I would walk with her, but I was done showing respect for the sake of it. "Let me put on some clothes."

I fully expected her to have a photo shoot waiting down the street, some "Passionate Prosecutor Puts Family First" scene. But she didn't. We walked quietly for a bit, shuffling along the sidewalk, enjoying the first cool day since I'd arrived.

"Where's that cat of yours?" she asked out of nowhere.

I gathered my shoulders toward my neck as protection. "Somewhere safe."

"Frankie, I'm not the bad guy," she said. "You can have the cat if you want."

Who was this person who looked like my mom? "For how long?"

"Forever," she said.

I blinked rapidly, afraid to take the treasure being offered, fearful it would be yanked away just as I reached for it. "You mean it?"

"Every girl needs a cat," she murmured by way of answer.

I recognized that tone of voice where she was talking to her past rather than to me, but I wasn't about to look a gift kitten in the mouth. "Thank you."

She nodded, went back to being silent for a while. Then she caught sight of the playground, and another bizarre thing happened, the most compelling evidence yet that she'd completely lost her mind: she leaned over to pull off her taupe pumps, shot me a grin, and ran across the grass in her stocking feet.

"We should swing!" she hollered over her shoulder.

I didn't want to smile, but I couldn't help it. There was something suddenly bright and vulnerable about her, like she'd been scrubbed clean and new. I ran after and hopped onto the swing next to hers. We both pushed back in the sand as far as we could on our tippy-toes, then released ourselves to swing forward with our toes pointed, pumping back and forth until we were flying toward the sky.

"Wheeeeee!" she yelled. She sounded so young. So happy.

"Wheeeeee!" I yelled back. At first I didn't want to, but it felt so good that I just kept doing it. We swung like that for a few minutes, held in the feel-alive air of a Minnesota summer. The temperature hadn't broken with a storm, not like it would have in California, but maybe that's how it was here.

When Mom stopped pumping, so did I, and we eventually slowed. She dragged her feet through the sand. They looked like Barbie doll toes, all joined together by her pantyhose.

"Why'd you leave Dad?" I asked.

Because she deserved that, too.

She seemed to have been expecting the question. At least, she didn't get mad right away. "I loved swinging when I was a kid." She pushed off a bit from the sand again but didn't start pumping. "I imagined myself flying away. Safe as a bird."

I caught a glimpse of her then, of the kid she'd been before the abuse had worn off her shine, a kid with an imagination and hope and a future outside this town. But I'd been through a lot. I was impatient. I needed answers. "I asked why you—"

She stretched her legs out like kickstands, holding herself in place.

"I got everything I wanted when I married your dad." She looked at me. Her eyes were as deep as quarries, deeper than I'd ever swum. "Once I had it, I realized I didn't deserve it. Do you understand?"

I held her gaze even though it was dreadful in its honesty. Because I *did* understand. She didn't only mean Dad. She meant me, too, and what an awful hand for a woman to be dealt.

Finally, I nodded. Who has words for things like that?

She nodded back, then returned her attention to her feet. I found myself wondering if the sand crystals were small enough to slip through the webbing of her nylons, if she was packing tiny dirt cakes between her toes.

"Frankie, I will burn down the world before I let happen to you what happened to me. That's why I got the Zloduks. Ronnie. Why I'll get them all."

I felt the tears burn my cheeks.

"That's also why I didn't have you visit me in Litani anymore after that first time," she continued. "And that's why I'm teaching you how to be tough now, how to make it on your own. If you don't need anyone, no one can hurt you. Do you get what I'm saying?"

I didn't nod this time. It's not that I didn't understand. It was that she was wrong. We *do* need people, every one of us. In fact, it's impossible to do the hard stuff alone. I was sorrier than anything that my mom didn't know that.

She stood up from the swing. Smoothed her skirt in the front and back. Shook her feet even though she was still standing in the sand. "But every girl needs a cat."

She took off slowly toward the house.

I waited a few minutes before following her.

CHAPTER 52

"I want to tell you what I did," Crane said softly. "Do you want to hear it?"

He and I were sitting in a witness conference room at the Carver County Courthouse.

It had been two weeks since Ronnie'd abducted me and Dawn had knocked him out cold, twelve days since my mom had shown me herself on the playground. I hadn't been allowed to see Crane that whole time, or Dawn, or any of the kids at the foster home. But today, finally, Crane was having his day in court. He'd asked to speak with me beforehand. It was all I could do not to hug his big, stupid face when I was ushered into the conference room.

I nodded at him. He looked so handsome in his shiny-at-the-elbows secondhand suit and too-wide blue tie. "I want to hear it," I confirmed.

"You know what my grandma and grandpa and aunts and uncles were charged with," he said, the words clearly hurting him. His hair was over his eyes, which made sense given the subject matter. "It's all true, what they're accused of. But what you might not know is they were doing it long before they were caught. First time I remember I was five." His voice cracked. "They told me it was a game."

I wanted to squeeze his hand but didn't know if it'd be okay, so I stayed still.

"I lived here, in Litani, with my mom. At the trailer park. She would drive me over to my grandma and grandpa's when she wanted to go out. It wasn't very often. Often enough, though," he said, his throat getting all stuffed up. He cleared it. "And my grandparents filmed it. At first it was just them and my aunts and uncles. Then they got other adults involved, like Ronnie and Patty."

His face twisted. "But like I said, I didn't have to go there more than two or three times a year, and I never told my mom what happened when I was there. I don't know why."

I did. Some truths feel like they'll kill you if you say them out loud.

"Then Sly moved to the trailer park." He scratched his chin, quick and nervous. "He and Mom got close. She let him drive me to my grandparents' once, and they must have recognized one of their own, because they invited him into those horrible games right on the spot. Eventually, he brought in his parents. It kept up until three years ago, when your mom started to ask questions. By then I was fourteen. I . . ." His voice cracked in agony. "I was old enough to say something, to fight back, but I was too scared. It sounds stupid, I know it does. I was already bigger than most of the grown-ups."

"Crane."

He jerked his head. "No, I should have said something. And I didn't, and so it kept happening. When my grandparents realized they were about to get arrested, they gave most of the movies to Sly for safekeeping. My grandpa kept only a handful of photographs for himself, all of them featuring Zloduk kids and Zloduk adults."

I didn't want to hear any more, but I couldn't tell him to stop.

"When your mom finally pressed charges, she could only prove the accusations against the people in the photos. Only Zloduks. I didn't testify about the other adults involved cuz my grandpa said Eula and Victor would show the world the movies I was in if I did. Frankie . . ." He pushed the hair from his eyes. They were blue and intense and begging me to understand. "I didn't care if the whole world saw me in them. I was just too scared to say anything against my own family. That's why this all kept going, why Ronnie and Victor and Eula and Sly got to stay free to keep doing what they did. It's all my fault." His voice cracked again. He glanced down at his clenched hands.

I could've told him I loved him, because I did. I could've told him I saw the mountains of goodness in him, because that was true, too. I could have told him none of it was his fault, not by a long shot, and that he didn't deserve for any of that to happen to him, no kid did. But a story like his called for only one thing, and that was a tale of equal pain.

"I accidentally killed my dad," I said.

His head jerked up, and he gazed at me with surprise and agony and something else I couldn't name. Hope? Then it all spilled out, everything I'd told Ronnie at the brewery. And of course it felt so much better this time because I was telling it to somebody who loved me back. It all showed in his eyes, which were brimming with tears.

Both of us sat in the trembling, sad space, closer than a hug could ever bring us.

"Crane, where's your mom?" I asked after we'd been quiet for a bit.

He shrugged. "She left when they took the rest of the Zloduks to trial. She sends me money. It's better than what happened to my cousins whose parents were in on it. They're in foster homes all over the state."

"It sure is a lot of work being a kid these days," I said.

It was a dumb thing to say, and I instantly regretted it, but Crane didn't seem to be listening. His face had lit up. "Frankie, you know what this means?"

I wasn't sure what he was referring to. "What?"

His voice was both thoughtful and amazed. "Now that we've told our stories, we don't have to live in theirs anymore."

CHAPTER 53

I was so proud of Crane as he testified.

He shared the facts straight and clear, even the ones that would hurt him. There was more detail than I could almost stomach at some points, but he spoke with courage and conviction. I wished the reporters hadn't been allowed in, to sketch him, to hear him, to sell his words, but nobody could take away the magic of what he was doing.

His testimony and those videos told the whole story. Wagner Zloduk had recruited Josiah Rosewood, Ronnie and Patty, and Wagner's own wife and children. Crane's mom brought in Sly by accident, who recruited Eula and Victor Vogler. Sly had also gotten Karen, Darlene, and Crystal's mom, Carmen, to look the other way. They were the only adults involved.

I could tell Crane was nervous, but he had the truth on his side. The only part of his testimony that scared me was when my mom asked why he hadn't turned out like most of the rest of his family.

"You had the same exposure, the same early training," she said, pacing as she asked, as if she were just coming up with the question on the spot. I had to admit, she looked and sounded like a smart cookie in court, even though she was apparently taking a real beating in the press for the handling of the case. You can't falsely accuse so many people, can't suggest satanic cults and murders and have nothing to show for it, and walk away smelling like roses.

"But"—and here she stopped for dramatic effect right in front of Crane—"you say you've never hurt someone else in the way you were hurt. How is it possible you chose that path rather than the life you'd been groomed for?"

He was quiet for several seconds. It grew uncomfortable for some. I could hear them shifting in their chairs, fanning themselves, making those little dry-throat coughs people make to prod you to speak.

But Crane seemed to be gathering something. All during his testimony, his hair had been falling over his face, and he'd been brushing it back to expose his beautiful features. Her question made him so still that this time his hair stayed tucked as it was behind his ears.

That meant his close-set eyes were visible when he finally spoke.

"I am not what happened to me," he said, his voice clear. Then he patted his suit coat pocket. Only him and me knew that the plant personality I'd sketched for him was folded up in there.

CHOOSE YOUR OWN PLANT PERSONALITY
YOU'RE CAPTAIN OF YOUR OWN DESTINY!
WHICH PLANT PERSONALITY DO YOU CHOOSE?

WEEPING WILLOW

Sturdy, strong, and sad, you wait.
For someone to see you have just what they need to salve their ache.

I'd given it to him right before he took the stand.

Everyone knew that the willow was nature's aspirin. Chewing on it relieved headaches, cramps, backaches, and arthritis, plus it prevented heart attacks. If you didn't want to gnaw on it, you could instead make a tea using two teaspoons of bark per cup of water. The bark turned the water a rad burgundy color, and it tasted crazy bitter. Dad said it was best to harvest the bark directly from the willow branches in the early spring rather than taking it from the tree trunk; otherwise you'd create an open wound that could destroy the tree.

That was Crane: gentle, vulnerable, kind, and, best of all, a protector.

The evil of what had been done to Crane and the choices he'd made because of it were living inside him, just like I'd have to carry around forever everything I'd survived and done. That's the way it was, I was realizing. Every person carried some bad, and we all had some good. Our job was to figure out how to let only the good stuff steer.

I wished it could be different, that a slate could be wiped clean, but I had a good guess that nothing was pure in life after age five.

Earlier if you lived somewhere like Litani.

CHAPTER 54

The courtroom buzzed after Crane's testimony.

The judge called a recess.

Mom hung out in the hallway just outside the courtroom to take questions from the press. She wasn't going to be able to make the whole world safe for me, but she was about to lop seven poison branches off the tree. There was no way Victor, Eula, Ronnie, Patty, and to a lesser extent Dawn's, Crystal's, and Michelle's moms could go free, not with Crane's testimony and the videos (which it turned out he'd stolen from Sly's trailer; he didn't trust Mom or the police to get the videotapes out in time, and good thing because Eula and Victor would have gotten there first if not for his quick thinking).

It was a good day for Mom. Her trial was going well, and the journalists crammed in the courtroom hallway were throwing her softball questions that she was batting out of the park. There would probably be a million better times to ask her what I wanted to ask her, but I needed to know now. Since our talk on the playground, I knew there was some room for me to be myself. Not a lot, but some.

I got her attention, waving my arm until she spotted it over the heads of journalists. I wasn't even nervous anymore. Sometimes it's like that when you know exactly what you're supposed to do.

She wove through the small crowd and approached me with a smile. I'd assumed that she wouldn't be able to ignore me with journalists watching her every move, but when she reached me, her warm expression was genuine.

"Yeah, Frankie?"

"I need to talk to you," I said. "In the conference room. It'll only take a couple minutes."

"Sure." She turned to the press. "My daughter needs me. I'll be back to answer questions shortly."

They ate that up, and I was okay with it. It didn't cost me a thing, and for the first time, I suspected there was some truth to it. Mom really did care. She just showed it in a profoundly messed-up way. I led the way to the same conference room where me and Crane had swapped stories right before his testimony. Some of our melancholy love still glittered up its corners.

She closed the door behind her. "Crane was so brave!" she said. "His testimony is going to help everybody. I just wish he'd had the courage to share it earlier."

We had limited time, so I let that one lie.

What I wanted was the true story of Benny's drowning.

I'd heard enough bits to know Mom had danced around the truth when she shared her version. I needed to put the matter to rest, and to do that, I required the facts. For better or worse, Mom was the only one who could give it to me.

"Mom, tell me what happened the day Benny died." I was proud of how strong and clear my voice sounded. "Everything. If you come clean now, it won't leave this room. If you don't tell me, though, or you tell me some whitewashed version, I will never stop searching for the truth."

Her face tensed for a moment, but she smoothed it over as quick as if she'd hot ironed it. "I don't know what you mean."

I wasn't going to argue. I was going to wait until I got what I wanted. I was my mother's daughter, after all.

She opened her mouth and then closed it. I didn't know what deals she was making in her head, the pros and cons she was weighing. I knew only that I'd been honest when I told her she could either tell me now or I'd dig until I found out later.

"Fine," she finally said.

She composed herself and dived in, her voice flat. "I loved your dad from the moment I met him."

They'd met on the first day of third grade. He offered her his jacket when she was cold and shivering on the playground. He didn't like her, not like that, and she didn't think he ever really did. "Not even after we were married," she said, without a hint of irony.

But he was always so kind to her that he felt like home. She waited for him to notice how she felt and reflect it back to her, but that never happened. He had eyes only for Darlene. "She was different back then," Mom said. "Joyful. Sunshine in a jar."

Mom loved Paul, who loved Darlene, who loved Paul—a terrible, lonely chain if you were Mom. She was faithful to her unrequited love for Dad for years, but on that scorching day by the river, when they were all hanging out and Benny tagged along, she'd finally given up.

Not forever, she swore that wasn't it. Just for a moment. And in that moment, she let Ronnie separate her from the group, take her into the woods, and do what he wanted.

"He'd been after me for years," Mom said by way of explanation. "And I'd been drinking that day. He wore me down."

When Ronnie dragged Mom off, Dad was sitting with Darlene near the truck, listening to Darlene bubble up about something with one eye and keeping the other on Benny.

"That boy worshipped Paul, followed him everywhere. And Paul loved him back." Mom massaged her cheek, her voice gone hoarse, the first emotion she'd shown since we'd sat down. "Benny had to pee. That must have been what happened. That's the only way he would have left Paul's side. The only explanation for how he stumbled onto me and Ronnie."

She shook her head, her eyes shiny. "'Be quick,' I'd told Ronnie. He knew I loved your dad. Everybody did. But Ronnie didn't make it quick enough, because there stood Benny suddenly, horrified. I yanked up my pants, but it was too late. Benny turned and ran toward the river, and all I could think was that if he tattled about what he'd seen me and Ronnie doing, I'd never stand a chance with Paul."

My skin grew cold as the horror of what she was telling me began to coat me, the chill sinking deeper with each breath.

"I hollered at Ronnie to make sure that Benny didn't tell, and then I ran in the other direction to find Paul, figuring I could cut Benny off at the pass if he took a shortcut. I found Paul chatting with Darlene and Mike, and I blurted out to Paul the first thing that came to mind, which was that I needed to talk to him about something private."

She laced her fingers together. "Paul said he needed to wait until Benny came back. I said Darlene and Mike could wait for the kid, or better yet, they could go find Ronnie because Ronnie was with Benny. Paul still didn't want to come with me, so I pulled out the big guns and started crying. Your father could never resist a woman's tears," she said, smiling ruefully. "I got him into the woods and confessed what my own father had been doing to me. I hadn't planned to, but I had no other story to offer."

She shuddered. "Your dad listened to every word I said, and he held me, and I started to believe that's what I'd meant to do all along."

She was staring off, her eyes vague.

"Honestly, I forgot that I'd told Ronnie to make sure Benny didn't tell."

I could see that she, at least, believed she was telling the truth. Whether Ronnie followed her command out of love or boredom or to feed his own monster didn't really matter.

"Next thing I know," Mom said, drawing a deep breath, "Darlene is screaming about Benny being lost. Ronnie and Mike are beside her, and they look grim."

Her hand went to her throat before she thought better of it and let it flutter to her lap. "The next time we saw Benny, they were dredging him out of the bottom of the river. Your dad never forgave himself." She smiled a stiff smile. "He had to be institutionalized for a bit. Ronnie visited him. Drove him home from the hospital, in fact, if I recall correctly. But your dad couldn't wait to move away from Litani, from us. We all reminded him of what he'd lost. I couldn't let that happen, though. I loved him too much."

I nodded. I understood loving him that much, understood it better than anyone else in the world.

Mom rose to her feet. "We will never speak of this again," she said firmly.

"Mom," I said. "I killed Dad. His heart was bad. I knew he needed to go to the hospital, but rather than force him, I gave him some of the experimental medicine he'd been taking. It killed him."

It seemed to me the air froze, her face picking up and then discarding several costumes. Finally, she chose one. To my lasting surprise, it was sympathy. "Honey, your dad knew he had a heart condition. If he mixed up some forest medicine rather than bring himself to the hospital when it got bad, that's not your fault, and it'd kill him all over again to know you thought otherwise." She rapped her hand on the table, drawing my gaze. Her expression was . . . motherly. "I know your father, and I know you. Don't make his mistake yours."

The warmth that flooded me dropped into the earth, growing roots.

CHAPTER 55

Litani High School was quite a thing come that fall. We were each of us walking wounded. Not everyone had been hit by the bomb, but we'd all felt the explosion and were each paying in our own private ways. For me it was regular nightmares so terrifying that I'd begun sleepwalking to escape them. The good news was I got to see Crane most days, even if it was only a high five as we passed in the halls. He'd dropped out with two weeks to go at the end of his junior year. Given his extraordinary circumstances, they'd let him cram in his makeup work over the summer and start on time for his senior year.

Mom had made some noises like she was going to send him to a foster home because of his age, but it was all for show, and anyhow, he turned eighteen at the end of September. Michelle moved in with her dad in Wisconsin shortly after that, no one told me where Crystal went, and Dawn was still at Grandma Jenny's until a more permanent home could be found for her.

In the meanwhile, besides allowing Wort to move back in with us for good, Mom let me invite Crane and Dawn over some nights for homework. Crane was a mostly good student, but Dawn needed *a lot* of help. She'd have terrible outbursts, screaming, ripping up her papers, and who could blame her?

Tonight was one of those nights she'd broken down. I'd been going over her math homework with her when she exploded, chucking her book across the room. I wanted to get mad right back, but I knew from experience that wouldn't work. Instead, I begged her to bundle up and go to the playground with me, told her I'd go down the slide with her even though I hated the slide. She agreed. We were both happy to meet Crane en route. He'd been on his way to my place, so we all headed to the playground together. The best part was that we weren't the only kids there.

Litani was gradually, so gradually, becoming less scary.

We had the best time at the park. There was no one better than Crane for pulling Dawn out of one of her black moods. He suggested a game of TV tag where rather than yell the name of the television show, we'd have to act out the main character real quick before we got tagged. When he squared his shoulders and impersonated Mr. T from *The A-Team*, Dawn and I laughed so hard that I peed my pants a little.

Once our noses were red and running, we skipped to my place and relaxed in front of the television. The three of us were taking turns playing with Wort and half-heartedly taking a swing at our individual homework when the local news out of Minneapolis came on. The top stories were the end of the drought and Ronald Reagan's landslide win over Mondale, and then out of nowhere, the anchor mentioned Litani.

We stopped what we were doing, our faces snapping toward the screen.

"All seven have been sentenced," the anchor intoned, "and Carver County prosecutor Linda Jubilee is currently under investigation for ethical breaches."

"Change the channel," she hollered from the kitchen.

I obliged. Mom had been tight lipped about work in the months since the trial. She was at a crossroads, I knew that, where she'd have to choose what sort of prosecutor she wanted to be moving forward. I hoped she chose right.

Mom's career fork in the road also meant I was more grateful than ever for the stability of Theresa, who let me drop by whenever I wanted. She was determined to do something positive for Litani despite all the town had been through, and somehow, she'd pulled off the time capsule project on schedule. The normal stuff went into it—a yearbook, newspaper articles, an antique beer can from the Engle Brewery. But something real dear to me had gone into it, too. When I showed Theresa the drawings I'd done of Wort, Darlene, my mom, Dawn, Sly, and her, she insisted they go in the time capsule with the rest of the stuff. I was fine with that. Better than fine, actually. They'd paint an honest picture of what life had been like when I was growing up there, and that was important to me.

I hadn't told anyone except Crane about the sketch I'd discovered tucked in a flap of the journal's cover that I'd never known was there. It was the only plant personality Dad had created all on his own, and his drawing skills weren't great. (Honestly, neither was his poetry.)

But that didn't matter, one bit.

It was me as a plant.

CHOOSE YOUR OWN PLANT PERSONALITY
YOU'RE CAPTAIN OF YOUR OWN DESTINY!
WHICH PLANT PERSONALITY DO YOU CHOOSE?

ALOE VERA
The most wounded should rejoice
because you help even the quietest to find their voice.

I slept with that page under my pillow.

I was thinking about it, chewing on my pencil eraser, when Dawn sneezed, which made Wort jump eight directions all at once. She landed in front of the television all puffy, like a dandelion floof.

Dawn, Crane, and I all started laughing, our hoots out of proportion to Wort's goofiness. But we weren't only laughing at the kitten. We were laughing because we'd survived something no kid should have to. Our hard-won strength and understanding were now our blood, bone, and armor, and they made us into something more.

Not just the three of us. Lots of kids.

And we'd always recognize each other, and even in the pain of that knowing, we'd realize we weren't alone.

LITANI EDITING PLAYLIST

- Simple Minds—Alive and Kicking
- Pet Shop Boys—It's a Sin, 2018 Remaster
- Pet Shop Boys—Always on My Mind
- They Might Be Giants—Birdhouse in Your Soul
- They Might Be Giants—Your Racist Friend
- Depeche Mode—Personal Jesus, Original Single Version
- Depeche Mode—Never Let Me Down Again
- Depeche Mode—Just Can't Get Enough, 2006 Remaster
- Violent Femmes—Blister in the Sun
- INXS—Suicide Blonde
- INXS—Don't Change
- The Lightning Seeds—Change
- Dexys Midnight Runners—Come On Eileen
- Crowded House—Don't Dream It's Over
- Men at Work—It's a Mistake
- Eurythmics—Here Comes the Rain Again
- Bow Wow Wow—I Want Candy
- Prince—Let's Go Crazy
- Rick Springfield—Jessie's Girl
- The Cure—Just Like Heaven
- Suzanne Vega—Left of Center
- Howard Jones—Like to Get to Know You Well
- Howard Jones—No One Is to Blame

- Erasure—A Little Respect
- The English Beat—Mirror in the Bathroom
- The Go-Go's—Our Lips Are Sealed, Single Version
- Duran Duran—Hungry Like the Wolf
- Eurythmics—Sweet Dreams (Are Made of This)
- The Icicle Works—Birds Fly (Whisper to a Scream), Single Version
- Squeeze—Tempted
- World Party—Ship of Fools
- Big Country—In a Big Country
- Wang Chung—Dance Hall Days
- The Church—Under the Milky Way
- Blondie—Heart of Glass
- The Bangles—Walk Like an Egyptian
- Joan Jett and the Blackhearts—Bad Reputation
- Cyndi Lauper—Girls Just Want to Have Fun
- Cyndi Lauper—Time After Time
- Pat Benatar—Hit Me with Your Best Shot
- Pat Benatar—Invincible
- Tina Turner—The Best
- Salt-N-Pepa—Push It
- Diana Ross—I'm Coming Out
- Soul II Soul—Back to Life (However Do You Want Me)
- Kate Bush—Running Up That Hill (A Deal with God)
- The Pointer Sisters—I'm So Excited
- Selena—I Could Fall In Love
- Simple Minds—Don't You (Forget About Me)
- Culture Club—Do You Really Want to Hurt Me

ACKNOWLEDGMENTS

I'm a child of the '80s. The crime-based media I consumed as a teen, from the *Friday the 13th* movies to *Miami Vice* to the real-life Richard Ramirez trial, centered on either the predator or the police. I couldn't get enough of it at the time, but as I grew older, I became more interested in the experience of the injured person over the criminal or the cop. Ordinary people living their lives, fighting the daily battle and digging out joy where they could, when evil swooped in.

Part of my interest in the innocent was my own difficult childhood, one that centered the perpetrators and erased the children (I got to tell that story in *Unspeakable Things*). The other piece is this: once I move past the gruesome curiosity, I find most predators' stories fairly predictable. They've been hurt, and so they hurt others. Conversely, I find the healing journey deeply compelling, the three-steps-forward, two-steps-back trek of a person determined to overcome an unfair burden, someone who is going to not only survive but find a way to alchemize their pain.

Those are the narratives—and the people—I'm drawn to.

Still, these stories are difficult to write. The research is heartbreaking, and I feel every liquid ounce of the fear and the powerlessness as I draft. This is especially painful when I'm writing about children, so believe me when I tell you I couldn't do it alone. My early editors, Jessica Tribble Wells, Jessica Morrell (an army of Jessicas!), and my agent, Jill Marsal, help me to go into these dark but necessary places. Thanks to all three of them as well as the entire superstar Thomas & Mercer team, with a special shout-out to Charlotte Herscher, Sarah Shaw, Liz Pearsons, Jon Ford, and Kellie Osborne.

I'd also like to thank Lori Rader-Day for providing the '80s-inspired playlist that got me through the editing of this book (songs listed above), Carolyn Crane for being the best parallel writer/taskmaster an author could ask for, and Tony for his illustrations plus for making me watch *Venom*, not knowing that it would help me untangle a problem I'd been working on in this manuscript. And I'd be lost—in life as well as in writing—without an amazing, weird, funny, wholehearted, brilliant group of people who travel in my lifeboat: Zoë, Xander, Suzanna, Shannon, Catriona, Susie, Erica Ruth, Christine, Cindy, Terri, Linda, Johnny, Sandy, Tam, Allison, Tamara, and Patrick.

I'd also like to thank the mystery community, which is a wonderful, supportive crew to roll with. Finally, thank you, the reader. Together, we can open the door a little wider and let the sunlight in.

ABOUT THE AUTHOR

Photo © 2018 CK Photography

Jess Lourey is the Amazon Charts bestselling author of *Bloodline*, *Unspeakable Things*, *The Catalain Book of Secrets*, the Salem's Cipher thrillers, and the Mira James mysteries, among many other works, including young adult, short stories, and nonfiction. An Edgar, Agatha, Anthony, and Lefty Award nominee, Jess is a tenured professor of creative writing and sociology and a leader of writing retreats. She is also a recipient of The Loft's Excellence in Teaching fellowship, a *Psychology Today* blogger, and a TEDx presenter. Check out her TEDx Talk for the inspiration behind her first published novel. When she's not leading writing workshops, reading, or spending time with her friends and family, you can find her working on her next story. Discover more at www.jessicalourey.com.